What readers are saying about

The Perfect Life

'A **compelling** and **twisty** thriller – I was **hooked**'
Joanne, *Netgalley*
★★★★★

'A **great** read – found myself doing that "**just one more chapter**" thing'
Stephanie, *Netgalley*
★★★★★

'**I couldn't put this down**'
Lisa, *Netgalley*
★★★★★

'**Loved** this one! So easy to read and **lots of twists and turns** along the way'
Kelly, *Netgalley*
★★★★★

'Oh my! **Hooks** you right from the start. **Suspenseful** and **twisting** – simply **brilliant**'
Cathy, *Netgalley*
★★★★★

'Full of **mystery** and **drama**'
Shabana, *Netgalley*
★★★★★

'**Fast-paced** and **thrilling**. Nuala Ellwood knows how to get the reader **enthralled** from the start'
Julie, *Netgalley*
★★★★★

ABOUT THE AUTHOR

Nuala Ellwood is the author of three bestselling novels: *My Sister's Bones*, for which she was selected as one of the *Observer*'s 'New Faces of Fiction 2017', *Day of the Accident* and *The House on the Lake*. Nuala lives in York with her young son.

The Perfect Life

NUALA ELLWOOD

PENGUIN BOOKS

PENGUIN BOOKS

UK | USA | Canada | Ireland | Australia
India | New Zealand | South Africa

Penguin Books is part of the Penguin Random House group of companies
whose addresses can be found at global.penguinrandomhouse.com.

First published 2021
001

Copyright © Nuala Ellwood, 2021

The moral right of the author has been asserted

Set in 12.5/14.75 pt Garamond MT Std
Typeset by Integra Software Services Pvt. Ltd, Pondicherry
Printed and bound in Great Britain by Clays Ltd, Elcograf S.p.A.

The authorized representative in the EEA is Penguin Random House Ireland,
Morrison Chambers, 32 Nassau Street, Dublin D02 YH68

A CIP catalogue record for this book is available from the British Library

ISBN: 978-0-241-98909-8

www.greenpenguin.co.uk

MIX
Paper from
responsible sources
FSC® C018179

Penguin Random House is committed to a
sustainable future for our business, our readers
and our planet. This book is made from Forest
Stewardship Council® certified paper.

Dear Reader,

I wanted to make some content notes available for you to inform yourself, if you wish — but some readers may consider these spoilers, so please skip the rest if you would rather not see.

This story touches on some difficult topics, including sexual assault. I have tried my best to portray these issues delicately and I hope this comes across as you read *The Perfect Life*.

If these are topics that you are sensitive to, please be aware.

Nuala x

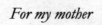

For my mother

'Fairy tales do not tell children the dragons exist. Children already know that dragons exist. Fairy tales tell children the dragons can be killed.'

– G. K. Chesterton, *Tremendous Trifles*

Prologue

Goring-on-Thames – August 2018

'What a view,' says the estate agent. 'I'd imagine you can see right across the county from here.'

Her eyes flash with delight. She'll be thinking of the possible commission, a hefty sum on a property this expensive.

'It's stunning,' I say as I look out on to the milky-blue river and clear, unpolluted sky. 'So tranquil.'

'Yes,' she says, stepping away from the window. 'The only noise you'll hear is the sound of birdsong and the trickle of water. Quite a change from the bustle of London.'

I nod my head, smiling. How surprisingly easy this has all been.

'The current owners are retiring and want to downsize,' says the estate agent as she leads me through to the drawing room. 'As you can see, this has been a wonderful home for them. Now it's ready to be passed on to another family.'

She gestures to the huge seating area, which is larger than the average London flat. Plush moss-green velvet sofas surround a beautifully crafted bamboo coffee table, which is piled artfully with a spread of books and a vase overflowing with freshly picked hydrangeas.

'You said you had three children, is that right?'

'Oh yes,' I say. 'Two boys and a girl.'

'How lovely,' she says, smiling warmly. 'I bet they keep you on your toes.'

'I love them but they're hard work; the boys are so naughty sometimes. That's why I thought I'd make this trip alone,' I say, running my hands over the soft velvet armchair. 'But my little Lavender is an angel, and I wouldn't swap any of them for the world.'

'I bet they'd love the space to run around here,' the estate agent continues, selling this idyllic place to me even though my heart already knows what it wants.

'Oh yes, Freddie would go mad with all this space to play football and Barclay would run wild and most likely break an arm like he did on his ninth birthday last year! He's forever getting into trouble,' I chuckle.

'Imagine the birthday parties you could give them here,' she says, unlocking a side door that leads out to a sweeping stone terrace.

I step outside and breathe in the crisp morning air. As I stand on the terrace the air fills with children's laughter. I see trestle tables groaning with party food, guests bearing brightly coloured parcels, music filtering out from the kitchen, balloons and bunting and candles on a cake, birthday wishes to be made.

'It's perfect,' I whisper as the estate agent leads me back into the house. 'Just perfect.'

But as we walk back through the living room and head towards the hallway, a chill ripples through me. What would Connor say if he could see me?

'Now,' says the estate agent, consulting her brochure. 'Let's show you the first floor, shall we, Imogen?'

I nod my head.

If only you knew, I think to myself as I follow this poor, unsuspecting young woman up the winding staircase. *That there are no children, no birthday parties, no prospect of a commission. That Imogen isn't even my real name. That all this is a perfect lie.*

PART ONE

1. Now

Wimbledon, South West London
August 2018

I sit in my sister's living room, sipping coffee from a cup that says MUM, though I have no children to call my own, my eyes transfixed by the laptop screen in front of me. I know I shouldn't have logged on, know that this addiction will be the ruin of me, but nothing else will help tonight, nothing else will stop the dark thoughts invading or stem the fear that is creeping like poison through my body.

I think back to five days earlier, the momentary happiness I had felt as I walked up the driveway and saw the topiary animals and the griffins, smelt the faint scent of honeysuckle in the air. I think of the look on his face as he answered the door, the smile that didn't reach his eyes.

Don't think about it, I tell myself. Not tonight. Tonight, I need to escape it all. So I let the memory fade and, instead, try to focus on the website, wincing as I take a sip from the coffee that has now gone tepid. Nothing new has been added in the last few hours, but simply seeing the familiar listings is reassuring.

'Everything okay?'

I look up and see my sister standing in the doorway. She's wearing her oversized navy-and-white-striped apron. The smell of roasted vegetables wafts through from the kitchen. Georgie is a great cook, like my mum was. I, on the other hand, can just about rustle up a basic pasta if I have to.

'Yes, all fine,' I say, minimizing the window on my screen. 'Just having a look at some job sites. Seeing what's out there.'

Georgie gives me that look, the one I've become accustomed to these last few weeks: a mixture of sympathy and bewilderment. A look that says *How did my ambitious, confident little sister get herself into this state?* It's a question I've been asking myself a lot too.

'Dinner won't be long,' she says, wiping a strand of dark hair from her face. 'I'm making stuffed peppers.'

'Thanks, Georgie,' I say, aware of the fact that she is trying her best to perk me up. 'They smell delicious.'

She goes to speak but is interrupted by a loud hammering on the door. My heart leaps in my chest as she goes to answer it.

Breathe, I tell myself; try to focus back on the page I've been looking at.

I hear muffled voices in the passageway and my throat tightens. I scroll down the page, cast my net a bit wider. Draining the last of the coffee, I try to think of somewhere new, somewhere I've never been before. But my brain is muddy, nothing will come, so instead I close my eyes and type a random letter into the search engine. *G.* I shiver at its meaning, then quickly click on the first suggestion – Gloucestershire – before his face has a chance to appear in my head.

I've never been to Gloucestershire but now, through the power of the internet, I can. My skin tingles as I enlarge the picture and step into a golden world. A world where everyone is wealthy and secure, where the floors are polished and gleaming, the gardens manicured and bursting with fragrant plants and flowers. A world of laughter and sunshine and families gathered together at outdoor tables, an abundance of food and drink. It should be making me feel better, but as I wander through this fantasy land, it only reminds me of what I have lost.

'Come through.'

Georgie's voice cuts into my thoughts and I look up. What I see makes the room constrict and my hand, poised over the computer mouse, starts to shake. There are two police officers standing in the doorway, one male, one female. Behind them I see my sister's face, all colour drained away.

'Iris Lawson?' says the male officer, his eyes fixed on me.

The name sinks like a stone in my stomach, but I nod my head all the same.

Georgie pushes past them and comes to stand next to me.

'There must be some mistake,' she says, placing her hand on my shoulder, her voice solid and commanding, ever the older sister. 'Her name is –'

'Shh,' I interrupt, shrugging my sister's hand away. 'It's okay, Georgie.'

'I'd like to ask, Miss Lawson,' continues the officer, a flabby-faced man who looks to be in his mid-fifties, 'if you know a man named Geoffrey Rivers?'

I look up at him. His eyes are the colour of damp autumn leaves. I turn from him to my sister. She shakes her head. We both know the significance of the name.

'Yes,' I whisper, my hand still hovering on the mouse. 'Yes, I do.'

The officer nods his head then takes a step forward.

'Well, in that case, Miss Lawson,' he says, his voice hardening, 'I'd like to ask you to accompany me to the police station. We need to ask you a few questions.'

'Why do you need to do that?' cries Georgie. 'What's happened?'

'I'm afraid Mr Rivers was found dead at his home in Hampstead,' he replies, his voice steady.

I hear my sister inhale sharply. In front of me the screen darkens, obliterating Gloucestershire and polished floors and perfect lives, leaving me only with the stark truth of what I have done.

2. Then

July 2017

The hooded figure rises from its haunches and creeps towards the unsuspecting young woman. She is looking up at the stars, trying to pick out Venus. So lost is she in her stargazing, she doesn't sense the shadow that has just crossed her path. Somewhere in the distance an oboe strikes up, playing a single note. It's an ominous sound, funereal. It gets louder and louder as the hooded figure bears down on the woman and clasps its bony hands around her throat. She tries to break free, but the figure is stronger than she is and soon she's overwhelmed. Her body loosens and flops backwards like a limp rag doll. In her final moments she turns her head to look at her killer, but her eyes are full of starlight.

'Bloody hell,' whispers Lottie, in the seat beside me, as the curtains close and the audience strikes up a reticent applause. 'The things you make me do, Nessa.'

She starts to giggle.

'Puppet theatre for adults?' she says, shaking her head. 'I mean, really?'

'Oh God, I'm sorry, Lottie,' I say as the lights come up in the auditorium. 'It got such a good write-up in the *Observer* too. Still, at least we didn't have to pay for the tickets.'

'Murderous gothic puppets,' says Lottie, her eyes widening.

She looks at me and her face is so astounded that we both burst into fits of giggles. A woman with cropped grey hair and a batik-print jumper, sitting in the row in front, turns to us with an expression of dismay.

'Come on,' I say, sliding out of the seat. 'Let's get out of here before they do an encore.'

'Christ, yes,' says Lottie, stumbling behind me.

When we reach the exit I turn and take Lottie's hand and, released from the deathly quiet auditorium, we explode into loud laughter.

'Remind me to thank Georgie for the tickets,' says Lottie as we make our way down the corridor to the bar. 'I wonder why she passed them on to us.'

As senior curator of a successful independent art gallery in Mayfair, my sister is always being given free tickets for exhibitions and theatre shows of the more experimental kind. Tonight's murderous puppets were part of a six-part show produced by a Danish theatre company who specialize in something called 'Puppetry of the Macabre'. I smile as I imagine Georgie trying to convince Jack, my rugby-loving, no-nonsense brother-in-law, to go and watch a puppet show. 'Give the tickets to Vanessa,' he would have said. 'She likes fairy stories.' He would have been right about that. I do. Though, if I'm honest, there was something about the puppet show that got under my skin.

'Next time, I get to choose,' says Lottie as we walk into the rather crowded Royal Court Theatre bar. 'And I'm going full-on musical theatre. You're going to have to sit through two hours of *Mamma Mia* or *9 to 5* to make up for that, agreed?'

I smile. Lottie really is the light to my darkness. It was the same at university. I loved Emily Brontë, she was more Jane Austen. I liked listening to PJ Harvey – whose records Georgie had introduced me to – while Lottie loved cheesy pop. On paper, we shouldn't be friends, but somehow we balance each other out.

'Agreed,' I say as we spot two vacant seats by the bar. 'Now, what can I get you to drink?'

Lottie purses her lips. She always does this when she has a decision to make. Or, at least, when she feels she has to look as though she's making a decision. I know for a fact that after a minute's deliberation she will say, 'A glass of Merlot, please.' Her usual. The drink she always has. Yet she will still give herself a moment to weigh up the options.

'Er . . . I'll just have a glass of Merlot, please,' she says, pushing her hand through her thick red curls.

'What a surprise,' I say, shaking my head. 'Dry-roasted nuts?'

Lottie smiles widely. One of the great things about our friendship is the fact that we know and understand the little things, the things that other people might not find important, but mean everything to us. I know that Lottie always drinks Merlot on a night out but has to have a packet of peanuts with it to line her stomach. She knows that I have to drink my coffee when it's steaming hot because tepid coffee makes me feel queasy. And I know never to engage her in conversation or ask important questions of her before eight in the morning because it takes at least two coffees and a shower before her brain is able to function. Little things. Silly things, some would say. But remembering these things and honouring them is what, I have always felt, has kept our friendship going for so long. We're like a married couple, just without all the boring relationship complications.

'So,' I say when the drinks arrive. 'How was today? Craig behaving himself?'

She rolls her eyes. Craig is her colleague and desk partner at the children's charity where Lottie works as case manager. She'd always got on well with him until last week when he got very drunk on an office night out and told Lottie he thought he was in love with her.

'He's been very quiet, thankfully,' she says, taking a sip of wine. 'Though it's tricky when you're sharing a desk. I keep catching him staring at me.'

'Awkward,' I say, taking a handful of nuts from the opened packet. 'That's why I'm glad I have an office to myself.'

'Yeah, well, we can't all be super executives like you,' says Lottie, tapping me playfully on the arm. 'My mum says you're like Melanie Griffith in *Working Girl*. We watched it together on her birthday. Pure eighties yuppiedom.'

'I'm hardly a yuppie, Lottie,' I say with a laugh. 'My office is no bigger than a cupboard. *Yuppies*. I remember my mum using that term to describe my dad's sister, my Aunt Yvonne. She worked in the City and used to wear trouser suits with huge shoulder pads.'

'She sounds ace,' says Lottie. 'I bet she drank Campari and lemon. We should be more yuppie.'

'Yeah, I'd like to see you try that in your office,' I say, feeling merry with wine. 'What was the name of the guy Michael Douglas played in that film? The one where he says "lunch is for wimps"?'

'Gordon Gekko!'

We both remember the name at the same time and collapse into giggles.

'Lowering the tone as ever, Miss Adams?'

I look up and see Damian Astley. He's the finance officer at Luna London and the man I go to when I need extra cash for my — as he likes to call them — 'ambitious' marketing campaigns. He's in his late fifties but keeps himself so trim and groomed he could easily pass for a man in his forties, though I would never tell him that or his ego would go through the roof.

'Fancy seeing you here,' I say as he approaches the bar. 'I didn't think theatre was your thing.'

'It isn't,' he says, smirking. 'We're here for the booze.'

He gestures to his friend, who is standing on the far side of the bar, to join us.

'We were just talking about you, actually,' I say with a smile. 'Gordon Gekko. Remember that old eighties film, *Wall Street*?'

'Old eighties film,' he says, shaking his head. 'Thus spake the millennial. It's an absolute classic, though I'm guessing it came out before you were born.'

'A few years after,' I say, watching as Damian's friend comes towards us, a bottle of beer in each hand. He's very attractive, with dark curly hair and deep-brown eyes. He smiles as he approaches and I find myself blushing.

'Guys, this is Connor,' says Damian, pulling out a bar stool for Connor to sit down. 'Connor, meet Vanessa Adams, our marketing miracle worker, and . . . sorry, love, I didn't catch your name.'

'It's Lottie.'

'Ah, Lottie. Same name as my wee niece, I'll remember that,' says Damian, his old Northern Irish charm surfacing. 'What do you do, Lottie?'

While Lottie and Damian discuss Lottie's job, Connor pulls his chair further towards me.

'Nice to meet you, Vanessa,' he says. His voice is deep, with a trace of northern accent. 'Damian speaks very highly of you.'

'Ah, that's good to know,' I say, taking a sip of wine. 'I always feel bad for getting him to loosen the company purse strings for my ad campaigns. How do you two know each other?'

'Damian was a friend of my dad's,' says Connor. 'They were at uni together. When Mum and Dad split up, Damian stuck around for me. He's a sort of unofficial godfather.'

His eyes glisten slightly and I get an urge to reach out and touch his arm, reassure him. It's an odd feeling. I've only just met this man yet I want to protect him. Beside us I hear Lottie telling Damian about the 'murderous puppets'. She's laughing and doing impressions, much to Damian's delight.

'I read about that show in the *Observer*,' says Connor, leaning in to me and raising his voice above the din of the bar. 'It sounded interesting. What did you think?'

'I actually quite enjoyed it,' I say, edging my seat away from Lottie. 'Though I feel bad for subjecting Lottie to it. It was a bit dark for her tastes.'

'Why would you feel bad?' he says, a frown passing across his face. 'It's not your fault she didn't enjoy it.'

'I guess not.'

'What did you like about it?' he says, flinching slightly as Damian lets out a roar of laughter at something Lottie has said.

'It reminded me of the children's stories I enjoyed when I was a kid,' I say. 'You know, the Grimms' fairy tales, ghost stories, that sort of thing.'

'Yeah, ghost stories were a big thing when I was at primary school,' he says, staring at me intently. 'The girls loved them, though I could never see the appeal. Remember those Holly Maze books?'

I breathe in sharply. For a moment the memory of my mum driving into sharp sunlight flashes in front of me. I can't allow myself to think about that, not tonight.

'No, I don't remember those. I was more into *The Demons of Winter Valley.*'

'Sorry, I interrupted you,' he says, touching my arm. 'You were saying?'

'The show just reminded me of those stories,' I say, the wine loosening my tongue. 'Good versus evil, morality lessons, if you like. The main character wasn't as sweet as she made out. She was playing with the audience, hiding her true nature from them. But the hooded figure, the one we imagined was bad, was actually her guilty conscience. And when he . . . oh, I'd better not spoil the ending for you in case you go and see it.'

'No, do,' he says. 'I'd like to hear.'

'Well, in the end, the hooded figure kills her.'

'Ah, hence the murderous puppet?' he says, gesturing to Lottie.

'Yes,' I say. 'But the murder was . . . well, it didn't look like he was killing her. The way the puppeteer worked the

17

puppet's hands made it look like he was embracing her, like he was, in some weird way, saving her.'

'Saving her from herself, I suppose,' he says, fixing his brown eyes on me.

'Yes, exactly that,' I say excitedly.

It's a relief to talk about the show like this. I love Lottie but she can be so fixed in her likes and dislikes that sometimes I feel I have to adapt my own to suit her.

'I'm a bit of a nerd when it comes to theatre,' he says, placing his beer bottle on the bar. 'Though it's the look of the stage that really intrigues me. I studied set design at college before changing tack and going into art direction. That dress you're wearing, for example. It caught my eye immediately because it brings out the shade of your eyes. Blue is definitely your colour – Christ, that probably makes me sound rather vacuous.'

'Not at all,' I say, my stomach fluttering as I look down at my dress, a pale-blue Zara number I've had for years. 'I know a lot of people think that about my work in cosmetics. People view the beauty industry as something frivolous and lightweight, but for me it's about storytelling, creating different characters for each occasion.'

'It sounds like you love your job,' says Connor with a smile. 'You're lucky. There are so many people trapped in jobs and lives that they hate.'

'You're right,' I say, feeling myself relax. 'Before I got the job at Luna London I'd spent years temping. God, some of those places were really dire. I remember one time I was working on the reception desk of a marketing company in the City and the boss asked me to sew a button on his shirt.'

'Christ, what a dinosaur,' he says, shaking his head.

'Yep,' I say, remembering those years. Jobs like that had left my confidence battered. 'It was the last straw. A couple of days later I saw the job ad for Luna London and decided it was now or never.'

'What do you mean?'

'Well, I've always been rather shy,' I say. 'When I was a kid I used to be scared of meeting new people, putting myself out there, even when it was for my own good. I realized I was still doing that after university. I was playing it safe, not daring to go for what I wanted in case I made a fool of myself.'

'I understand that,' he says, taking a sip of beer. 'Those first few years after uni are pretty tough. You have to develop a thick skin.'

'I knew I'd have to do that or else spend the rest of my life trapped in dead-end jobs,' I say, recalling how nervous I'd been when I turned up to the interview at Luna London. 'Though I still felt like an imposter those first few months.'

'That's interesting,' he says, narrowing his eyes. 'Do you still feel that way?'

'No,' I say. 'And that's down to Anne.'

'Anne?'

'My boss. She's amazing, a real inspiration. She took a chance on me, someone with very little experience, and spent the next year mentoring me in every aspect of the job. I'll always be grateful to her for that.'

'Everyone needs an Anne in their life,' he says, smiling. 'She sounds great.'

I go to speak but I'm interrupted by Lottie tapping my arm.

'Sorry to be a pain but our table's booked at Rossi's for 9 p.m.,' she whispers. 'Unless you want to cancel it.'

She darts her eyes towards Connor and smiles. I feel my cheeks redden.

'No, of course we should go,' I say, draining my wine. 'It was really nice to meet you, Connor.'

'Likewise,' he says, running his hand through his hair. 'We should have a drink sometime, maybe.'

'Um, sure,' I say, watching as he takes his phone out of his pocket.

As I give him my number, Damian appears behind me.

'Nice to see you two getting along,' he says, placing a hand on my shoulder. 'Connor's a lovely chap.' He whispers this last bit in my ear and I get a waft of beer and peanuts.

'See you on Monday, Damian,' I say, shaking my head as he winks playfully at me.

As we walk out of the bar, Lottie squeezes my arm.

'God, he was a bit intense, wasn't he?' she says, rolling her eyes. 'I would have rescued you, but Damian was telling me a long-winded story about his sister who works for an animal charity in Tanzania.'

'I actually kind of enjoyed talking to him,' I say, aware, as we step out on to Sloane Square, of an invisible gap widening between myself and Lottie, like I don't really want to break the spell by telling her the way Connor made me feel. 'Anyway, let's get a move on or we'll be late to dinner.'

As we hurry towards the restaurant, Lottie chattering beside me, I feel an overwhelming sense of loss. I could quite easily have talked to Connor all evening. He had made me feel so at ease, like I could be completely myself. It was strange and lovely in equal measure.

When we've ordered our food, Lottie takes her phone and shuffles up next to me.

'Come on then, let's check him out,' she says, opening up Instagram and holding the phone up so I can see. 'Your Mr Wonderful.'

'Oh, don't be so dramatic,' I say as I take a sip of sparkling water. 'He was just a nice guy, no need to stalk him.'

'This isn't stalking,' says Lottie, looking up at me, her large amber eyes sparkling in the half-light. 'This is trying before you buy.'

'Oh God, Lottie, that's terrible,' I say, shaking my head. 'How the hell did people manage before social media?'

'Er, they got big surprises,' she says, raising her voice above the Ed Sheeran song that has just started up. 'Like, "Ooh, I had no idea Colin used to be morbidly obese. He never had any old photos lying about."'

'You're evil,' I say, laughing, as she thrusts the phone at me.

'Here we are,' she says as Connor's Insta profile looms in front of me. 'Connor Dawkins. Art Director @Turner-MathersPR. Foodie. Runner.' His profile photo shows him standing against a tiled doorway. It looks like Spain or Portugal. He's tanned and wearing sunglasses and a crisp white shirt.

'Right, let's see his dirty secrets,' says Lottie, scrolling further down the page. 'God, it's all work stuff. Drawings of sports people and banners. Ooh, hang on, what have we here?'

She passes me the phone. There's a photo of Connor, with shorter hair, wearing a navy suit and holding hands with a slim, blonde-haired woman. She's wearing a tight-fitting, shimmery pink dress and is holding a glass of champagne. It looks like they're at a wedding as she's got what must be an order of service in her hand. I barely know this man yet I get a twisted feeling in my stomach looking at him holding hands with a woman.

'Well, he definitely has a type,' says Lottie, taking the phone from me. 'Blonde, blue-eyed, slim. Let's see when this was taken. Ah, January of this year. And no other photos of women since. Looks like he's single, at least. Now, what about Facebook.'

'That's enough, Lottie,' I say as the waiter arrives with our food: Spaghetti Carbonara for Lottie, Penne Arrabiata for me. Our usual. 'I feel awful stalking the poor guy like this.'

'Try before you buy,' she says, raising her glass of water at me. 'It's the only way.'

Later, when we've paid the bill, Lottie heads to the loo. I'm just getting my coat on when my phone vibrates. It's a text.

> I was going to play it cool and wait a few days but then I thought, sod it, I've never been cool. Would you like to have brunch with me tomorrow at 11? At the cafe in Battersea Park? Do tell me to piss off if you want, Connor

My stomach does a little fluttery dance as I type out my reply.

> Ha! I've never been cool either. Brunch sounds perfect. See you then.

I quickly put my phone away as Lottie returns to the table, but she has clocked me.

'Who was that? Surely, not Mr Dawkins? If it is, he's certainly keen.'

'No, it was just Georgie, asking about the play,' I say as we make our way out of the restaurant.

I feel bad for lying to Lottie. I don't even know why I did it, exactly. I just know I want to keep him to myself. Just for a while.

3. Now

West Hampstead Police Station

I can see Georgie through the glass panel. She is pacing up and down the corridor, her phone clasped to her ear. When the police told me I had to go to the station to be interviewed under caution she totally lost it. I'd never seen her like that before. My calm older sister suddenly screaming and shaking her fist, remonstrating with the officers as they led me to the car, telling them that they had made a dreadful mistake, that my name was Vanessa Adams, not Iris Lawson, and that I had nothing to do with the murder of Geoffrey Rivers.

If only that were true, I think to myself, as DS Alan Bains shuffles in his seat on the other side of the table, his arms folded across his chest.

'So, Miss Adams,' he says, fixing me with a stare so cold I flinch. 'Now that we have ascertained your real name we would like to continue to interview you under caution. Do you understand what that means?'

I nod my head, remembering what I was told when I got here: the fact that I have not been arrested, that this is a voluntary interview, that I am assisting the police with their enquiries. It all sounded a lot less terrifying than I had imagined but then, as we sat down at the desk, Bains had stated the phrase that I'd only ever heard on cop shows – *You do not have to say anything, but it may harm your defence if you do not mention when questioned something which you later rely on in court. Anything you do say may be given in evidence* – and I had started to shake. Defence. Court. Evidence.

'As you have now consulted with your legal representative,' continues Bains, gesturing to the elderly man beside me, Frank Solomon, a family friend of Jack's, 'we can commence the interview.'

I glance back through the glass panel and see Georgie, still talking on her phone. When I'd been placed into the back of the police car she had run up to the window and mouthed to me that she would get in touch with Frank, and that all would be fine. 'He's the very best,' she'd said, her lips visibly trembling. 'He'll get you out of there.'

I'd nodded my head as I was driven away, though inside I felt an odd sensation, one I hadn't felt since childhood in the weeks after my mother's death. It was a feeling not unlike weightlessness, as though I had left my body and was floating above the scene, calmly observing myself and the police officers and my frantic sister.

As Bains sets up the tape recorder I think back to the afternoon of the 11th of August. The sunshine pouring on to the driveway, the talismans of my childhood lined up along the path, Geoffrey's smiling face as he opened the door.

Then I remember something.

The glass bird.

The bird that all Geoffrey's readers would have been familiar with, as each story was narrated by it: 'The Bird of Truth'.

I hear Frank Solomon clear his throat; Bains clicks a button on the tape recorder but I'm not in the room any more. I'm back there, at Holly Maze House, remembering. I see sunlight pouring through the window and the glass bird looking at me from its perch on the sideboard.

'Miss Adams.'

Bains is speaking and gesturing to the tape recorder but all I can think about is the bird.

'Miss Adams, are you ready to start the interview?'

I nod my head and fold my hands in front of me as he begins to speak.

'Miss Adams, can you tell me where you were on the afternoon of the 11th of August 2018?'

Bains fixes me with an unblinking gaze as he asks the question. I look down at my hands, which are clasped in front of me, as a fleeting image of the body appears before my eyes. I try to block it out, try to summon a comforting image, but all I see is him.

'Miss Adams, could you answer the question?'

I try to speak but my throat is dry. I would like a glass of water but I dare not ask, for if I speak at all then this nightmare becomes real.

'We believe that you visited the offices of Price Burrows Estate Agency in Hampstead at 1 p.m. that day,' he continues. 'Is that correct?'

I look beside me at Frank Solomon. He shakes his head. At our brief consultation half an hour earlier he told me that I was not under arrest but here voluntarily and was under no obligation to answer any questions, though failure to do so might add to their suspicions. Does the shake mean I shouldn't answer?

'Miss Adams, it's a simple question,' says Bains with a sigh. 'You would be doing yourself a favour if you work with us on this.'

I catch his eye for a moment. His expression lifts. He thinks I'm relenting but instead I look down at the desk and shake my head.

'Okay,' says Bains. 'Perhaps this might jog your memory.'

He takes his iPad, swipes the screen, then pushes it into the centre of the table for me, and Frank, to see.

'For the benefit of the tape I am showing Miss Adams CCTV footage from inside the offices of Price Burrows Estate Agency, Hampstead, taken at 1 p.m. on the 11th of August 2018.'

The footage is clearer than I imagined and I flinch as I watch a woman, clad in a pale-pink sundress, enter the office and stride over to the desk. She talks to the estate agent – a young man called Edward Carter-Vaughan – for around five minutes. The footage then shows him making a call, while the woman sits at the desk opposite him.

'Do you remember now?' asks Bains, zooming in to my face.

Of course I remember. I remember every little detail. The layout of the office: two desks on either side of the room, one for sales, one for lettings; the smell of lilies and fresh coffee. The ringing of phones and the cut-glass accent of the lettings agent as she answered each call: 'Good afternoon, Price Burrows, how may I help you?' And Edward finishing the call then looking up at me with a smile: 'We're in luck. Mr Rivers is free to show you the property at 1.30. Does that work for you?'

'Miss Adams?'

I don't reply, though it's clear to anyone with a pair of eyes that the person on the screen is me.

'Okay,' says Bains, shaking his head and grabbing the iPad. 'I'd like to show you another piece of CCTV footage, this time from the northern end of Hampstead High Street at 2.14 that afternoon.'

My stomach knots as Bains opens up a new screen then places the iPad back on to the table, pushing it towards me.

'Miss Adams,' he says, emphasizing my surname as though it's a lie, 'I believe this footage shows you running down Hampstead High Street after leaving Holly Maze House. You look to be in a state of extreme agitation.'

He leans across, pauses the film, then zooms in.

'Can you see?'

I nod my head. Beside me, Frank Solomon shuffles uneasily in his seat.

'For the benefit of the tape, Miss Adams, was that nod of the head an affirmation? Are you confirming that the person on the screen is you?'

I freeze. Why had I nodded my head?

We sit in silence for what seems like an eternity before Bains takes the iPad and switches it off.

'Miss Adams,' he says, shuffling forward in his seat, 'we have CCTV footage of you entering the offices of Price Burrows Estate Agency on the 11th of August 2018, where you booked an appointment to view Holly Maze House at 1.30 p.m., using the false name Iris Lawson, though you – helpfully for us – gave your sister's address.'

I wince as I recall Edward Carter-Vaughan asking me for a contact address. I knew I'd have to give him a valid one, despite the fake name, but I had thought it was just a formality. No one was going to follow up this appointment or make use of Georgie's address. But then, I had no idea what was about to happen in Geoffrey's house and that the police would come looking for me.

'You are then shown emerging on to Hampstead High Street via the side street that leads to Holly Maze House,' continues Bains, his eyes fixed on me. 'You are clearly in a state of agitation and distress.'

I stare at the table where the iPad had been, watching the space as though the film is still playing. And if it was, it would show me running to the tube, terror and panic burning inside me, tears running down my face.

'The estate agent who dealt with you, Edward Carter-Vaughan, tells us that he remembered you because you were making rather a lot of fuss about viewing the house.'

Bains's words rip through me as I sit staring at the empty space.

'Mr Carter-Vaughan says that you told him, and I quote, "It's rather important I see it as soon as I can. It's a matter of urgency."'

I flinch as I recall myself saying that to the bemused young man. But it was true. It *was* a matter of urgency that I saw Holly Maze House.

'It really is in your best interests to answer these questions, Miss Adams,' says Bains, his voice softening somewhat. 'The evidence is right here in front of us. You were there in the offices of Price Burrows Estate Agency at 1 p.m. on the 11th of August, using a false name, and you were there on Hampstead High Street one hour and fourteen minutes later. Weren't you?'

I look up at him. His face is getting more flushed. I'm exasperating him.

'Miss Adams, your refusal to cooperate and to answer these very simple questions is rather concerning,' he says, his eyes bulging now. 'Particularly as we have clear evidence of your being in the vicinity of Holly Maze House in the hours surrounding Geoffrey Rivers's murder. Miss Adams, I shall lay this out for you in basic terms. According to the pathologist, Geoffrey Rivers died some time between 1 p.m., when he spoke on the phone to Edward Carter-Vaughan, and 3 p.m., when Mr Rivers's window cleaner spotted his body through the window.'

His voice is getting louder and louder. It's scaring me. I want him to stop.

'Between those two things occurring – Rivers talking to Carter-Vaughan at 1 p.m. and his window cleaner arriving at 3 p.m. – you, Miss Adams, were booked to view Holly Maze House, which I strongly suspect you did, as you were shown on CCTV running like the clappers back on to the high street from the direction of the house.'

'Stop,' I whisper, digging my nails into my forearm. 'Please stop.'

'Oh,' says Bains, clapping his hands together. 'So you do have a voice? That's wonderful. Now, maybe you can use that voice to tell me what happened at Holly Maze House because it appears, Miss Adams, that you were the last person to see Geoffrey Rivers alive.'

It is 1996. I'm ten years old and have just woken up in my yellow bedroom. I like the way the sun, coming through the yellow curtains, makes the room look sepia tinted, like an old photograph. I love old things: historic houses, ghost tales, antique furniture, things with a story attached to them, a meaning. The past is a comforting place. A safe one. It is the present — school in particular — that I find most problematic, though I've never told my mum that. I always say everything is fine, that I've had 'a lovely day at school, thank you very much'. I don't want to worry her. I want her to think that I'm happy. But the truth is that friendships, and all the things involved in making and keeping them, are a mystery to me. It feels like everyone else has received a set of instructions on how to be, what to say, how to dress, what music to like, how to navigate life, and I have somehow missed the memo.

4. Then

30 September 2017

'Happy birthday, baby.'

I feel Connor's breath on my neck as I lie curled up against his chest. It's still dark outside though I can hear the faint throb of Sunday-morning traffic on Queenstown Road.

'That was a very lovely birthday surprise,' I say, recalling the heat of Connor's body as we made love earlier, his fingers exploring every little part of me. I've never had this kind of physical chemistry with a man before. There was Tony, back at university, who I'd been quite serious about before he decided he wanted to go travelling in Australia to 'find his purpose'. After that I had a few short-lived relationships and a succession of disastrous dates but I wasn't all that bothered as I had a job I loved and a great flatmate in Lottie. I knew that one day I would find the person I was meant to be with but I could never have imagined it would feel like this. It's like some strange and powerful drug.

'What? Lovelier than Lottie's surprise?' he says, gesturing to the silver-and-pink helium balloon floating, ghostlike, at the end of the bed. It had arrived in a box delivered by courier last night while Connor and I were having dinner. A card was attached to the string of the balloon. Inside, Lottie had written: *Happy Birthday, you old fart! Now hurry up and come home. Love you, Lottie xx*

It was typical Lottie, masking her true feelings with humour. Yet it's true I've been spending more and more time at Connor's place these past couple of months. Most of my clothes are here, hanging in his large wardrobe, and I've got duplicate sets of toiletries and make-up in the bathroom. I'm still paying rent on the flat I share with Lottie and I make sure I spend at least three nights a week over in Fulham but when I'm away from Connor it feels like I'm missing a limb. It's a strange feeling, one I've never experienced before.

When we met for brunch that day in Battersea Park, the morning after the Royal Court play, I knew that something incredible was happening. I'd ordered my staple fare of toast with jam and orange juice, and he'd smiled and said that when he was a little boy his mum would make him toast with strawberry jam if he was feeling ill. 'Sugar lifts the spirits,' he said, taking a piece of my toast and feeding it to me, almost without thinking. After brunch we went to the little petting zoo in the park and spent the afternoon watching the otters playing. When I tried to tell Lottie about it later that day, it had sounded trite and uneventful. That's the problem with love: it makes no sense to anyone but the two people in it.

Beside me, Connor has fallen back to sleep. I gently ease myself out of his arms and get out of bed. It's a cold morning. I take Connor's fleece dressing gown from the hook on the back of the door and wrap it round me, then head down the passageway to the narrow galley kitchen. The kitchen has a little door that leads out to a small but beautiful roof terrace. I unlock the door and let in a blast of morning air as I fill the kettle. While I wait for it to boil I go outside and sit on the bench, looking out across the rooftops of Queenstown Road and Lavender Hill.

The sun begins to creep above the skyline and as I watch the sky turn from deep violet to pinky blue my thoughts turn, as they always do on my birthday, to my mother.

'Thirty-two, eh, Mum?' I whisper into the air, hoping it will carry the message to wherever she is. 'Who would have thought it?'

The kettle clicks and I get up and head back into the kitchen, thinking how complete this day would be if Mum were here to share it. If she could see me, her little nervous, shy Vanessa, happy, with a great job, good friends and a man she loves. How perfect would that be?

I close the door, shutting out the memories of my mother, for it does me no good to dwell on them, only makes me ache for her. I make two big mugs of coffee and take them to the bedroom. When I place Connor's mug on the bedside table he opens his eyes and smiles.

'You shouldn't be making the coffee, not on your birthday,' he says, pulling me down on top of him. 'That should be my job. You'll have to let me do something for you.'

'I can think of one thing,' I say, kissing him gently on the cheek and feeling him harden beneath me.

He sits up, takes my face between his hands and kisses me deeply. Almost three months in, it still feels like the first time when he kisses me.

Afterwards we lie in each other's arms, warm, content, neither of us wanting to get up and break the spell.

'I wish you could stay here today,' he says, stroking my hair with his fingers.

'I know,' I sigh, nuzzling the soft fuzz of his chest hair, inhaling his musky scent. 'But the birthday lunch with Georgie and Lottie is a bit of a tradition. They like to make a fuss.'

Connor is quiet but I can feel his chest rising and falling. Every part of me wants to stay in bed with him, to chat, have a lazy brunch, make love, watch a film. Time seems to go so fast when we're together. Morning comes too soon.

'I think Lottie's getting a bit pissed off that I'm not spending much time at the flat,' I say, recalling her curt comment of, 'Oh, hello. I thought you were a burglar,' when she walked into the kitchen and saw me having breakfast last week. She's been making comments like that almost every time I've seen her recently.

'That's rather childish of her,' says Connor, stroking my hair. 'Don't feel bad. You're allowed to have other people in your life besides Lottie, you know.'

'I know. Anyway, thankfully, it's only lunch,' I say, sitting up. 'It'll be three, four hours max.'

'Don't worry, baby,' he says, leaning back and watching me as I get out of bed and take the dressing gown from the floor where I dropped it earlier. 'Of course they want to see you. It's your birthday. It would be selfish of me to want you all to myself. Anyway, it'll give me a few hours to get everything ready.'

'Hmm, that sounds intriguing,' I say, pausing at the door to look at him, to drink him in.

'I love you, Vanessa Adams,' he says, his face serious for a moment. 'You know that, don't you?'

I nod my head and smile. I do know that. I can feel it in my bones.

'Make a wish!'

I close my eyes but as I prepare to blow out the candles I realize that this year, for the first time, I have what I've always wanted. So I make a wish for the happiness I feel to last for ever.

'Hurrah!'

I open my eyes and see Georgie and Lottie, their faces beaming.

'Happy birthday, darling,' says Georgie, wrapping her arms around me. 'I hope this is a wonderful year for you.'

'Thanks, Georgie,' I say, smiling as I open the card she has given me. It's a picture of a little girl sitting in front of a mirror, lipstick smeared over her face.

'Oh, and Dad and Lynda send all their best,' she says, a hint of hesitation in her voice. 'They're at the cottage this weekend but Dad said he'll call you when they get back.'

'Hmm,' I say, shrugging my shoulders. 'In other words, when Lynda gives him permission.'

I think about my dad. He had always been a distant figure even when Mum was alive but now he's a stranger to me. When he and Lynda got together she made it clear that she should be his priority and though he made half-hearted attempts to be a dad it was Georgie who stepped in and looked after me when Mum died. Once I left for university he took early retirement and bought the holiday home in France with Lynda. On the rare occasions when we do meet up the atmosphere is awkward and the conversation stilted. Over time Dad has slowly retreated from my life. It's sad but I can't mourn for a relationship that never was.

'Oh well,' says Georgie, taking a sharp knife from the wooden block and handing it to me. 'It's their loss. I just can't believe my baby sister is thirty-two. That makes me feel so old.'

'Don't be silly, Georgie,' says Lottie, taking a photo on her phone of me slicing the cake. 'You look amazing for your age. Like Nigella Lawson.'

'Ha, thanks, Lottie, but Nigella's a lot older than me,' says Georgie, handing us all a plate. 'Still, she looks great and I doubt she's plagued with crow's feet like I am. Right, coffee time.'

'If I look as good as you when I'm your age I'll be a happy girl,' says Lottie, laughing as Georgie heads back into the kitchen. 'So, Vanessa, what did Connor get you?'

'He's giving it to me tonight,' I say, taking a bite of the cake that Georgie must have spent most of yesterday baking. It's the same recipe Mum used for all our birthdays. Strawberry milkshake cake, she called it, made with a spoonful of milkshake powder and lots of pink icing. Funny how Georgie still feels she has to do this for me, even though I'm thirty-two now and she's got two grown-up kids of her own. But then traditions, particularly when you lose a parent so young, are hard to give up.

'Well, Roger and Herbert and I are missing you at the flat,' says Lottie, picking at a piece of strawberry icing. Roger and Herbert are the nicknames we made for two potted spider plants that live in our bathroom. 'It would be nice to see you some time.'

She says it playfully but I know she's feeling sidelined. I wish I could split myself in two.

'So, when am I going to meet this new man of yours?' says Georgie, bringing in a tray laden with mugs, sugar, milk and her favourite antique pewter coffee pot. 'Lottie was telling me about him before you got here. He sounds interesting, and very good-looking by all accounts.'

I'm intrigued to know what Lottie told Georgie about Connor. On the few occasions they've met since that night at the Royal Court, the conversation has been rather stilted between them, which is a shame as I really want them to get on. Still, I suppose that's just wishful thinking on my part.

'He's wonderful, Georgie,' I say, indulging in the kind of straight, honest speaking that only a big sister can bring out. 'We get along really well. He loves art and theatre and I can talk to him about anything . . .'

'Art and theatre, my arse,' says Lottie. 'What she means is the sex is great.'

I shake my head at Lottie. I know she's convinced that it's all just a physical thing with me and Connor but she's wrong. It's more than that, much more.

'Well, you certainly look good on it, whatever it is,' says Georgie, pouring the coffee. 'You look really well, better than I've seen you look for a long time.'

'That'll be the sex, eh?' says Lottie, winking at me.

'Sex?' says Georgie, smiling ruefully. 'Can someone remind me what that is?'

We laugh but I detect a hint of sadness in Georgie's voice. She's still young though she had to grow up fast when Mum died. I think the pain of losing her made Georgie determined to have a family of her own as soon as she could. I remember how shocked I was when she got pregnant a year after Mum's death, yet having Imogen didn't stand in the way of her career – if anything, becoming a mother made her even more ambitious. When Harry came along two years later her family was complete and she and Jack became a force to be reckoned with in their respective fields. Now, however, she looks rather lost, as though Imogen and Harry leaving home has diminished her somehow.

'But all joking aside, darling,' she says, placing her hand on mine, 'I'm delighted for you. If anyone deserves a happy ever after, it's my Nessa.'

It's almost six o'clock by the time I get back to Connor's flat. As I walk up the stairs I hear the faint sound of music and breathe in the smell of spiced roast chicken, my favourite.

'Is that you, baby?' Connor calls from the kitchen.

'Yes, home at last,' I reply, then check myself. Home? When did that happen?

'Come outside,' Connor says as I take off my coat and hang it on the hook in the living room.

I walk through the kitchen and out on to the roof terrace where I'm greeted with a sight so lovely it brings tears to my eyes.

There are candles on every surface, fairy lights threaded round the railings, soft cushions scattered on the ground and, on the table, a feast fit for a queen: a whole roast chicken with blackened crispy skin, just as I like it, bowls of couscous with pomegranate seeds scattered over it like tiny jewels, platters of roasted vegetables and flatbreads, hummus and salads. The little South London terrace has been transformed into a Moroccan souk.

'Oh, Connor, it's magical,' I say, kissing his cheek, inhaling his peppery scent. 'What a lovely surprise.'

'Well, we were talking about going to Marrakesh next year,' he says, handing me a glass of Laurent-Perrier rosé champagne, another favourite. 'So I thought I'd give us a little taster. Happy birthday, baby.'

He kisses me and his mouth tastes of champagne. As we draw apart I recognize the song that's playing.

'God, I haven't heard this for years,' I say, sitting down on the cushions. 'It was Mum's favourite.'

'I know. I remember you saying so I dug the album out on Spotify,' he says, taking a knife and carving the chicken into thin slices.

I take a sip of champagne and listen as Massive Attack's 'Unfinished Sympathy' rings out into the crisp autumn air, remembering how Mum used to play it over and over in the car on the way to school. I pause the memory as the song fades and I take Connor's hand. I want to be in the moment now; want to allow myself to be happy.

'Oh, before we eat,' says Connor, getting up from the cushions and heading inside, 'I've got a little something for you.'

He disappears indoors. I feel my phone vibrate in my pocket. Taking it out, I see two texts from Lottie. The first, sent while I was on my way home, reads:

Nice to see you today. I'd forgotten what you looked like.
Hope you have a good evening.

The second, which she has just sent, is more terse:

> Sorry to be a pain but could you transfer your share of the
> gas bill ASAP. It needs paying this week.

She knows I always pay my share on time, making sure it goes into her account on the same day each month. But then I realize, this isn't about the gas bill, it's about Connor. She doesn't like the fact that I'm spending so much time with someone other than her.

'Everything okay?'

I look up and see Connor standing in the light of the kitchen doorway. He has his hands behind his back and his eyes are twinkling in the moonlight.

'Yes,' I say, sliding my phone into my pocket as he comes to join me. 'Everything is fine.'

'Right, I want you to close your eyes and hold out your hands,' he says playfully.

I do as he asks and he places a small parcel into my palm.

'Happy birthday, baby,' he says.

I open my eyes and my stomach does a little lurch. It's a box, beautifully wrapped in rose-gold paper; a ring-sized box.

'Connor, I . . .' I say, my hands trembling.

'Open it,' he says, sitting down next to me.

I carefully peel away the paper and take out a blue velvet box. *Surely, it can't be*, I think to myself. It's too soon. But as I lift the lid I see, not an engagement ring, but a pair of square sapphire earrings.

'Your birthstone,' says Connor, taking the box from my hands. 'And art deco, according to the woman in the shop.'

He laughs in that nervous way people do when they're unsure if they've got the gift right, then hands the earrings to me.

'They're just a little token to say how much I love you and how happy you've made me these last few months.'

'They're beautiful,' I say, putting them on. 'What do you think?'

I push my hair out of the way and turn my head this way and that.

'They suit you,' he says, kissing me lightly on the neck. 'I'm glad you like them. Now, let's eat.'

Three hours and two bottles of champagne later, we're still out on the terrace. Connor has located a couple of herringbone-patterned wool blankets and we sit huddled up together on the bench, looking up at the night sky.

'Thank you for this evening,' I whisper. 'It's been a wonderful birthday. One of the best I've had for a long time.'

'You're welcome,' he says, nuzzling my hair with his mouth. 'I love being with you, Vanessa. I just wish that . . . No, it doesn't matter.'

'No, go on,' I say, pulling him closer. 'What were you going to say?'

'I just wish we could always be like this,' he says, stroking my arm lightly. 'I hate it when you have to go back to Fulham. Waking up without you, it's horrible. I know it's crazy, because we've only been together for a few months, but you're the person I want to be with, Vanessa. I know that. What I'm saying is, how about we just go for it? How about you move in here properly?'

He sits up straight and looks at me. Everything about the evening feels right: the air, the food, the music, the champagne and the warm fug it has enveloped me in.

'I want that too,' I say, and his expression relaxes into a broad smile. 'I want to be with you all the time. God, sometimes I'm even jealous of your colleagues because they get to see you more than I do. Waking up next to you each morning would be heaven.'

'You mean it?'

'Yes, I mean it,' I say, reaching out for my glass to drain the last of the champagne. 'I love you, Connor. And you're mine. You're all mine.'

5. Now

West Hampstead Police Station

'It isn't me.'

I hadn't meant to speak but Bains was goading me, pushing me to admit that I was there, that I had something to do with Geoffrey's death. In the end, the words just spilled from me without my consent.

'Honestly,' I say, trying to keep my voice steady, though my legs are trembling. 'That person on the CCTV. It isn't me. Like you said earlier, that woman's name is Iris Lawson.'

'No, Vanessa,' says Bains, his eyes widening as though he can't quite believe how crazy I am. 'That is what you told our friend Mr Carter-Vaughan your name was.'

I shake my head.

'It wasn't me,' I say, as beside me Frank Solomon clears his throat. 'It's just . . . just someone who looks like me.'

'A doppelgänger?' says Bains, leaning back in his chair. 'That's an interesting theory. Straight out of a fairy story. But then, you're rather fond of stories, aren't you, Vanessa?'

He stares directly at me, his lips pursed. I shiver under his gaze then look away.

'You particularly like inventing characters, don't you?' he says, his voice hardening. 'So much so it would seem like you missed your vocation. You could have been another Geoffrey Rivers. A bestselling novelist.'

'I don't know what you're talking about,' I say as Bains riffles through a bundle of papers. 'I swear to you that the person on the CCTV is not me. I'm not Iris Lawson. I have no idea what any of this is about.'

'I could believe that, Vanessa,' says Bains, straightening out a piece of paper on the desk in front of him, 'if only I hadn't had statements from at least a dozen estate agents up and down the country with CCTV footage of you doing this same thing over the last six months. Now, do any of these people ring a bell?'

My body goes cold as he recites the list of names.

'Tabitha Richardson; Elsie Summers-Allan; Eleanor Hawkins; Monica Holmes; Imogen Hartley.'

The names make me cringe. How does he know?

'I can see by your reaction that you're familiar with them,' says Bains.

He stops reading and places the piece of paper to one side.

'We've all done it, Vanessa,' he says, leaning forward, his voice softer now. 'Looked at something we have no intention or means of buying. I mean, I spend my Lotto win in my head every Saturday night before the draw. A place in the Bahamas, new car, that kind of thing. My missus used to like viewing those new-build show houses, back when they were a "thing". We used to go and have a look at them, imagine ourselves living there with all the snazzy furnishings.'

I don't know where he's going with this but I try to keep my face still.

'What I'm saying is that we all do it,' he says, shrugging his shoulders. 'We all dream, imagine other lives for ourselves. Only, you went one step further, Vanessa. You actually created different personas for yourself – posh Tabitha Richardson, tree-hugging Eleanor Hawkins. You admit that, don't you?'

I glance at Frank Solomon.

'You don't have to answer,' he says, shaking his head.

I turn back to Bains. He has another set of notes in front of him now.

'Estate agents are used to this,' he says, flicking through the notes with his index finger. 'I mean, they're wise to the time wasters, aren't they? The people who just want to have a nose around a posh house with no intention of buying it. That must be really annoying for those estate agents. Most of them are on commission, aren't they, poor sods?'

I don't respond but as he speaks I feel a creeping dread rise up my spine.

'It was a Mrs Ros Coverley from the Whitstable branch of Harrison and Uttley Properties who put the warning out,' says Bains, his deadpan voice cutting through my thoughts.

At the mention of that name I'm taken back to the disastrous viewing of an eco house in Whitstable, Ros Coverley watching me like a hawk as I walked from room to room.

'Mrs Coverley noticed, right at the beginning of the viewing, when you opened your purse to put away the business card she'd given you, that the name on your credit card was not the name you had given her: Eleanor Hawkins.'

I flinch as I recall that viewing. Ros Coverley's eyes watching me.

'After you left that day, Mrs Coverley did a cursory search of your name and found that you were not a wealthy financier but a marketing manager for a cosmetics company. Yet when she contacted the company – Luna London – to ask about you, they said that you no longer worked for them.'

My cheeks burn as he continues.

'She'd heard, from colleagues in other offices, of a woman doing the same thing – wasting their time, using fake names – so she put an email out to them, flagging you up and telling them to be aware. One of the agents, Jane Treadwell, recalled a viewing she'd conducted a few months earlier with someone who matched your description. She was shocked because the woman she had met had seemed – how did she put it? – "so convincing".'

I feel sick with shame.

'Of course, there's no crime in doing what you did, Vanessa. But the amount of planning and subterfuge involved is quite something. And we can now safely say that it was you who visited the offices of Price Burrows Estate Agents on the 11th of August using the name Iris Lawson, can't we?'

There's no crime in doing what you did. His words roll around my head. There's no crime. He just wants to ask me some questions, rule me out.

He takes my silence for affirmation.

'So now that's clear,' he says, putting his hands to his temples, 'how about you tell me what happened that afternoon at Holly Maze House?'

'I didn't go to the house.'

The lie drops easily from my lips, though somewhere inside me a voice is screaming: *What are you doing, Vanessa? This is going to make it so much worse.*

But then I haven't been able to do what's best for me for a long time now.

'I'm sorry, could you speak up?' says Bains, pushing the Dictaphone into the centre of the table. 'I didn't quite catch that.'

Come on, Vanessa, urges the voice inside me, *just tell him the truth. Don't dig yourself in deeper.* But I can't do it. I can't admit that I was in that house.

'I said, I didn't go to Holly Maze House in the end,' I say, staring down at my clasped hands. 'I . . . I was on my way out of the office when I remembered I'd arranged to meet my sister for lunch and –'

'Hang on, I'm confused,' says Bains, putting his head in his hands. 'You leave your sister's house in Wimbledon first thing Saturday morning to travel to Hampstead to insist on booking an appointment to view a house you are in no position to buy. Then, once you've booked it, you suddenly remember you have to meet your sister for lunch?'

I feel bad for lying and even worse for bringing Georgie into all of this.

'Yes,' I say, trying to sound composed. 'She . . . she works in Mayfair. We'd arranged the lunch date the night before but in all the excitement of – I mean . . . after seeing Holly Maze House was up for sale I just got carried away and it slipped my mind.'

'Miss Adams, you can see why your behaviour may be confusing to others, surely?' says Bains. 'Like I said earlier, we all have our moments of escapism – spending lottery

48

wins in our head, pretending we're Elton John when we get on the karaoke down the pub, that sort of thing – but the way you have gone about creating whole new personas for yourself, duping estate agents and travelling up and down the country to view multi-million-pound properties you cannot possibly afford has been calculated and, may I say, somewhat disturbing. Not just that, but you'd become more than a menace to a lot of hardworking estate agents.'

'It's not like that,' I say, my voice cracking. 'It was just harmless curiosity, that's all.'

'Harmless curiosity?' says Bains, nodding his head. 'You see, Vanessa, I don't think this is just harmless curiosity, as you put it. I think you visit these houses to torture yourself with what you can't have.'

I shake my head. I don't know what he's getting at but his voice is growing loud and menacing.

'And what happens when you can't have something, Vanessa, hmm?' he continues, spittle gathering at the corner of his mouth. 'You get angry, don't you?'

'I don't know what you mean,' I say, my voice dry and reedy.

'Well, let me make it a bit clearer,' he says.

He reaches across and opens the cardboard folder, licking his finger as he flicks through the pages.

'It seems, Vanessa,' he says, laying the folder flat in front of him, 'that you've had a rather eventful few months.'

'I have no idea what you're talking about,' I say.

'You left your job at Luna London after increasingly erratic behaviour,' says Bains, looking down at a sheet of paper. 'Spiralled into depression. Couldn't pay your rent. And then there are these violent altercations.'

'What? Who has told you all this?' I say, panic rising in my voice.

'The truth is you're not satisfied with what you've got,' says Bains. 'You think you deserve better, is that right?'

'No, that couldn't be further from the truth,' I say, trying desperately to see what is written on that piece of paper.

'I think it's a lot closer to the truth than you will admit,' says Bains, a sick smirk spreading across his face. 'That's what all this is about – the fake names, the fantasy world, the inability to stick at a job – it's because you feel superior to others, don't you? So superior you think you can fool everyone with your lies. In fact, I've been told that you have admitted to people that you enjoy creating different characters to suit different situations.'

I flinch as I recall saying that to Connor when we first met. But I had been talking about work, about using make-up for different occasions, not actually becoming different people.

'Look, I know what this is about,' I say, my chest burning with anger. 'You've been talking to my ex-boyfriend. He has an axe to grind because I ended the relationship. He wants to get back at me and he's made all this nonsense up to frame me. This is bullshit.' I spit the last word out.

Bains's mouth turns down. I've walked right into his trap, losing it like that. I need to calm down.

'Geoffrey Rivers had what you didn't,' he says, his voice laced with contempt. 'Financial security, a big house, a successful career. All the things you've observed in your little trips across the country, viewing spectacular properties, seeing how perfect life can be. But on those trips you had an estate agent with you so your anger had to be curbed. No matter how furious you were that the Georgian pile in Surrey or the eco mansion with the sea view could never be yours, that anger had to be held in, didn't it? Yet that afternoon at Holly Maze House something changed. You'd had enough. You couldn't deal with being inadequate any more. So, when you met Mr Rivers, you – what, threatened him? Got into an argument? What happened, Vanessa?'

As he speaks I'm back there in the house. Geoffrey is telling me something then stops mid-sentence. 'I'm awfully sorry but will you excuse me?' I remember watching him as he walked out of the room. And then . . . My skin prickles at the memory but I can't let Bains see that I'm cracking.

'I want to know what it was about Geoffrey, about that house, that sent you over the edge,' he says, leaning forward in his chair. 'There's more to this than you're letting on, Vanessa. This is more than just jealousy, isn't it? What was it that made you snap?'

'This is crazy,' I say, trying to keep my voice calm. 'You're actually saying I had something to do with Geoffrey Rivers's murder?'

'I'm saying that you have a temper, Vanessa,' says Bains, tapping his fingers on the table. 'When things don't go your way you lash out. That's what happened to Jackie Dawkins, isn't it?'

At the mention of Connor's mother my legs buckle. If he's told them what I did to her then it's all over for me. I'm finished.

I get out of bed and make my way across the landing. I can hear you singing along to the radio in the kitchen. Radio 2. Terry Wogan's breakfast show. You're singing along to a song. It's an old song. One that Terry Wogan must really like because he's always playing it: 'January, February' by Barbara Dickson. You seem to like it too because I hear you turn the radio up so the song fills the house. I stand holding the banister, glowing with contentment. It's the first day of the summer holidays. There's no school to worry about, no cross-country runs, no wandering round the edge of the playground wishing I was somewhere else. I don't have to worry about any of that because I am at home with you.

I go downstairs and as I walk into the kitchen you look up at me and smile. Your teeth are sparkly white and you have a gap between the front two that you have always been self-conscious about though I think it makes you look pretty.

'Morning, my darling,' you say, your green eyes twinkling. 'Fancy some breakfast?'

I nod my head, a deep feeling of contentment filling my bones. There is nowhere else I would rather be than here with you.

6. Then

2 October 2017

I've only just arrived back at the flat when I hear the key in the lock. Work has been tough today – a backlog of emails to deal with, a disgruntled Damian who needed to be placated when I presented him with my monthly budget forecast, three of my team of five off sick – but I know, as I hear Lottie's footsteps coming up the stairs, that the toughest part of the day is yet to come.

'Hello, stranger,' she says, bounding towards me with her arms outstretched. 'Oh, it's so good to see you. I was steeling myself for a night alone with Netflix and a take-away. Speaking of which, do you fancy Chinese?'

I nod politely as she dumps her bag and coat then goes into the bathroom to change her clothes. I feel wretched as I hear her take a shower, perform her nightly just-home-from-work ritual. Lottie and I have lived together for years. Boyfriends have come and gone; we've sat up through the night with each other when one of us has been ill or heartbroken or both. We've made this rather poky little flat into the closest thing either of us have had to a home. And now I have to tell her that I'm moving out, drawing a line under this period of our lives, and I feel sick with dread.

'Shall I Deliveroo then?' she says, returning to the living room with wet hair, loose-fitting yoga pants and her favourite, now badly faded, Nirvana T-shirt. 'You definitely want Chinese?'

'Yes, that would be great,' I say, trying my best to sound upbeat.

I watch as she opens the app. She looks so happy. I feel like the worst person in the world having to do this.

'I'll fix us some wine while you order,' I say, getting up and heading to the kitchen, guilt twisting inside me.

How can I do this to her after everything she has done for me? I remember how she brought me out of my shell that first, terrifying freshers' week at Durham University when I thought I was going to end up spending the whole term locked in my room. I can still see her bright smile and mass of red, corkscrew curls as she bounded over to me in the corridor of our shared dorm.

'Hi, I'm Lottie, fancy a cup of tea?'

Ten minutes later we were happily ensconced on beanbags in her room, sipping Yorkshire Tea, nibbling chocolate Hobnobs and telling each other our life stories.

Lottie had been brought up in Edinburgh with her mum, a human rights lawyer. Her dad had died when she was nine and, though she hadn't been as close to him as I had been to Mum, she understood, more than anyone, the loss I had experienced. Not that she was one to dwell on sadness. No, Lottie was the perfect antidote to my natural shyness and introspection. If she sensed I was having a low day she would spring into action; organize a day of shopping in nearby Newcastle or a trip to the coast in her battered little car. And though I would usually be reticent at first, I always felt better afterwards. Whatever dark clouds had been gathering were blown away by Lottie's positivity and exuberance.

'Men come and go but your friends are a constant.' I remember Georgie telling me that when I was drowning in misery at the end of my first year at Durham. I had just come out of a rather intense six-month relationship with Tony, a man I thought was my soulmate but who had decided to relocate to Australia. The temptation to spend the whole of that summer wallowing in self-pity was overwhelming until Lottie stepped in and suggested a trip away. We ended up having the time of our lives working in a vineyard in the South of France, where we were paid in sumptuous meals and gallons of wine to crush grapes and stick labels on bottles. It was fun and exhausting and we spent so much time laughing that by the end of the summer my broken heart was healed. Georgie had been right.

I owe Lottie so much, and now here I am about to put a man ahead of our friendship. What kind of person am I? But then I think of Connor and how happy he makes me feel.

Come on, Vanessa, I say to myself, pouring two glasses of wine. *Be strong. Life can't stay the same for ever. It's not a crime to fall in love and want to be with that person.*

I take the wine into the living room where Lottie is curled up on the sofa with her feet tucked underneath her. She looks up from her phone as I walk in.

'I ordered Szechuan prawns and egg-fried rice for you. Your usual. It's going to be about fifteen minutes.'

'Great. Thanks, Lottie,' I say, handing her the glass.

I sit down on the ancient, squishy armchair opposite her, take a sip of wine and steel myself.

'Listen, Lottie,' I say, putting the glass down on the table. 'There's something I need to talk to you about.'

She looks up at me, her eyes widening.

'What is it, Ness?' she asks, leaning forward, her hands clasped. 'Is it Connor? You two haven't been arguing, have you?'

'No, it's not that,' I say, my heart thudding in my chest. 'The opposite, in fact. Like I said, I've never felt this way before. We . . . we love each other and . . . we were talking and we both feel like we want to be together all the time.'

'You already are together all the time,' says Lottie, with a snort. 'I've barely seen you these last few months. Sometimes I've come home to the empty flat after a particularly bad day and it's been tough not having you to chat to.'

I nod. Lottie's job as case manager for a charity dealing with displaced refugee children is emotionally as well as mentally demanding. It's a wonder she can stay so upbeat with the amount of tragedy she has to absorb week in week out. I feel even worse now, imagining Lottie sitting alone in the flat with no one to talk to.

'That's why I'm so looking forward to Christmas,' she says, taking a sip of wine. 'I know it's a couple of months away but you know how I like to plan. It'll be heaven to just switch off for the holidays and be with my best friend, watching *Love Actually* and stuffing our faces. That reminds me, we'll have to order the turkey well in advance. Remember how quickly they sold out last year. Will Georgie still be doing her Boxing Day lunch, do you think?'

'Lottie, what I'm trying to tell you is –' I begin, my stomach twisting. I'd forgotten about Christmas and how Lottie starts planning it as soon as the clocks go back. Now I feel even worse. 'Well, it's just that, like I said, Connor and I were talking and we feel like we're ready to take the next step.'

Lottie looks at me, her smile fading.

'Which is why ... which is why I'm going to have to give my notice on the flat,' I say, forcing the words out. 'I'm so sorry to have to do this, and I will stay until you find a new flatmate. I'll help you find one. There's a lovely woman called Claire who's just started at Luna. She's moved down from Newcastle and is really sweet and –'

'Hold on,' says Lottie, visibly shaken. 'Can you slow down, please. Have I got this right? You're telling me you're moving out?'

'Yes,' I say, my cheeks burning, as always happens in stressful situations. 'I ... I love him, Lottie. I want to be with him.'

'This all feels really rushed,' she says. 'I mean, we've only just renewed our lease. You could have said then that you were planning this.'

'That was six months ago, Lottie,' I say. 'I hadn't even met Connor at that point.'

'But you hardly know him,' says Lottie, raising her voice. 'Like you said, you only met him a few months ago.'

'It feels right,' I say, trying to keep my voice calm. 'I can't explain ... it's just, well, I love him and I want to be with him.'

'You see him all the time,' she says, her eyes blazing. 'Why do something as extreme as move in with him?'

'Lottie, I thought you'd understand. I thought you'd be happy for me,' I say, feeling increasingly on edge. 'I don't know why you're being like this. It's not like I'm ending our friendship or anything.'

'It just feels wrong that we've lived together for years and you're abandoning me for someone you've known for five minutes,' she says, shaking her head.

'It's not like that,' I say with a sigh. 'Things are serious with Connor and we want to build a life together. I'm thirty-two years old, for God's sake. I can't put my life on hold so I can carry on having girlie sleepovers with you. We're not students any more, Lottie.'

'I'm aware of that, thanks, Vanessa,' she says, her voice hardening. 'I think my fifty-hour working week and pension scheme will attest to that, you patronizing cow.'

'Oh great, we're resorting to cheap insults,' I say, getting to my feet. 'It's crazy that you're making me feel guilty for wanting to move on.'

'Move on?' she says, shaking her head. 'With some dickhead you've only just met.'

'Dickhead?' I cry, my voice cracking with upset. 'How dare you? Who the hell do you think you are? Just because you can't find anyone to put up with your childish crap, you want to make sure no one else finds happiness either.'

I know by the darkened expression on Lottie's face that I've crossed a line.

'Childish crap?' she cries, jumping up so forcefully her phone clatters to the floor. 'Do you know something, Vanessa? There have been times over the years when I have been dog tired after a gruelling week at work, dealing with kids who've seen their parents die in front of them, and I've come home to find you sobbing about some bloke, or something Georgie has said or done that you didn't like, or the fact it's your mum's birthday, and I have sat and listened and poured wine and been there for you. How's that for childish crap? And I've done that because I was brought up to never let friends down.'

'Oh, Lottie, don't be so dramatic,' I cry as she rushes into her bedroom and returns wearing her heavy wool coat. 'You know how much I value our friendship and I always will, it's just that Connor and I –'

'Come first,' she snaps as she hurries down the stairs. 'I get that. Though it'll be a different story when you're crying your eyes out over him in a couple of weeks. Anyway, forget it. It doesn't matter. I'm going out.'

'You can't go out, you've got wet hair. You'll freeze,' I say, following her down the stairs, but as we reach the door the bell rings and, with a heavy heart, I remember the takeaway.

Lottie opens the door to a skinny, bearded Deliveroo cyclist holding a bag of delicious-smelling Chinese food.

'Lottie, wait,' I say as she squeezes past the man. 'At least let's eat and talk about this.'

'Forget it,' she says, turning back to me with a wounded expression. 'Why don't you take it to Connor's? In fact, why don't you just move in with him tonight? And I don't need your help finding anyone to live here either. I can look after myself.'

7. Now

Bains turns the page of his notes, centres them, then looks up at me with an unblinking stare.

'So, would you like to tell me about Jackie Dawkins?'

Memories of that evening blindside me. Connor's mother screaming. I just wanted it to stop. I look at Frank Solomon, beside me. He shakes his head.

'Okay,' says Bains. 'Maybe I can fill you in.'

He looks down at his notes and starts to read.

'The attack on Mrs Dawkins came right in the middle of your viewing spree, didn't it?'

He looks up at me, waiting for a response. I won't give him the satisfaction. Instead, I look at my hands. My nail polish is chipped and has left a red crescent moon on my thumbnail. I stare at it as Bains continues.

'You were still viewing houses you couldn't afford,' he says, his flat, northern vowels digging into my skull. 'You were angry, full of frustration. I'm right, aren't I?'

I scratch at the red crescent moon until it starts to disappear, leaving a pink stain on the nail. I don't want to hear what Bains is about to say. I want to block him out, but I can't.

'You walked in that day and found Jackie Dawkins at the flat. She was there to comfort her son, your ex-partner, Connor, because he was at the end of his tether.'

I dig my nails into my palms, willing myself not to respond, not to lose my temper.

'He'd had weeks of erratic behaviour from you,' continues Bains, slamming his hand down on the desk. 'Going AWOL, drinking heavily, causing arguments, losing your temper. He was trapped in a toxic, abusive relationship and he had no one to turn to but his mother. But Jackie wasn't scared of you. She confronted you about your behaviour. Asked you why you were treating her son so badly, and you, Vanessa, you snapped, didn't you?'

I shake my head.

'You didn't like being told a few home truths,' he says. 'Particularly from a woman so close to Connor. Because Connor was your property, wasn't he? You wanted him all to yourself, didn't you? That's what you used to tell him, "You're mine." And here was Jackie Dawkins getting in the way of that. You didn't like that, did you?'

'He's twisting my words,' I say, unable to hold back any longer. 'He's doing this on purpose. To get me back for ending the relationship.'

'Oh, you ended the relationship?' says Bains, a sly smirk creeping across his face. 'Well, that was very decent of you. Not many men would stand by their girlfriend after she attacked their mother.'

'I didn't attack her,' I say, trying to keep my voice steady. 'She was . . . she . . .'

It's no use. I can't do it. I can't tell Bains the truth.

'You were angry at Jackie for interfering,' he says, his eyes narrowing. 'And you launched a disgusting attack on her, a defenceless, middle-aged woman, which resulted in an injury to her face.'

'That is not true,' I cry. 'It wasn't like that. Connor is lying. He's twisting it.'

'Did you or did you not hit Jackie Dawkins, causing a bleed to her face?' says Bains, leaning forward so far that I can smell the stale coffee on his breath. 'Tell me.'

I nod my head.

'Right,' he says. 'You attacked your boyfriend's mother because you didn't like what she was saying. Did you also lose your rag when Geoffrey Rivers said something you didn't like? Maybe he sussed you out like Ros Coverley did. Maybe he was about to report you and you got angry and –'

'DS Bains, my client does not have to answer this line of questioning.'

The sound of Frank Solomon's voice makes me start.

'She is here voluntarily,' he continues. 'And regarding the case of Mrs Dawkins, I understand the assault was not reported to the police. I can't see how an unreported and therefore alleged domestic matter can have anything to do with the Rivers case.'

'Unreported, yes,' replies Bains, his eyes still fixed on me. 'But Miss Adams has just admitted to the incident, so not alleged.'

'DS Bains, you have to charge my client with an offence or let her go,' says Frank Solomon, his voice rising passionately as though he had spent the entire interview biding his time, waiting for his chance to silence this man.

I wait for Bains to reply, watch as he consults his notes. Beside me, Frank Solomon shuffles in his seat. Outside, a car door slams and the noise brings a memory hurtling back: his body hitting the ground with a thud, his blood on my hands.

'Miss Adams, I will ask you once again,' says Bains, placing the papers into a neat pile. 'What happened that afternoon at Holly Maze House?'

I look up at him but it's not Bains's face I see, it's Geoffrey's. Purple, bloated, eyes wide open. Dead.

I sit at the wood-panelled breakfast bar and watch as you take the white sliced loaf out of the wooden bread bin and put two slices into the toaster. It's a white toaster with orange flowers on the side. Rather old-fashioned for 1996 but it had belonged to Gran and you kept it because it has sentimental value. You never throw things away, do you, Mum? Dad says you're a hoarder but I think you just like holding on to things that have a story to tell. You wink at me as you go to the fridge and take out a carton of orange juice — the one with bits — and a jar of strawberry jam. Toast with jam and a glass of juice. I've been having that for breakfast since I was a toddler.

'Ooh, listen to this,' you say, putting the plate of toast down in front of me. 'He's interviewing a children's author.'

I take a bite of toast. You lean across the breakfast bar and turn the radio up then we sit and listen to a man with a soft West Country accent describing the latest book he's written.

'These stories,' he says, his voice soothing and hypnotic, 'were written for any child who has ever felt out of place. Who has ever stood on the edge of the fairground, looked at the dazzling lights and felt themselves unworthy of it all. For any child who has ever worried about not fitting in, my stories are a reminder that there are other worlds, other lives, other dimensions, beyond this one. And it is there, in those magical spaces, that you will find wonders beyond your imagination; that you will find yourself.'

'Well, that sounds right up your street,' you say, smiling. 'And what a lovely voice he's got too. Listen.'

I do listen. It is impossible not to. It's as though this man has reached inside my head, taken all fears and insecurities, and thrown them aside: 'There are other worlds, other lives.'

'Catch his name, Nessa,' you say, scrambling for a pen and paper. 'I'll pop into town later and get you that book.'

8. Then

November 2017

'The number you have called has not been recognized.'

So it's official, I think to myself as I end the call and stare out of the window at the Number 22 bus crawling along the King's Road, *Lottie and me are finished*.

I think back to the last time I saw her, the hurt in her eyes when I told her I was moving out. Hurt that quickly turned to anger. We'd had arguments before, lots of them, but we'd always made up eventually. The fact that Lottie has gone as far as changing her number means that this time is different.

The office is quiet. Rose and Gemma are still off sick and the rest of the team are out for lunch. I have a pile of emails to deal with still and an online presentation to prepare but I need to hear a friendly voice, need to feel reassured that I'm not the bad person Lottie has made me out to be.

Picking up my phone, I click on my sister's name and wait.

'Hello, darling, what're you up to?'

Hearing Georgie's voice makes me feel suddenly emotional. I swallow back the tears and try to sound as upbeat as I can.

'Hi, Georgie. I'm fine, thanks. Just wondered if you fancied meeting up for lunch tomorrow. Connor and I are going to be in Chelsea and I thought it's probably time the two of you met.'

'That would be lovely,' says Georgie. 'Jack's away on a golfing trip this weekend so I'd be glad of the company and I'm dying to meet Connor.'

'Great,' I say, typing a reminder to myself on my laptop. 'I'll book a table at Rossi's.'

'Nessa, is everything okay?' says Georgie, ever the vigilant big sister. 'You sound a bit down.'

'I'm fine,' I lie, flicking a piece of fluff from my jacket sleeve. 'Just a bit swamped at work, that's all. But I'm looking forward to seeing you tomorrow. It's been ages.'

'Me too, darling,' says Georgie. 'What time shall we say? One-ish?'

'Perfect,' I say. 'Connor's dying to meet you too.'

'Well, I shall be on my best behaviour,' she laughs. 'See you then, darling.'

'See you, Georgie,' I say.

Talking to my sister usually lifts me but for the rest of the afternoon all I can think about is Lottie. Fourteen years of friendship, gone. Just like that.

'It's sad,' says Connor over breakfast the following morning. 'But not entirely unexpected. From what I could see, Lottie was rather controlling. She wanted you all to herself. I could tell that from her body language in the Royal Court bar that night. It was like watching one of those overbearing parents, a helicopter parent. Hovering over you, telling you when it was time to leave. That's not healthy, Vanessa. Friends should let you be happy.'

'I know,' I say, spreading the last of the strawberry jam on to my toast. 'And there were times when I used to feel I had to go along with what she wanted to do even if I wasn't enjoying it. Still, to change her number like that. It feels rather extreme.'

'Yes,' says Connor, watching me as I bite into my toast. 'But that's her choice and she's made it. It happens a lot with friendships though. I don't want to sound harsh but some of them just run their course. I had a big group of friends at Bristol who I saw all the time during my three years at uni. We were inseparable. When we graduated we all went our separate ways but a few of us ended up in London. For the first year or so I would meet up with a couple of the guys, for old times' sake, but something had changed. We'd outgrown each other. It got to the point where we were all making excuses not to meet up. It's brutal but it's just the way life works out. Certain friendships only make sense at a particular time in your life and you have to let go. You and Lottie are a case in point.'

'You're right,' I say, getting up from the table and brushing off the toast crumbs from my dressing gown. 'And I have to remember that it's not a crime to move in with your boyfriend when you're thirty-two years old. Anyway, we've talked about this over and over. Let's move on: would you like a coffee?'

I turn round and see Connor plugging in the vacuum cleaner.

'Just getting rid of those toast crumbs before they build up,' he says, smiling. 'Coffee would be great, thanks.'

I go into the kitchen and open the cupboard. Connor's been working from home the last few days and it appears he's also been hard at work in here. All of the items in the cupboard have been lined up neatly. The half-empty packets of rice, bran flakes, pasta and biscuits have been decanted into plastic tubs and labelled. When I open the fridge to get the milk I see that he has done the same in there.

'Someone's been busy,' I say, handing him a cup of coffee.

'Ah, yes,' he says, looking rather sheepish. 'It's embarrassing really but I'm just a bit of a neat freak as you'll have probably gathered. And I love you to bits but you can be a little . . . messy.'

He looks like he's treading on eggshells as he says this, like he's terrified of offending me.

'Oh God, I'm sorry,' I say, sitting down on the arm of the sofa. 'I guess I've just got stuck in a rut. Lottie was pretty messy round the house and we'd just let things slide then do a big blitz on the cleaning every couple of weeks. I know that's not the best approach.'

'I'm not criticizing you,' says Connor, rubbing my hand. 'Far from it. I'd hate it if you changed. It's just I can't function if things are chaotic. I need to know where everything is and, well, mess just sets me on edge. I should loosen up, shouldn't I?'

'No,' I say, leaning forward to kiss him. 'Don't do that. I love you as you are.'

'You mean that?' he says, touching my face lightly.

'Yes,' I say. 'I do. Now, I'd better go and get ready. I want to have enough time for shopping before we meet Georgie.'

*

'Remind me what we're looking for again?'

Connor has trailed after me for almost half an hour now yet I still haven't managed to find anything.

'Well, it's nothing specific,' I say, pausing outside Cos to take a closer look at the window display. 'I've got a presentation next week. We've managed to secure a meeting with a major US manufacturer. I need to look my best but I'm not sure what I should be aiming for.'

'Can I give you some advice?' says Connor, taking my arm.

'What's that?' I say, turning to look at him.

'You're not going to find the right outfit in one of these high-street shops,' he says, guiding me away from the window. 'This is a big presentation, right?'

'Yes,' I say, nodding my head.

'And you've probably been working on it for, what, weeks? Months?'

'A few months, yep.'

'And every little detail has been perfected over those months,' he says. 'Every point has been scrutinized.'

'Yes, it's a big deal. If we secure this client it will take the company to another level.'

'Right,' he says. 'So, after all that hard work, why fall at the final hurdle by turning up in a cheap, high-street dress? You need to think about your image, what kind of message you're sending out.'

'I know,' I say, feeling rather awkward. 'But for years the high street's been my only option. My salary at Luna

London just about covers bills and rent. I can't afford expensive clothes.'

'Look at it this way,' he says, smiling warmly. 'If you add up the cost of all those cheap clothes you've bought over the years, which you probably ended up chucking in the bin because they fell apart, you could spend the same amount on a few select pieces that will last.'

'I guess,' I say, thinking back, shamefully, to the number of cheap dresses and T-shirts I've thrown away.

'It's true,' he says. 'Now, how about you let me find something for you? If you don't like what I choose then, fair enough, we'll go to Zara. Agreed?'

'Agreed,' I say, feeling relieved that the decision has been taken out of my hands.

'Great,' he says, taking my hand. 'I know just the place.'

Forty-five minutes later we are all done and sitting in Rossi's drinking Chianti and waiting for Georgie.

'I'm feeling rather nervous,' says Connor, wiping his forehead with the back of his hands. 'What if she doesn't like me?'

'Don't be silly,' I say, taking a breadstick and snapping it in two. 'Here, have this. It'll calm your stomach.'

'Sorry I'm late, darling.'

I look up and see my sister rushing towards us. Her hair is smooth and shiny, as though she's had a blow-dry, and I notice she's wearing more make-up than usual. It seems she's just as keen as Connor to make a good impression.

'Don't worry, we've only just arrived,' says Connor, getting to his feet. 'I'm Connor. It's lovely to meet you at last.'

He shakes Georgie's hand and, as he gestures to the waiter for an extra menu, Georgie gives me a wink.

'I arrived in town early and decided to pop into the gallery, which was a huge mistake as I ended up getting caught by Bill, who had a barrage of questions for me about the new exhibition,' she says, shrugging off her coat and handing it to the waiter. 'You know what he's like. Ooh, look at this lovely menu. I think I might have the bream.'

I smile to myself. Georgie is talking nineteen to the dozen as always. It takes a bit of time for new people to get used to this. Connor, however, seems unfazed.

'Exhibition?' he says, taking a sip of wine. 'What are you showing?'

'It's a retrospective of Paula Rego,' says Georgie, helping herself to a breadstick. 'We're putting it together in collaboration with the Tate.'

'Paula Rego? Wow, no way. She was the subject of my dissertation,' says Connor, his eyes widening.

'Really? How wonderful,' says Georgie. 'Well, you should come over and see it.'

'I'd love to,' says Connor, his voice brightening.

'I tell you what,' says Georgie, pausing as the waiter arrives with her wine. 'How about you come over one lunchtime when it's quiet? Bill, my curator, is something of an authority on Rego. He'll give you a private tour, so to speak.'

'Thanks,' says Connor, smiling. 'That would be amazing.'

'So, Vanessa tells me you grew up in Harrogate,' says Georgie, taking a sip of wine. 'That's a lovely part of the world. Do your folks still live up there?'

'Er, my mum does,' says Connor, brushing his hair out of his eyes. 'My dad lives in the States.'

His voice alters when he mentions his dad. It's clear the divorce is still a sore subject.

'You'll have to take Ness up to Yorkshire,' says Georgie with a laugh. 'She's a great hill walker, aren't you, Ness?'

'Very funny,' I say, rolling my eyes. It's a running joke between me and my sister that I'm not really suited to country pursuits.

'I will,' says Connor, squeezing my hand under the table. 'Though my mum has rather erratic working hours so it's tricky to nail her down for a visit. But we'll definitely do it soon.'

He squeezes my hand again and I feel a flutter through my body, like a surge of electricity.

'Ooh,' says Georgie. 'Look at all those bags. What have you been buying, Nessa?'

I tell her about the presentation and how Connor had advised me to buy a few statement pieces.

'Alleluia, thank you, Connor,' says Georgie, rolling her eyes. 'I've been trying to get this one to give up her disposable fashion habit for years. Let's see what you've got then.'

I take out the main outfit. It's a simple shift dress made of pale-blue silk. When I'd tried it on it fitted me like a second skin. The price tag made me wince but, as Connor said, it will last me for years.

'That is beautiful,' says Georgie, reaching out to touch the fabric. 'And so right for the presentation.'

I put the dress back into the bag just as the food arrives and as we sit and eat, Georgie filling in Connor on the details of the Rego exhibition, I feel a deep sense of contentment. After Georgie excuses herself to go to the bathroom my phone vibrates in my pocket. I take it out and see Georgie's name on the screen.

He's a keeper. I'm so happy for you, darling.

And in that moment I decide to stop feeling bad about Lottie. Connor is my best friend now and I'm not going to lose him.

9. Now

'DS Bains,' says Frank Solomon, clasping his hands together. 'You have to make a decision. Charge my client or let her go.'

Bains leans back in his chair, his eyes still on me, silent. He is waiting for me to snap again, to say something I will regret, but I'm not going to give him the satisfaction.

'That will be all for now, Miss Adams,' he says eventually. 'Though we may need to speak to you again should more evidence come to light. Which it will.'

I feel light-headed as I get up from the table. I can sense Bains's eyes on me as Frank Solomon guides me out of the room.

Once I have been signed out I take my phone and call Georgie.

'Hello,' she says, answering at the second ring. 'Vanessa? What's happened?'

'Can you come and get me, Georgie?' I say, trying to suppress my emotions. 'They've finished questioning me but the tube has stopped for the night.'

'I'll be right there, darling,' says Georgie. 'Stay inside the police station, okay?'

'Okay,' I say. 'See you in a bit.'

I end the call and sit down on a plastic chair. The duty officer looks over at me from behind her desk, her expression chilly.

My body feels limp with exhaustion. The effort of having to keep the truth from Bains has taken its toll. I close my eyes but all I see is Geoffrey staring back at me. Asking *Why?*

I need to get out of here, I think to myself, looking up at the posters on the walls: 'Have you been a victim of crime?' 'See it. Say it. Sorted.' I feel like I'm being watched, like Bains is hidden somewhere behind those posters, waiting to pounce.

'Nessa, darling.'

I look up. Georgie is rushing through the main doors towards me. As I see her, the tears I've been trying to hold back all evening come rushing forth. It feels like I'm four years old again and I've just spotted my mum waiting for me in the playground after my first day at school.

'I'm sorry,' I say as she wraps her arms around me. 'I – I'm so sorry.'

'Come on,' she says, gently guiding me towards the doors. 'Let's get you home.'

Georgie is silent as we cross the dimly lit car park. I feel a prickle of unease as I look up into the night sky. *This isn't over yet*, I whisper to myself, *this nightmare. It's only just beginning.*

Georgie unlocks the car door and doesn't say a word until we are on the road heading for the common. Then she turns to me and asks the question I've been waiting for.

'Tell me what happened, Ness. Why did you go to that house?'

I know I should be honest with her. She's my sister. And though there's thirteen years between us, we have always been close. She's always been there for me. But as we drive through the deserted London streets I can still feel Bains's gaze on me, accusatory, judging. If I tell Georgie the truth now she will never forgive me. Never. So, instead, I close my eyes and let the lie slip out.

'It was all a misunderstanding, Georgie,' I say, my voice cracking slightly. 'I wasn't there. It wasn't me. They got me mixed up with someone else.'

'But I thought they said —'

'They got it wrong,' I say firmly. 'And they've let me go. I'm so sorry you've had to come out at this time of night, and that I've worried you. I'll make it up to you. I promise.'

'You don't have to make it up to me, Nessa,' she says as we pull up in front of her imposing double-fronted Victorian terrace. 'Look, I don't know what happened between you and Connor but you haven't been yourself lately, even before the split. Jack's noticed it too. You've always been so sensible, so focused and together, but recently, well, it's . . . it's like you've turned into a different person.'

She switches off the engine and turns to face me. Her black hair is falling messily out of its bun, her face — free of make-up — pale and lined. For the first time I see that my sister is getting old and that makes me feel scared. Time is rushing like a torrent, unrelenting and out of control.

'If there's anything you want to tell me,' Georgie continues, 'you can. You know that, don't you? After Mum, we all . . . well, you know what happened. But sometimes I think we should have looked after you better. The fact that you were so studious and sensible made us think you were stronger than you were.'

The mention of Mum brings the tears to my eyes again. I blink them back, then turn to my sister and smile.

'I'm fine, Georgie,' I say, unclipping my seat belt. 'Honestly, I am.'

'Oh, there's Jack,' she says, waving.

I turn to see my brother-in-law standing in the doorway, the light from the hallway pouring out on to the small front garden and the street.

'He's been very worried,' says Georgie, getting out of the car. 'He'll be so relieved to have you back.'

It doesn't look like that to me, I think to myself as I follow Georgie up the path. In fact, the look on Jack's face is more anger than relief.

'Vanessa, what on earth was all that about?' he says, ushering us inside.

'It's fine, darling. It was all a big mistake,' says Georgie, taking his arm. 'They just wanted to ask her a few questions and now they've let her go. No further action.'

He doesn't look convinced, but slowly follows Georgie into the living room.

'I'm going to head up to bed,' I call, tiredness gripping my bones now. 'Thanks again for picking me up, Georgie, and I'm sorry for being such a pain.'

Georgie comes to the door of the living room. Her face is drawn but she smiles warmly.

'Okay. Well, goodnight, darling,' she says, blowing me a kiss. 'Get a good rest and we'll chat some more in the morning.'

She goes back into the living room and, as I walk up the stairs, I hear Jack's voice. 'You know I had poor old Mr Allen at the door? He'd seen the police car pulling away and got worried. Good grief, what's she playing at, Georgie?'

Jack is tired of me, and rightly so, I think to myself as I walk into the bedroom and shut the door. They don't need all this trouble and turmoil. I gaze up at the ceiling, in the centre of which is a beautifully ornate ceiling rose.

I remember Georgie commenting on the rose when she first viewed the house, back in 2000. It was a renovation project but she and Jack put every penny they had into restoring it to its former glory. I remember the first time I visited, with Dad and his new girlfriend. Lynda. God, just thinking about that woman makes me feel tense. She had worked alongside Dad at the stationery company and had offered him consolation after Mum died, though if the whispers I overheard between Jack and Georgie were anything to go by it seems Dad and Lynda had been growing close long before Mum's death. I just hope Mum never knew. That would be too much to bear. I hope, instead, that she went to her death feeling loved and secure.

I was fourteen years old when I first set foot in this house and was already feeling like an outsider. Dad had sold the family home and moved to a new-build bungalow in the centre of Reading. 'Lynda thinks it's time for a fresh start,' he told me when I said I didn't want to leave. 'And she's right, Vanessa. It's not healthy to dwell on the past.' And so I did as I was told and left everything I loved – my yellow bedroom, the kitchen where Mum and I had danced around to Radio 2, the walled garden with the birds she had talked to like old friends – Mr Robin and Mr Sparrow off on their morning stroll – and went to live in a bland, soulless house with my dad and a woman who made it clear that three was a crowd.

Seeing Georgie so happy with her family in her beautiful house made me feel even more alone, though she always did her best to make me feel like I was part of the family, that I was loved and cared for. But I remember vowing, as I played with little Imogen in this bedroom, that one day I would have a home that was all mine, and nobody would be able to take it away from me.

And now I'm back here, trapped like a cornered rat.

I close my eyes and I'm just about to drift off to sleep when there's a knock on the door.

'Come in,' I call, my voice reed thin.

The door opens and I see Jack's figure silhouetted in the darkness.

'Oh, sorry, V,' he says. 'I thought you might still be awake. I'll leave it.'

'No, it's okay, Jack,' I say, sitting up in the bed and switching on the lamp. 'What is it?'

'Just a parcel,' he says, stepping into the room. 'It came for you while you were . . . er, at the police station. Or rather, I saw it sitting on the doorstep when I opened the door to Mr Allen. I'll leave it here.'

'Thanks, Jack,' I say, watching as he places the square parcel on the chest of drawers.

'No problem,' he says in his usual clipped fashion. 'Right, I'm off to bed. Night, night.'

'Night, Jack.'

I wait until he has closed the door, then get out of bed. The parcel is wrapped in plain brown paper and has no postmark. My name is written in blue biro. Big, angry capital letters. I peel it open and see a flash of pink. Inside the box is a pile of papers wrapped in a thick pink satin ribbon.

I take one out and unfold it. It's a letter, written in messy, childish handwriting.

My handwriting.

I read the first couple of lines.

Dear Angus, I hope you are well. I think you are the luckiest boy in the world to live somewhere as magical as Holly Maze House.

I continue to read. It's a letter to Angus.

A boy with piercing blue eyes and a sad smile.

Angus was the protagonist of the Holly Maze books. Like me, he had lost his mother and he felt so different because of this that he found it difficult to make friends. He lost himself in a world of fantasy, just as I did. He was a male version of me really, a twin. And the more I read the Holly Maze books the more I felt that Angus wasn't an invention, that he was real. I started writing him letters, telling him about my life and how sad I was feeling with my mum gone. I had forgotten all about them until now.

As I sit here, a chill courses through me, though it's a warm summer's night. Who has sent me these?

I can hear Dad filling the kettle to make a cup of tea. The ITN news headlines echo through the house. Dad always turns the news on when he comes in from work. You still haven't got back from the shops. You told me you would pop to Bee's Books in town to buy Geoffrey Rivers's book before you went to do the weekly shop at Sainsbury's. I try to block out the sound of the news and concentrate on my latest book: The Demons of Winter Valley. *I borrowed it from the school library before the holidays and I'm almost finished. I curl up on my polka-dot beanbag in the corner of my bedroom and let myself be whisked away to a land of snow and ice and enchanted forests, much more exciting than interest rates and politics.*

I'm so engrossed that before I know it two hours have passed. I can hear voices downstairs. You must be home. I put the book down and walk out on to the landing but it's not your voice I hear, it's another woman's, half obscured by a crackling radio. Dad is with her. His voice is shaking. The woman asks him if he'd like to sit down.

10. Then

We wait until the Americans are safely in the lift before letting out a collective squeal of delight. The presentation went better than I could have expected and Luna London has now acquired Loris International as a major new client.

'Gosh, well done, everyone,' says Anne, taking a bottle of champagne from the tiny fridge in the corner of her office and bringing it over to the table. 'Six months of blood, sweat and tears, and look what we've achieved. I'm bloody proud of each and every one of you.'

She opens the bottle and as it pops there's another round of applause from the team. Anne looks thrilled as she hands us all a large glass of fizz.

'You were amazing today, Vanessa,' she says, coming to sit next to me. 'Your knowledge of the US cosmetics market shone through. You could see how impressed they were. Brilliant. Bloody brilliant.'

'Thanks, Anne,' I say, feeling heady as I take a long sip of champagne. 'I put everything into this presentation. I'm just so glad it went well.'

'Great choice of outfit too,' says Anne, gesturing to the silk shift dress Connor picked out for me last week. 'I must say, I've noticed a change in you these last few months.

You're looking great. You've got more confidence. It's like you're blossoming in front of my eyes. It's wonderful to see. It really is.'

'Thanks,' I say again, feeling rather emotional. 'That means such a lot coming from you.'

'I think I know the reason why you look so good, Vanessa.'

I turn to see Damian, beaming at me from the other side of the table, his champagne glass held aloft.

'She's found the love of a good man,' he says, laughing.

'Oh,' says Anne, smiling awkwardly. As a lifelong champion of women, it's not her nature to think that success stems from being with the right man. 'Well, you've certainly made us all proud here, Vanessa. Well done.'

She gets up and walks across to Colette, her PA, who has appeared at the door with Anne's diary.

'Hey, I didn't mean to embarrass you there,' says Damian, sitting down in the chair she has just vacated. 'And Anne's right. You did a brilliant job today. I can't believe it. You've actually brought money in for once. Just kidding.'

'Thanks, Damian,' I say, draining my glass. 'And, you know, you're right about Connor. We're really happy.'

'It shows,' he says, smiling warmly. 'And I meant what I said. Connor's a good 'un. I've known him since he was a kid and he's always had a big heart. It's great that he's found a good 'un too. Right, enough of this schmaltz, I'm off to crunch some numbers.'

Later, as I'm walking back over Albert Bridge, I feel a deep sense of relief and contentment. Today was a good day, a brilliant day. We all pulled together and secured a major client. And throughout the presentation I'd felt relaxed and confident. As I stood up to speak I could hear Connor's words in my head – 'You can do this. You know you can. I believe in you, Vanessa' – and it felt like he was there in the room with me, cheering me on.

I thread my way along the outskirts of Battersea Park and on to Queenstown Road, thinking about the day and how I should swing by Sainsbury's and pick up a bottle of champagne to celebrate, but as I reach the corner of Ingelow Road, two streets away from the flat, I see a large 'For Sale' board outside a red-brick Victorian terrace. It's a house I've noticed as I pass by on my way to work, as it has retained its original iron railings and has a fox-head door knocker. I take a closer look at the board: 'Two bedroom, split-level ground-floor flat with garden. Open Day: Saturday November 11th at 1 p.m.'

A garden flat. My mind goes into overdrive, imagining me and Connor planting flowers and vegetables in our own little garden. I take out my phone and go to the estate agent's website, scrolling down until I find the listing. The flat is on at £500,000 which, for this area of London, is a bargain. And I actually think we could maybe afford it. For a while now I've been thinking about how amazing it would be to have our own little home, and something about this just feels right.

My mind is whirring with all the things we could do to the flat as I make my way back. I'll put together a mood board, I tell myself, get Jack to give me some architectural advice, see if it has its original flooring. By the time I get in I've got a fully formed picture of our future home in my head.

'Is that my brilliant girlfriend?'

Connor comes out of the kitchen and hands me a glass of champagne. He's wearing an apron and the air smells of cumin.

'See,' he says, clinking his glass against mine. 'The outfit did the trick. I told you.'

'Yeah, thanks for helping with that, baby,' I say, following him into the kitchen, which is a bit of a squeeze for two.

I open the door to the roof terrace and step outside. It feels wintry tonight, despite the outdoor heater. As I sip my wine I think about the garden flat. According to the description on the website it has a dining kitchen. I start to imagine the Le Creuset pans we could buy and the big farmhouse-style table with a bench. And flowers, lots of flowers, peonies and hydrangeas which I'll put in little jam jars and vintage milk jugs.

'It's lovely seeing you look so happy,' says Connor, coming out to join me.

'Well,' I say, putting my glass down on the table. 'It's not just the US deal that has made me happy. I think I've found us a flat.'

'What are you talking about?' he says, his smile fading. 'We've got a flat.'

'No, we rent this place,' I say. 'It's not ours. Anyway, when I was on my way back I saw a "For Sale" board outside that little house on Ingelow Road. You know, the one I've pointed out to you before, with the original iron railings?'

'I think so,' he says, his voice flat.

'Well, the house is divided into apartments. The ground-floor garden flat is for sale. And guess what?'

'What?'

86

'It's on at five hundred thousand,' I cry, waiting for his eyes to light up. 'I mean, that's a total bargain for round here.'

'That's a huge sum of money, Vanessa,' he says, shaking his head. 'We're in no position to buy a flat and certainly not anything that expensive.'

'I did the sums and I think it's doable if we make a low offer,' I say, handing him my phone with the details of the flat on the screen. 'Have a look at the photos. With our salaries combined we could get a mortgage and there's the building society money that Mum left for me. She left it with strict instructions that I should use it to put towards "a home". We could use that as a deposit. Plus, after today I reckon Anne will give me a pay rise when it comes under review next month.'

'Slow down, Vanessa,' he says, holding his hands up. 'You're getting overexcited. First of all, I want to continue saving for our deposit. The money your mother left is yours. I wouldn't feel comfortable using it as a deposit. Plus, the repayments on a mortgage like that would be huge. We'd have no money for anything else.'

'But it would be a home,' I say, rubbing his arms. 'I mean, this place is lovely but it's tiny. We could really expand, have friends over for dinner, have a vegetable garden.'

'No, Vanessa,' he says, handing the phone back. 'It's also a renovation job. Look at the photos. It's the kind of place a property developer will snap up and turn around in a few months. It's for someone with the money to do it, not us. Those kind of places are notorious money pits. It's too much of a risk.'

He gets up and heads inside. Then, probably sensing my disappointment, he comes back out and kisses my head.

'Our perfect home is out there somewhere, baby,' he says gently. 'But we just have to wait a little while. And as we both know, the best things come to those who wait. I waited years to find you. Right, give me ten minutes and I'll have dinner ready.'

'Okay.'

When he's back in the kitchen I get out my phone and retrieve the estate agent's web page. I think back to this afternoon, how confident I had been when I delivered the presentation, how I had felt in control of my own destiny. *This flat could be the next step in taking control*, I think to myself as I scroll through the photos. Just as I have outgrown disposable fashion, so I should be moving on from renting. I need to start thinking about the future, need something to show for all my hard work.

As I sit contemplating the flat my phone beeps. Sixteen Instagram notifications. I click on the app and see a stream of photos from Luna London, tagging me and the rest of the team, and congratulating us on our success. I smile. Today is a meaningful day. I'm about to click off the app when I see a post from Lottie, whose account I still follow. It's a photo of the interior of a plane; a window to the left shows billowing clouds. I read the words underneath the photo with a heavy heart: 'Off to find new adventures in South Africa.' Accompanying the post are a series of hashtags and the name of the South African branch of the children's charity Lottie works for.

So that's it, I think. She's got a new job in a new country and didn't even have the decency to tell me or to even attempt to clear the air before she left. It's then, in that moment, that I make my mind up. Connor and Anne are right: I *have* changed. But I've changed for the better. It's time to stop living in the past and move on.

I hear Connor dishing up the food. He'll be out here any minute so I'll have to be fast. I open up the estate agent's website and, before I know it, have added my name to the list of viewers for tomorrow's open house. As the confirmation email pings into my inbox I feel a surge of excitement. This could be the beginning of a whole new life for us. If the flat is as perfect as I imagine it is then I'm sure I can talk Connor round.

When I arrive at the flat just before 1 p.m. there is a large crowd of people already assembled outside. I join the back of the queue and when I reach the front a rather harried-looking young man, holding a clipboard and wearing a lanyard round his neck with JAMIE RICHARDS printed on it, asks me my name.

'Ah, yes, there you are,' he says, running a stubby finger down the list. 'Vanessa Adams. Do go through, Miss Adams. We're showing people round in groups of six. My colleague Dawn is inside and will happily answer any questions.'

'Thanks, Jamie,' I say, stepping into the rather dank hallway.

I can see Dawn standing by what looks like the kitchen door with a group of men and women. One of them, a suited, balding man in his late fifties, looks like a property developer. The rest are couples in their twenties. Dawn, a petite black woman, seems to be a lot more in control than Jamie on the door. I catch her talking about the flat's 'amazing potential' as I join the group.

As Dawn walks us from room to room I realize that Connor was right. This flat needs renovating from scratch. The floorboards are rotten, there are green damp patches climbing up the walls, there is a substance that looks suspiciously like asbestos hanging from the ceiling. Dawn suggests we see the garden but I hang back. Seeing it would only make me feel worse. I know I shouldn't be taking this to heart so much – after all, this is only the first flat I have viewed – but I'd had such a good feeling about it. I'd let myself get carried away and created a fantasy of it in my head. Of course, the reality was never going to match up.

Still, as I stand at the window of what appears to be the main bedroom, watching Dawn pointing out various features of the garden to the group, I can't help thinking how time is slipping away from me. My parents were much younger than me when they bought their first place. Granted, house prices weren't as insanely high when they were young and there was a lot more job security, but still I can't shake the feeling that the home life I've been searching for since I was ten years old will never materialize.

I step back from the window and look around the room, narrowing my eyes as I try to imagine Connor and me lying in bed in here. The thought of my neat-freak boyfriend even setting foot in this hovel makes me giggle. Someone has lived here though, I think to myself, as I see a stack of boxes piled up by the door. Probably an old person, judging by the dated kitchen units and peeling wallpaper. I take a peek into one of the boxes. It's full of books. I read a few of the spines: *Delia's Complete Cookery Course*, *Jane Fonda's Workout Book*, *The Day of the*

Jackal. It's an eclectic mix. All headed for the charity shop by the looks of it, I think as I riffle through. There's a small paperback wedged at the side of the box. I pull it out and a shiver flutters through my body. 'Good grief,' I whisper as I run my fingers over the embossed letters on the cover: *The Spirits of Holly Maze House.* I open it up and see that it has been signed by the author, Geoffrey Rivers.

'Mum,' I whisper as I turn the pages and see those quirky line drawings I had loved so much as a child.

The day after Mum's funeral Georgie had come upstairs to find me. I had barely left my room since the accident. I didn't want to talk to anyone. I wanted to hide away and pretend it had never happened, that Mum had just popped out somewhere and was going to be back soon. Georgie tried to make conversation but I turned away and faced the wall. I heard her put something on the side table, then she said, 'The police found this in Mum's car. I think she must have bought it for you.' After she'd left the room I turned over to see what she had put there and when I saw the book I felt my heart burst into a thousand pieces. But then I remembered Geoffrey's words – '*These stories were written for any child who has ever felt out of place*' – and I picked up the book and started to read.

Once upon a time there was a boy called Angus. Now, young Angus was sad because he was all alone. I don't know if you've ever felt alone before, truly alone, without a friend in the world. You see, when you are alone, the world can seem like a terrifying place, a cold place, with ghouls and monsters hiding at every turn.

Even now, all these years later, I can still remember whole sections of that book. I read it over and over again those first few months after Mum's death until I became so familiar with the characters and the house and the story, I convinced myself they must be real.

What I found reassuring, as I read the book again and again and again, was that unlike real life, which was scary and unpredictable, stories were safe. I knew where I was with a story. It had a beginning, a middle and an end, a clear direction. Real life, on the other hand, was like being lost in the woods with no map and no hope of finding the way home.

I knew that Angus, a motherless child like me, would find solace at the end of the story. He went on adventures with three little ghost children, who had died in the house in 1680. They had returned from the dead to help Angus learn how to live without his mum and they were helped on this quest by a strange glass blackbird who sat on the sideboard inside the house and mysteriously came to life whenever the children and Angus needed him. It sounds quite dark now, but back then I didn't find anything scary about it. It was comforting.

I remember wishing that I had a bird like that, a protector who could take me to another world, even for just a few hours. However, I knew that could never happen so the world inside the book became the next best thing. I used to dream I'd been inside that house, walked along its corridors, climbed its wooden staircase, talked to Angus and the ghosts. In my grief, I convinced myself they were real.

This book had been the only light in my life during the dark weeks and months following her death. And now, just when I'm feeling despondent, it has found me again. It's like Mum is watching me, telling me everything is going to be all right.

I hear footsteps outside the room. Dawn is bringing the group back in. I quickly slip the book into my bag and head out of the flat, heart thumping with exhilaration. Jamie taps my arm as I hurry down the steps. 'Miss Adams, what were your thoughts?' he says, gripping his clipboard tightly.

'Oh, it will make a lovely home for someone,' I say, feeling the reassuring bulk of the book in my bag. 'But it's not for me.'

11. Now

Angus looks up and sees that the sky is on fire. Golden snakes wriggle and squirm in the air before exploding into glittering rain. He stands for a moment, marvelling at the colours, the way the rockets look most beautiful in the final moments before they die.

Delicious smells fill the air. His mouth waters as he smells the heady scent of hotdogs with crisp fried onions, candyfloss, hot plum juice.

The garden is alive with people, most of them dressed in white; painted-faced men walk on stilts and ghost women breathe orange fire. Catherine wheels spin on the ancient wall while little spirits weave in and out of the maze, their eyes reflecting the lights in the sky.

'Who are all these people?' says Angus as the air rings with laughter. 'Where have they come from?'

'Why, these are your guests,' says the bird. 'Come now, children, step forward and greet your host.'

Angus's heart thuds as two boys step out of the crowd.

They are dressed in the clothes of days gone by – like the Cavaliers Angus likes to read about in his storybooks – their hairstyles long and curled, their necks concealed by white ruffs, their feet clad in polished buckled boots.

'At last,' says the taller of the two, who, the bird whispers, is called Tom. 'We've been waiting for you.'

'We have to go and find her now,' says the other, who, the bird informs him, is called Cecil.

'Find who?' says Angus as the boys take his hands in theirs and guide him to the maze.

'Why, Iris, of course,' say the boys in unison.

The maze seems to go on forever and Angus is certain he will take a wrong turn and lose his way. His feet are leading him on, seemingly independent of his body. As he reaches the end of the maze he feels the air grow thinner. He has lost the boys somewhere in the centre and is now heading out alone. He looks up and sees, to his amazement, that the sun is blazing in the sky, the day has come.

I open my eyes and see a figure standing by the window. Bright sunshine, golden walls. Iris is here in her blue smock. But then, as I come to, I see it's Georgie. She's wearing a pale-blue blouse, the light from the window making the fabric shimmer. And the walls aren't golden, it's just a trick of the light.

'It's a beautiful morning,' she says. 'Why don't we go and have a walk on the common?'

The dream is still with me, attached to my consciousness like a second skin. That had always been my favourite part of the story, the moment Angus meets Iris at the end of the maze. It always made me tingle; the fact that Angus had walked from darkness into light in a matter of moments. I remember the feeling of excitement as I read the story, holding my breath as Angus prepared to meet his friend, his Iris.

'What time is it?' I mutter, sitting up in bed and wiping the sleep from my eyes.

'Just gone ten,' says Georgie, stepping away from the window. 'I thought . . . after everything you went through yesterday you could do with a lie-in. I've got the day off so I thought the two of us could do something together. Have a walk on the common, maybe have lunch in the village.'

The thought of going into the village and facing all those yoga-trim Yummy Mummies who frequent its shops and cafes makes my heart sink but I know staying in bed, enclosed inside four walls, is not what I need right now.

'A walk would be good,' I say, putting on my best 'everything is fine' face for Georgie. 'Give me ten minutes to get ready.'

She smiles though she can't hide the worried look in her eyes. I feel wretched for what I put her through last night, having to see me being led away by the police like that. I'll make it up to her, I tell myself as she leaves the room and heads downstairs. Buy her lunch in that new French place that's opened up in the village. I look down and see the letters scattered on the floor. A feeling of dread rises up inside me as I look at my childish writing. All I can think is that Dad must have found them in the loft or something and he's decided to return them to me now in some misguided attempt at recovering our relationship. I need to get them out of my sight. I climb out of bed, then scoop the letters up and put them into the bottom drawer, underneath a pile of winter sweaters.

Fifteen minutes later, washed and dressed, I accompany Georgie along the narrow lane that connects their row of houses to the wild expanse of Wimbledon Common. The sun beats down on us as we cross the road, weaving in and out of dog walkers and families who have been lured out of their houses by the glorious weather.

'Summer's last hoorah,' says Georgie, lifting her face to the sky. 'Things always feel better when the sun shines.'

She turns to me and takes my arm gently.

'I meant what I said last night, Nessa,' she says, pausing as a young black spaniel bounds across the path in front of us. 'Whatever is going on, whatever it is that's bothering you. You can tell me. Keeping things bottled up is never a good thing in the long run. I know that more than anyone.'

Her smile fades and as she looks into the middle distance I remember those months after Harry's birth when we thought we'd lost her. Becoming a mother to Imogen had emboldened Georgie but Harry's birth seemed to diminish her. I remember how she had folded in on herself, barely eating or sleeping, talking in a strange, stilted fashion, sitting motionless on the old armchair in the living room. None of us knew what had happened to her, couldn't work out where our bright, extroverted Georgie had gone. Only when she was diagnosed with postnatal depression after almost a year did it all make sense. She later said that the trauma of Harry's birth – he was breech and Georgie was given an emergency Caesarean – had sent her into shock. Professional help was sought and after a few months of medication something of the old Georgie was returned to us. Yet she had left a part of herself behind in that maternity ward. The carefree fearlessness had been replaced with a seriousness, a sense that the world was something to protect against rather than explore. I couldn't understand it at the time, how someone could change so much, but then I look at my own life over the last year and feel the same sense of disconnect. Who was that sensible, happy girl and where did she go?

'I know you worry about me, Georgie,' I say as we head across the vast stretch of scorched grass. 'But really, everything's fine. All that stuff with the police, it was just a mistake. They got it wrong.'

She turns to me, and I see my reflection in her mirrored Wayfarers.

'But of all the people,' she says, lowering her voice as two giggling young girls walk past us. 'Geoffrey Rivers. We all know how much he . . . well, how much solace you got from his books after Mum's death.'

The sun is reaching its height and as it burns into my face I see him, standing at the door, and I shiver, despite the heat.

'I told you, Georgie,' I say as we join the overgrown path that leads to the village. 'It was all a misunderstanding.'

As I walk, Geoffrey's face appears in my mind.

'Look, I know it can't be easy for you at the moment,' says Georgie. 'With the break-up and all that. And it's such a shame because you and Connor seemed so happy. It's sad to see things fall apart.'

She takes my arm again and, as we continue to walk, Geoffrey's face dissolves in the sun.

'Yes,' I say, watching a procession of young horse riders from the village stables skirt the road alongside us. 'But Connor and I just weren't right for each other. We can't all be like you and Jack.'

'God, if we're the poster kids for a happy relationship then you're all screwed,' she says, laughing. 'Try sharing a bed for more than twenty years with someone who snores like he does. That's surely grounds for divorce.'

'If the only complaint you have in all that time is the fact that he snores, then I'm sorry, dear sister, but I have no sympathy for you.'

'True,' she says, holding her hands in the air. 'But he also leaves the milk out, which is a sackable offence, surely?'

We laugh and for a few moments it feels like old times again. Back when I was Vanessa, the successful marketing manager leading a team of five in my plush office in Chelsea, and I would spend my Saturdays catching up with Georgie over a bottle of dry white in the village. That feels like a different planet now, that time, that life.

'There really is nothing to worry about,' I tell her. 'I've had a bit of a blip but I'm coming out the other side. I can feel it.'

'Good,' says Vanessa, squeezing my arm. 'It hurts me to see you so low.'

We reach the end of the common and as we stand waiting to cross the road I see something up ahead, a flash of yellow. As we draw closer I see a satchel that looks just like the one I bought Lottie for Christmas a couple of years ago. And then I recognize the tight red curls, the broad shoulders.

'It's Lottie,' I say, quickening my step. 'Over there by the bookshop, look.'

'Where? I can't –'

As she's speaking, a dark figure springs in between us. In the strobed light it looks like a horned demon.

'What the hell?' I scream, staggering backwards.

Then, as the sun disappears behind a cloud, the figure takes form and I hear sniggering.

It's someone dressed up as a cartoon horse.

'Sorry to scare you,' it cries in a cut-glass accent. 'Just after some spare change. It's all for a good cause. The folks at the riding school are raising funds to provide new facilities for disabled kids.'

I watch as my sister takes out her purse and places a five-pound note in the collecting tin.

'Thank you, ladies,' chirps the horse. 'Have a lovely day.'

As it departs, Georgie shakes her head and laughs.

'Are you all right?' she says, taking my arm. 'You got an awful shock.'

'I'm fine,' I say, feeling rather foolish.

'I don't think that *was* Lottie,' says Georgie as we head past the bookshop where I thought I'd seen her. 'She wouldn't come to Wimbledon without getting in touch to say hi, surely? After all, it was just a silly quarrel.'

I think about Lottie's face when I told her I was moving out, the way she changed her phone number, the fact that she had left the country for a new life and not got in touch. Lottie hates me for what I did. If it was her I've just seen, then it's further proof that our friendship is over. To be back in the UK and still not get in touch. That means something.

'So, how about lunch in the village?' says Georgie as we reach the high street. 'Maybe even a sneaky bottle of Chablis for old times' sake.'

It sounds heavenly and the old me would be there like a shot, ordering a plate of moules and spending the afternoon putting the world to rights, but the shock of seeing Lottie and then that horse springing up out of nowhere has shaken me. I think of Bains last night, his eyes boring into me, and suddenly it feels like everyone else is doing the same. Watching me. Judging me.

'I'm sorry, Georgie, but the sun's given me a headache,' I say, putting my hand to my temple. 'Do you mind if we go home?'

Georgie doesn't object, though I know she really wanted to have lunch and relax. As we turn and head back across the common, she slips her hand in mine and gives it a reassuring squeeze, just as she used to when I was a kid. That small gesture brings tears to my eyes, though I tell Georgie it's the sun and the onset of a migraine that is making them water. I don't know whether she believes me, but she doesn't press it, and when we get back to the house she busies herself getting me a glass of water and two painkillers.

Back in the bedroom I lie on the bed staring at the ceiling, my head full of Bains and Geoffrey. I need to know what is being said, how the news sites are reporting it. A flutter of panic courses through me as I imagine my name splashed across the internet. I sit up and take my phone from the bedside table then type the words 'Geoffrey Rivers' into the search engine.

RECLUSIVE CHILDREN'S AUTHOR FOUND DEAD: POLICE LAUNCH MURDER INQUIRY

No, I can't face it. Instead I click on a piece from the *Observer* in which the great and the good of the literary world have offered tributes and condolences. '*Geoffrey set the benchmark for those who followed . . .' 'A light has gone out today . . .' 'Geoffrey's stories will live on in the hearts of so many children . . .'* One writer refers to Angus, the child protagonist of the Holly Maze House books, as '*a modern-day Christopher Robin*'.

The tributes soon become overwhelming and I have to put the phone away. But as I lie on the bed, Geoffrey's face flashes in front of me, his eyes cold, as though with disgust. Then another memory assaults me: the sound of leather smashing against skin, the spurt of blood, the smell of sweat.

My heart starts to race and I sit up, try to remember the calming breathing exercises Anne taught us in the mindfulness session she ran last year. As I exhale I hear voices filtering up from the kitchen.

Jack is home from work. His voice is raised and I can hear Georgie trying to reason with him. They're talking about me. 'In bed?' I hear him say. 'But it's the middle of the day. This can't go on.'

I pull the covers over my head to block out his voice but in the darkness I see Geoffrey lying at the foot of the stairs, his eyes to the ceiling. I throw the covers off, jump up and go to the window. Outside the road is still and peaceful, the afternoon sun casting strange shadows on the walls of the houses across the way.

I can't allow myself to think of what happened. The sound of Geoffrey gasping for breath as he fought for his life. No, I must wipe it from my mind.

My phone begins to ring on the table next to me. The noise of it makes me jump. I pick it up and look at the screen. It says 'unknown number'. I answer it, tentatively.

'Hello?'

There's a pause, then I hear someone sigh heavily.

'Hello? Who's there?' I say. 'Who is this?'

There's another sigh and then whoever it is ends the call.

I stand at the window, holding the phone in my hands, trying to work out who it could have been. Connor? No, because his number would have shown up. It could just have been a sales call, I tell myself, putting the phone back on the table. These things happen all the time but because I'm in a heightened state I'm attaching more significance to it. I have to calm down.

Just then the front door slams. I look out of the window and see Jack storming across the common. Downstairs, I hear Georgie clattering dishes. I turn from the window and slump down on the bed, putting my head in my hands. This is all my fault.

12. Then

January 2018

'Vanessa. Dinner's ready.'

I grab my phone from the bathroom floor and look at the time. Eight p.m. on the dot. Sinking back into the warm bathwater, I wish that just for once Connor and I could have a takeaway or dinner in front of the TV. It's been a really tough week at work. The campaign for Mulberry Moment, the new Luna London lip shade for winter, is in full swing and my days have been wall-to-wall meetings from 8 a.m. to 7 p.m.

Tonight is Friday night and all I want to do, when I get out of this bath, is curl up on the sofa with something trashy on the TV and something equally junk-like on my plate: a slice of cheese on toast or a bowl of Frosties with milk. However, I know that won't happen as Connor is a stickler for both routine and for sitting round the table to eat. At 8 p.m. Every evening.

This is one of the things I have learned about him since moving in, along with the fact that he is obsessively clean, with a box and a label and a place for everything. No more throwing my clothes on to the bedroom floor or letting the laundry basket overflow. I found in the first couple of weeks that when I did that, the item in question would be magically put on a hanger and the washing machine would be on overdrive until the laundry basket emptied.

'I'm sorry,' Connor had said, when I caught him putting my trainers neatly away on the shoe rack one morning. 'I know I'm a bit anal but it's just the way I was brought up. When Dad left, Mum made sure I did my share of the housework.'

It had made me feel bad when I saw him folding up my clothes and putting my paperwork into neat piles. I'd worried that he would regret my moving in with him, that I had somehow intruded on his nicely ordered flat, trailing mess and chaos in my wake. But after a few weeks I started to take on some of his habits too. I like the fact that if I choose which outfit to wear for work the next day and lay it out the night before, then I will have more time to spend in bed with Connor in the morning, rather than rushing around like a headless chicken, looking for my shoes and bag and phone. I feel more composed, more in control. He's made me become a better version of myself.

'Vanessa, it's getting cold.'

Connor's voice trails up the passageway. With some reluctance, I get out of the bath and dry myself with a soft white towel.

'I'll be two minutes,' I call as I head into the bedroom.

I open the wardrobe to see what I can wear. My tired body wants nothing more than to sink into a pair of cosy pyjamas but Connor doesn't think wearing pyjamas for dinner is proper. And there is something quite fun about dressing up for each other. I pull out a black silk pleated maxi skirt. It has an elasticated waist and will be comfortable enough. I team it with the green cashmere jumper Connor got me for Christmas and slip a pair of loafers on my feet. Running my fingers through my hair to tidy it, I hurry along the passageway towards the kitchen.

'You look nice and relaxed,' says Connor, appearing at the open door. 'Dinner's ready and I've got the outdoor heater on.'

I step out on to the roof terrace which, weather permitting, has become our dining room. Connor prefers the space outside, because it feels less claustrophobic than sitting at the small table in the living room. And it is nice, eating under the stars – certainly more romantic than a greasy takeaway on the sofa. Still, I'm thankful for the outdoor heater, particularly on a chilly January night like this.

'I got some cod from the fishmonger's on Northcote Road,' he says, sitting down at the table next to me. 'So I thought I'd make a fish pie. Tuck in.'

I smile as I take a mouthful of the pie. It is rich and creamy and feels like a warm hug. Despite my initial desire to lounge on the sofa with junk food, this is exactly what I need.

'It's delicious,' I say, taking a sip of cold white wine. 'Where did you get the recipe?'

'From Mum,' he says wistfully. 'She used to make it all the time when I was a kid. Mums make the best meals, don't they? Oh God, sorry, that was insensitive of me.'

He squeezes my hand and smiles.

'Don't be silly,' I say, feeling the warmth of his skin next to mine. 'You know I'm fine with you mentioning your mum. I was lucky that my mum was a great cook too. She made everything from scratch. No microwave meals, no jars of pasta sauce, no takeaways. She loved cooking and she loved her family.'

'That's what home is all about,' he says. 'Warmth and love and food. Sitting round a table. I missed all that when I moved into this place.'

'I'd like to meet your mum,' I say. 'We should plan a little trip.'

'Yep,' he says, clearing his throat. 'We should. She's been really busy with work but she's dying to meet you. The divorce hit her pretty hard, which is why she threw herself into work. Coming home to an empty house must be tough for her. I never want to end up like that. Having you here, seeing your face next to me at the table, it's everything to me. I realized the other day when I was watching you sleeping that you're my family now.'

I smile. I feel the same way. Connor is my family and the next step should be to find somewhere we can grow.

Ever since I viewed the garden flat, my need to find a home has taken on more urgency. Connor doesn't understand this urge and constantly tells me that the rented flat we're living in is good enough for now and that we should concentrate on working hard to build up a solid deposit. I'd brought up the subject of the money my mother had left me again and he'd snapped at me and told me that he would not be using someone else's money and that was the end of it.

But it's not the end of it as far as I'm concerned, not by a long shot. I realize that I have wasted a huge chunk of my life just coasting along. Now that doesn't feel good enough. I think about Anne with her beautiful house in Muswell Hill, which she opens up for staff parties and get-togethers. That house is a solid symbol of all the hard work she has poured into her career. I want to have that too and I don't think it's a crime to go after what you want.

Since the viewing I have signed up for every property website I can find, entering my details, my budget, my search radius, what kind of property I'm looking for, etc. I've also become addicted to the interior design pages on Instagram and have started to follow hashtags such as #periodproperty #mydreamhouse #cosyhome #vintageterrace. Each page takes me further and further into a dream world but, unlike a story, these worlds are attainable.

Later that evening, when Connor is washing up the dishes, I sit, glass of wine in hand, and click on to Instagram. One of the hashtags leads me to a page called Dream Properties. Most of the 'dream properties' are in the million-pound-plus bracket. Still, it is nice to dream.

I scroll through the listings, which are mostly mock-Tudor houses and penthouse apartments. Nothing catches my eye. I hear Connor go into the bathroom and I'm about to click off when I see a house so beautiful it takes my breath away. It's described as an early Regency gem in the heart of Surrey. A red-brick building with a pillared porch and wisteria creeping round the door. Inside, it has retained its original features with stone floors throughout, sage-green panelled walls and a mulberry-painted music room complete with grand piano. To the rear is a sweeping terrace and, hidden away at the end of the grounds, a walled herb garden with a twisted willow pergola running down the middle.

It might be the wine but I decide to make an appointment to view the house. It is, of course, completely out of my budget, at £1.5 million, but I reason that if I go to see this house it will motivate me, give me a solid sense of what I can achieve if I carry on working hard. Also, I feel an urge to get out of London this weekend. Connor has forewarned me that he'll be working most of it as he has the branding for a big sports campaign to finish by the end of next week.

I bring up the 'Book an appointment' box on the website and I'm about to enter my name when I stop myself. As this property is well out of my price range, it feels silly to use my real name to view it. It would make more sense to come up with a pseudonym. But who can I be? I go back into the kitchen and refill my wine. As I make my way back to the sofa I've already come up with a name.

'Tabitha Richardson', I type into the form. Just the sort of person who would view this kind of house. I am so absorbed with Tabitha that by the time Connor comes back into the room to tell me it's time for bed, not only am I quite tipsy but I also have a fully formed backstory for Ms Richardson which sounds so plausible I almost believe it myself.

Two days later

Sitting on the 10.35 from Victoria to Epsom, I practise my introduction.

'Hellay, sooo pleased to meet you,' I drawl to myself as the train departs. 'My name is Tabitha Richardson. I'm here to view the Regency house.'

I repeat the lines over and over, easing my tongue across the words until they become part of me. Then, as we head into open countryside, I smile. I am no longer Vanessa. I have become someone else.

I have become Tabitha.

Tabitha Richardson is thirty-five years old, a little older than me, and a widow. Mother to two children, Bertie and Amelia. Tabitha's husband, a hedge-fund manager, tragically died in a skiing accident two years ago. 'It's been such a terrible time,' I mutter to myself as the train goes under a bridge. 'But now we're ready to move on. To sell the house in Chelsea and head to the country. It's going to be a fresh start for us. A chance to start again.'

Don't overdo it, I tell myself as the train pulls into Epsom station. *Just keep it simple.*

As I approach the door of Fairfax and Latimer Estate Agents, I practise my intro one last time, under my breath. 'Hellay, my name is Tabitha Richardson. I've come to view ... My name is Tabitha Richardson ... Oh, hello ... er ... hellay. My name is ...'

But as I walk into the office and see their faces my mind goes blank and I stand limply in the centre of the room, the eyes of half-a-dozen women fixed on me.

'Er ... hi, my name is ...' I begin. 'I've got an ... an appointment at 11.30.'

'Oh, you must be Mrs Richardson?' says a smiling blonde woman who looks to be in her early sixties. 'You've come to view Rosedale Manor?'

There is a hushed silence as she gets up from her desk and comes towards me, her hand outstretched.

'I'm Jane Treadwell,' she says warmly. 'Lovely to meet you.'

I nod my head but my mouth is dry as I shake hands with Jane, aware of the other women looking at me. Do they know what I'm doing? Can they tell it's a lie?

'Yes, I'm Tabitha,' I say finally as Jane Treadwell grips my hand. 'It's so good to meet you.'

I wonder if I should start with the bio now, tell Jane Treadwell a little more about myself, or rather Tabitha, but before I can say anything she has swept me out of the office and into the passenger seat of her car, a large, silver 4x4, and as we make our way along the narrow country lanes, she takes the opportunity to quiz me about my situation.

'You said in your email that you had been recently widowed, dear,' she says, raising her voice over the hum of Radio 4. 'A skiing accident. How awful for you.'

'Thank you,' I reply, speaking slowly and carefully. 'It was such an awful shock for me and the kids, er, sorry, the children, but we're finding our feet now.'

'And you're moving from London?' asks Jane, slowing down to let an elderly man cross the road. He's carrying a King Charles spaniel in his arms. 'Chelsea, you said?'

'That's right,' I say, watching as the man reaches the other side of the road and gently puts the dog on to the grass. 'London is just too much for us right now. There are too many painful memories.'

'I completely understand,' says Jane, nodding her head. 'I lost my husband five years ago. It was cancer, in his case, so we had time to prepare for it, unlike you, poor thing, but when he passed I knew I would have to sell up and find somewhere else. He loved to garden and seeing the empty greenhouses each morning was just too much to bear.'

'I know what you mean,' I say, relaxing a little in the wake of Jane's honesty. 'They say it's just bricks and mortar but houses are so much more than that, aren't they? They contain a whole lifetime of memories and stories. Oliver, my late husband, was so much a part of the Chelsea house. I can still see him sitting at the kitchen table when I come downstairs. It's like he never left.'

Beside me, Jane Treadwell nods her head.

'But after he died I remembered a conversation we had when we'd just got married,' I say, my chest tightening as the sign for Rosedale Manor comes into view. 'He knew how much I loved the countryside and that I'd compromised a bit by deciding to live in London with him. So he made me promise that if he died before me I would go and find my rural idyll.'

I feel terrible for lying to her but part of it is true. I think of my mother. She would want me to work hard and, one day, to have the chance to own a house like Rosedale Manor. My dream house.

'Oh, that *is* lovely,' says Jane as we sweep into the grandest driveway I have ever seen. 'Now let's hope Rosedale Manor is the one.'

She stops the car in front of the house and I have to restrain myself from gasping. The photographs had been impressive enough but in real life the house is magnificent.

'It's Grade II listed,' says Jane, taking a set of keys from her bag to open the door. 'So there'd be limits to what you could do to it.'

I wouldn't want to change a thing, I think to myself as we step into a circular entrance hall. The walls are painted sage green, in keeping with the Regency style, and there is a highly polished table in the centre with a tall glass vase of lilies on top.

'Rosedale Manor was built in 1820 and was home to four generations of the Hipsley family until 1910 when it was sold to Anglo-Irish politician J. P. Mulvey.'

I pretend to listen as Jane tells me the history of the house, but my eye is drawn to a framed picture sitting on the table next to the vase of lilies. The picture, a black-and-white photograph, shows a dark-haired woman with sparkling eyes and white teeth, her arms draped around a handsome man with cropped greying hair. In the fore-front, nestled in their daddy's arms, are an impossibly cute little girl in a floral dress, her hair tied in sweet bunches, and an older boy, around eight or nine, looking smart in his school uniform. I can't take my eyes off that family. It's as though they have stepped right out of my fantasy: a loved-up couple, two children healthy and thriving. It's a happy scene but the photo fills me with a sadness I can't quite put my finger on. It's the same sense of time running out I had when I viewed the garden flat in Battersea. I back away from the photo and go to find Jane, who is standing in the drawing room looking out at the sweeping countryside.

'Impressive, isn't it?' she says to me, her eyes gleaming. 'Just under eight acres of land. And it could all be yours.'

I smile but my initial enthusiasm has gone, the excitement drained away. I should go but, first, I really need to use the loo.

'Er, sorry, Jane,' I say, putting my hand on the woman's arm. 'I'm afraid I'm having trouble concentrating because I'm desperate for the loo. I don't suppose you could tell me where it is?'

'Oh, gosh, dear, of course,' she says, guiding me back into the hallway. 'I'm the same after a coffee or two. There's a bathroom at the top of the stairs to the left.'

'Thank you,' I reply. 'I won't be a sec.'

The bathroom is light and vast. A huge roll-top bath sits on clawed feet in the centre of the room and the casement window looks out on to landscaped gardens. There is a large vase of white hydrangeas on the window ledge. They were my mother's favourite flower. The sight of them makes me smile. I go across to the window. Leaning forward, I pluck a large sprig of hydrangea. Holding it to my nose, I take a deep breath of its soft scent and whisper a silent wish to my mother. Then, tucking it into my bag, I head back out on to the landing.

'Does that feel better, dear?' says Jane, smiling warmly as I walk down the stairs towards her.

'Yes,' I reply serenely. 'That feels much better.'

When I get back to the flat I hear the shower running. Connor must have decided to work from home rather than go into the office. I slump down on the sofa, the euphoria of the house viewing still making me tingle. I'm about to get up and make a coffee when I hear a beep. I look down and see Connor's phone on the coffee table in front of me. Its screen is lit up and I can't help but see the text message displayed.

From: Sara
Sterling work, darling! Loads of love xxx

Just then Connor comes into the room. His hair is wet and he's wearing a hoodie and sweatpants.

'How was Georgie?' he says, sitting next to me. 'Nice lunch?'

'Yeah, it was lovely,' I say, any guilt I was feeling about lying to him over where I'd been now cancelled out by the arrival of that message. 'Your phone was beeping.'

'Ah,' he says, reaching out to pick it up.

I watch him as he reads it, though his face remains expressionless. He places the phone back on the table then jumps to his feet.

'Fancy a coffee?' he says, heading for the kitchen.

'Er, who is Sara?' I say, following him out of the room.

He turns and looks at me, shaking his head.

'Sara is my work colleague. She's the senior art director, been there for donkey's years. And she's gay. Christ, she calls everyone "darling".'

He laughs dismissively and heads into the kitchen.

'Right, let's have a STRONG coffee, shall we?'

Later that evening, I lie in bed feeling deflated. Connor spent the whole evening working while I sat by myself on the roof terrace drinking wine. Eventually, I gave up and went to bed. When Connor came in I pretended to be asleep but now, as he lies snoring beside me, no sleep will come. I feel prickly and on edge.

I need a distraction.

I take my phone from the side table and tiptoe out of the room. Then, sitting on the sofa, I click on the Dream Properties app. The sight of all those beautiful houses soothes me as the hours tick away. And then I see it: an Edwardian Arts and Crafts house in Bishop's Stortford. I can feel the adrenaline returning, the same buzz I got when I saw Rosedale Manor advertised. This feeling is better than drugs or alcohol. It is pure euphoria.

'This will be the last time,' I whisper to myself as I type another fake name into the booking form, 'then no more. I promise.'

13. Now

I can hear the children but I can't see them. Their voices, high-pitched and merry, follow me as I try to find my way out of the maze. The holly nips at my skin as I turn left then right, stumbling into the ragged hedge. Above me, the sky explodes with red and blue and golden fire, and I clutch my chest in fright. I need to get to the centre of the maze before it's too late. Behind me the children's voices grow fainter and I realize I'm getting close. The air seems to get thinner with every step I take and I feel my lungs tighten. *Almost there, Vanessa*, I tell myself, just a few more steps. And then I see him. Lying there, spread-eagled like some ancient sacrifice. Legs jutting out at awkward angles, eyes bulging from his dead, grey face.

Geoffrey.

I try to turn back but the way is blocked by overgrown holly. It pierces my ankles, wraps itself around my chest until I can't breathe. I'm going to die and no one will know where I am. I push back at the sharp leaves, blood running down my arms. Then I feel something touch my shoulder. I turn and see Geoffrey. He's still alive. He's holding something in his hand. My blood runs cold when I see what it is. Then, all of a sudden, I feel a pressure on my neck. I try to scream but no sound will come out.

'Vanessa.'

I sit up in bed, sweat sticking to my forehead, my heart racing.

'Vanessa, are you okay? You were screaming.'

I look up and see my sister standing at the door, her eyes drowsy with sleep.

'I was dreaming,' I say as I slowly come to. 'What time is it?'

'Just gone midnight,' she says, leaning her head against the door frame. 'I was going to call you down for supper but when I looked in you were sound asleep, so I left yours in the fridge. Are you hungry? I can get you something if you like?'

'I'm fine, thanks, Georgie,' I say, trying my best to sound like I am. 'I'm really sorry I woke you.'

She stands for a moment, watching me, her face a mixture of fatigue and concern.

'Oh, don't worry about that,' she says, with what looks like a forced smile. 'As long as you're okay, that's the main thing.'

'I am,' I reply, putting my head back on the pillow. 'Just a bad dream, that's all. Night, night, Georgie.'

I hear her close the door. Then, once I'm sure she's back in bed, I reach across and turn on the lamp. The dream has left me feeling shaken. The image of Geoffrey's body lying in the maze, the holly wrapping itself around my chest, makes me feel sick. I look at my bare arms, sure there must be scratches and cuts, but there's nothing. It was just a dream.

Then I remember. The bird.

I get out of bed and pull open the bottom drawer. The first thing I see is the signed paperback of *The Spirits of Holly Maze House* that I took from the house viewing in Battersea. I lift it out and run my fingers along the indents of Geoffrey's handwriting. Then, setting it aside, I take out the glass bird. The bird I took from his house.

As I stare back at it, I tell myself that people lie all the time, they make up versions of themselves on Instagram and Facebook and job applications that bear no resemblance to who they really are. It's not a crime to want to be someone else, to live someone else's life. But it is a crime to take one, and as long as this bird and the book are in my possession then I am in deep trouble.

I place them back in the drawer and turn out the light. Tomorrow I will get rid of them, I tell myself as I get back into bed. Then, and only then, will I be safe.

I stand on the packed Northern Line train, holding on to the rail and trying to keep my balance. Sweat gathers on my forehead as the train doors open to let another wave of passengers on.

The doors close and, as the train pulls out of the station, I put my hand in my bag to check the book and the bird are still there. I know it's not a good idea to go back to the house, but I can't escape the feeling that if I just dump them somewhere then bad things might happen: karma, whatever you want to call it. The bird, particularly, has always possessed a strange power and now, more than ever, I can't risk it. By returning the bird to its rightful place, I feel I'm honouring it somehow, as well as atoning for my crime. As for the book, well, it was only going to be thrown away in Battersea. Best to take it with the bird, back to the place where it was written.

When the train pulls into Hampstead I join the crush of bodies surging towards the exit. It's only 10 a.m. but, according to my phone, the temperature is already in the high twenties. As I reach the top of the stairs the crush intensifies. I put my hand out to grab the rail but before I can get a grip someone shoves me in the small of my back. I lose my footing and half fall down the stairs.

'Are you all right, dear?'

I look up and see an elderly woman with short grey hair and red lipstick. She is standing above me, holding out her hand.

'That idiot could have killed you.'

'Who?' I whimper, taking her hand and hauling myself up.

'The man who knocked into you,' says the woman, shaking her head. 'He'd already nearly sent me flying as I got off the train. I don't know, you expect behaviour like that during rush hour but on a Saturday morning – well, it's just not on. Are you sure you're okay, dear?'

I tell her that I'm fine, then, as she walks away I stand for a moment to catch my breath. The fall has disorientated me. Then I remember: the bird. I thrust my hand into my bag and, to my relief, find it's still there, unharmed. The thought of it being crushed under a hundred pairs of feet doesn't bear thinking about.

I run my fingers along its smooth glass surface, then, taking a deep breath, make my way out of the station and on to the high street.

The sun is baking hot on my back as I cross the road, aware of the volume of people, their eyes watching me. I take a left down a narrow side street and breathe a sigh of relief as I leave the crowds behind.

But as I get closer, my optimism fades. Ahead of me I see a line of police tape sealing off the end of the street. Two patrol cars are parked across the entrance to the house.

I look around. The street is empty. I feel conspicuous. What if Bains is up there? How would I explain my being here? I need to get away. Fast.

I turn on my heels, the weight of the bird and book pressing on my shoulders, but as I reach the bustle of the high street and prepare to join the throng of tourists heading from the station, I tell myself that I have to hold my nerve. I have to finish this.

Then I remember something. The stones. The gravestones that Geoffrey stumbled upon on a walk, before he had even written the books. He had often said in interviews that the stones seemed to exert a force on him, drawing him in until he could read the names on them – Tom and Cecil. Then he saw the third stone and how the name had been scratched away, and he couldn't get them out of his mind. He decided to use those names for his ghost boys and came up with a new name and a new identity for the inhabitant of the mysterious third grave. And so Angus's great love, Iris, was created.

The patch of grass where the stones are laid is accessible via a little pathway to the left of the house. If I judge it right, I can be in and out in under a minute without being seen.

I turn back, my heart hammering in my chest. Any moment now, Bains is going to appear and then it's all over. But the road is still empty; the occupants of the police cars nowhere to be seen.

Without pausing, I turn left and find myself on a gravel pathway, overgrown with weeds. Only those who really paid attention to Geoffrey and his books would know of this shortcut. It was the focus of one of his lesser-known books, *Trouble at Holly Maze House*, which was published as a Christmas special in 1997. By then, Geoffrey's star had begun to wane a little and there was talk in the press that he was having trouble at home himself, though no one was really sure of the details. I know, because after Mum's death I did as much research into him as I could. After that he disappeared from view for a couple of years, returning in 1999 with a much-celebrated anthology of children's ghost stories before stepping away from the limelight altogether.

The air feels cooler as I head further down the path, the spindly branches of an elder tree forming a natural canopy above me. The noise of the high street feels a million miles away as I draw closer to the stones.

As I walk towards them more of the story comes back to me.

Angus liked to make model aeroplanes. His desk was covered in bits of cardboard and glue and scissors. He liked logic and patterns, and when he grew up he planned to be an engineer so he could save enough money to leave Holly Maze House and go home. Home was the little terraced house with the blue door in Mallison Street where Angus had lived with his mum and dad. But when his mum died, everything had changed.

In Mallison Street he had been an ordinary kid. One of the things he loved most was playing football in the park across the road – that and eating biscuits with Mrs Perkins, the nice old lady who lived next door.

Yes, Mrs Perkins! I remember her. She was the one who said that lovely thing about home, that 'a house is built on money; a home is built on love'.

Mr and Mrs Perkins were good people. Angus's mother loved Mrs Perkins because she had reminded her of her own mother, who had died just before Angus was born. They used to look after him when his mum was ill and Mrs Perkins used to help organize his birthday parties.

The birthday party, I remember that bit too. Angus's sixth birthday party, his last in Mallison Street. All his friends came and he danced wildly to his favourite song: 'Don't Stop Me Now' by Queen.

Mrs Perkins was at the party. That's right. My brain is moving faster than my feet.

He had loved the glass bird that sat on Mrs Perkins's mantelpiece ever since he was a baby. Mrs Perkins had told him that he could play with the bird and that it was special because its eyes were blue and sparkly just like his.

And when Mrs Perkins died, her husband had given Angus the bird, telling him that his wife wanted him to have it.

Her gravestone. Yes. It's all returning to me now.

Angus and his mum had gone to lay flowers on Mrs Perkins's grave and Angus had brought the bird along. He sat down next to the gravestone and told Mrs Perkins that the bird was their messenger, that if she had anything to say she could tell the bird and it would pass the message on to him.

How could I have forgotten that? It was such a big part of the story. I used to dream about that bird. It was just as real to me as Angus was. I can't believe I actually got to see it, to touch it, to hold it, to keep it for a little while.

And now I have to do the right thing and give it back.

Cecil and Tom are still there, though their stones are weatherworn and covered in moss and lichen. The third stone is gnarled and worn and sits in the shade of a large yew tree. As I stand here looking at it, I recall the opening line of the final chapter of the book where Angus has to say goodbye to his ghostly friends: '*The girl he loved lived in a shady spot, next door to the angels. Her protectors in this life and the next.*'

This stone is larger than the other two and is decorated with cherubic figures and musical notes. There are two stone vases on either side, empty of flowers. I kneel down in front of the stone, a deep sense of sadness enveloping me.

I take the book out of my bag first, rolling it up and pushing it into one of the vases. Next, I take the glass bird and place it in the palm of my hand. It looks smaller somehow. Its eyes have lost their sparkle.

'Goodnight, Geoffrey,' I whisper as I slip the bird into the second vase. 'I'm sorry for what I did.'

Sitting on the train as it approaches Wimbledon, I feel like a great burden has been lifted from me. As the train pulls into the station, I stand up and head for the door, enjoying the feeling. I press the button and step out into glorious August sunshine. I'll stop off at Waitrose on the way back and buy some food for supper. Georgie and Jack have been so good to me, it's about time I gave something back.

I exit the turnstiles and I'm just heading for the high street when my phone beeps in my hand. As always, I get a little flutter of hope that it might be Lottie, but as I stop by the pizza restaurant on the corner of the street I see that it's a Messenger notification from someone called G.

I can't quite make out the profile picture in the glare of the sun, but I'm sure that I don't have a Facebook contact called G. I'm rather cautious about adding people I don't know. Curious, I click open the message and what I see makes my heart freeze.

There is a photograph, clear and seemingly taken up close, of me placing the glass bird on Iris's grave.

But it's the message underneath that sends chills down my spine.

Found you.

I almost drop my phone in fright. I want to delete the message but I need to see who the person is. I click on their name and a Facebook profile comes up. G has no 'friends' and has shared no posts. The only photo is that of his/her profile image which, now that I'm standing in the shade, I can see clearly. My heart twists inside my chest as I enlarge the photo and see, looking back at me with vacant, open eyes, the dead face of Geoffrey Rivers.

14. Then

March 2018

It's Friday afternoon and the offices of Luna London are a hive of excitement. The younger interns and PAs are clustered round each other's desks, testing out some of our new make-up lines and getting ready for the night ahead. I smile as one of them, Layla – a strikingly attractive woman with long brown hair – swaggers up and down the gangway, pouting to the sound of Sia's 'Chandelier', which is blasting out across the office. This is their unofficial catwalk and as I watch them I feel a tinge of envy, remembering how Lottie and I would make a ritual of getting ready for a night out when we were at Durham. We'd pour a glass of wine and give each other's outfits the once-over. She'd do my eyeliner, which I was terrible at, and I'd tease her hair into big curls. I recall that strange butterfly sensation I used to feel in my stomach before a big night out, the thought that anything could happen.

Then I look at the image I have just pulled up on my screen – a five-storey Victorian townhouse in Highgate – and I think how the idea of creating a perfect home now outweighs any desire to go out drinking and clubbing. How did that happen? Is it an age thing? You reach your thirties and suddenly your needs change. I prefer to think that it's down to meeting Connor. Creating a home that we can be a family in is all part of that.

I click through a few more images of the Highgate house, imagining what I would do to it if I owned it. There's a secluded sixty-foot garden with a raised seating area. I picture the herbs I would plant in terracotta pots, the subtle lighting I would introduce. Inside the house there's a huge bathroom that would benefit from a roll-top bath and Moroccan-style tiling. As I'm lost in this reverie my phone rings on the desk beside me. I smile when I see Connor's name on the screen.

'Hello,' I say, minimizing the webpage on my computer. 'I was just thinking about you.'

'Good thoughts, I hope,' he says, his voice rather breathless.

'Always,' I reply. 'Where are you? You sound like you've been running.'

'I'm just on my way to Shoreditch,' he says, his voice momentarily drowned out by a piercing siren. 'Which is why I'm calling. There's a boxing match tonight. The company's sponsoring it. I meant to tell you about it earlier but I've been so busy this week . . .'

His voice cuts out and there's a fizzing noise on the line.

'Connor? I can't hear you.'

'Sorry, is that better? I've stopped in a doorway.'

'Yes, I can hear you now. What were you saying? Something about a boxing match?'

'Yeah,' he says. 'I meant to tell you but I got caught up with work. Anyway, it's tonight at 7.30.'

'Oh,' I say, feeling crestfallen. 'So you're going to be out tonight? That's a shame. We've hardly seen each other this week.'

'I know. Which is why I want you to come and join me. It'll be fun.'

'But you know I don't like boxing,' I say, flinching as one of the girls lets out a shriek of laughter. 'It makes me squeamish.'

'Oh, it's not a full-on bout,' he says. 'It's more of a corporate evening, an exhibition fight.'

'I'm not sure,' I say. 'I really wanted a night in with you this evening. It's been a long week.'

'It won't go on for long,' says Connor. 'An hour max and then we can go and have a nice meal somewhere. What do you say? I'd love it if you could come.'

I think for a moment, imagining the long evening ahead, all alone in the flat with just a bottle of wine and the Dream Property app for company. It's been like this for a few weeks now, I realize – Connor being out a lot. Not that I mind a quiet night in. But now he's inviting me along, and I know that I should make the effort. He's been to enough of my works gatherings and family lunches. And it's unfair of me to want him all to myself.

'Okay, I'll come,' I say, closing down my computer. 'What's the address?'

'That's brilliant, baby,' he says. 'I'll text you the details now.'

'I love you,' I say, but he has already clicked off.

One hour later I'm walking up and down Shoreditch High Street trying to find Redchurch Street, where, Connor informed me in his text, I will find a black-painted building with no number or signage. Huh, not very helpful. 'It's a pop-up venue,' he'd replied vaguely when I'd texted him from Sloane Square station expressing my confusion.

At last I find Redchurch Street and see what looks like the right building. I try the door but it's locked. Beside the door is a strip of buttons with no names next to them, again unhelpfully. I press the top buzzer and wait. After a minute or so I hear someone on the other side. The door opens and an elderly man with a goatee beard stands in front of me. He's wearing a grubby dressing gown and is holding a mug of tea.

'I'm sorry,' I say, taking my phone and bringing up Connor's message. 'Er . . . I'm looking for . . . this isn't the Ultimate Clash boxing event, is it?'

The man regards me for a moment then starts to laugh.

'I don't think so, love,' he says, shaking his head. 'Not with my knees.'

He closes the door and as I stand looking up and down the street it starts to rain.

'Shit,' I cry, huddling into a doorway. 'I just wanted a night in.'

I take out my phone and call Connor's number. It goes straight to voicemail. Then I see a group of men outside a grey building on the other side of the street. They are dressed in gym gear and one of them is holding a kitbag. I dash across the street, almost slipping on the wet pavement.

'Excuse me,' I shout as I draw level with them. 'I'm looking for the boxing event. Have I got the right place?'

One of them, a young black guy with cropped hair, smirks as he looks at my sodden trouser suit.

'Yep,' he says, gesturing to the door behind me. 'Down those stairs.'

I follow some of the men inside and find myself in a dark corridor. The air smells of sweat and cheap deodorant and the walls are covered in graffiti and torn posters.

'Through there,' says a voice behind me.

I turn. It's the young guy from outside. He gestures ahead of him.

'Thanks,' I say as I make my way into the gloom.

The corridor opens into a small, square room, with a large boxing ring in the centre. It's already heaving with people and as I squeeze through I see Connor standing with two men at the edge of the ring. He looks up as I approach and starts to laugh.

'Oh dear, what happened to you?' he says, pulling me towards him and kissing my cheek. 'This is Hanif and Bobby, by the way,' he says, gesturing to the two men standing next to him.

'It started to rain,' I say, smiling politely at the two men, who look more interested in the ring. I start to sway on my feet. The heat of the room is making me feel light-headed. 'And I got lost. You said it was a black building but it's grey.'

'Sorry about that,' he says, looking around the room distractedly. 'Anyway, you're here now and the fight's just about to start.'

'What?' I say, but my voice is drowned out by the sound of Rag'n'Bone Man's 'Human' blasting at full volume.

The lights go down and then a solitary spotlight falls on the entrance. I watch as a dark, hooded figure enters the room, bouncing on his feet like a springbok.

'That's Mark Fahey, the champion,' whispers Connor in my ear. His breath smells of stale beer. It makes me feel nauseous. 'The guy in the ring is Julius Morris, the contender.'

I look at the ripped guy standing in the centre of the ring. His eyes are blazing as he smashes his gloved fists together. There's a strange energy in the room that unsettles me, the prelude to something nasty.

The crowd starts to chant the name of the champion as he enters the ring. The chanting is accompanied by the stamping of feet that makes the ground beneath me vibrate. It's hot and airless in here and I feel something akin to travel sickness as the two men square up to each other, their noses almost touching.

'Come on, Fahey, fucking kill him,' yells a male voice behind me as the bell rings and the fight begins.

I glance at Connor. He's staring straight ahead, engrossed in the action. I notice he has his fists clenched. Behind me, the man who shouted is now providing a running commentary to the fight, screaming expletives as the two fighters skirt around each other.

The first punch comes from the contender, Julius Morris, and is so hard it makes me flinch. It unbalances Fahey and the crowd go wild. They're getting what they have come to see.

'Come on, Fahey, you fucking poof,' shouts the man behind me. 'End this sucker, for fuck's sake.'

And it looks like that's what Fahey is going to do. He ploughs into the contender like a machine, punching him in the side, and then, when Morris drops his guard, square in the jaw. Blood spurts from the contender's face, much to the delight of the crowd. The nausea that had been mild when I first arrived now intensifies. I turn to Connor. He's glued to the action. I shake his arm and he looks at me with an expression of irritation.

'What?' he hisses.

'I don't like this,' I say, raising my voice to be heard above the jeering crowd. 'You said it wouldn't be bloody.'

'It's a fucking boxing match, Vanessa,' he says, shaking his head and returning his gaze to the ring. 'I said it wouldn't take long and it won't by the look of it.'

'Connor, I really want to go,' I say, my stomach twisting. 'I don't feel very well.'

'Vanessa, please,' he says, pulling me closer. 'We have to stay. My company is sponsoring this fight. It'll look terrible if I leave in the middle of it. I told you we'd go and have drinks afterwards. Now shush and let me focus.'

I stand there, dumbfounded. He's never spoken to me like that before. I stare at the side of his head but he's completely oblivious.

Inside the ring, Morris is still taking a pummelling but he's on his feet, refusing to concede. His face is a mass of blood and swelling. It's a hideous sight.

Looking down at the beer-soaked floor, I close my eyes and try to think of the most innocent and pleasant image I can, something distracting. I momentarily land back in my old kitchen that final day with Mum. I see her face, her eyes twinkling as she listens to Geoffrey on the radio, see her grab for the pen to scribble down the name of the book. I hear her melodic, soft voice repeating it to make sure she got it right: '*The Spirits of Holly Maze House*. Ooh, that sounds right up your street.' But then a deafening roar goes up from the crowd and the memory fractures into a thousand pieces. *It must be over*, I think to myself. But as I open my eyes I see, in front of me, the horrifying sight of Morris lying on the floor of the ring, his face a mass of bloodied flesh.

It's horror beyond words, but it's not over. Within seconds, he's back on his feet, though he staggers from side to side like an injured animal. Fahey comes at him. Morris raises his gloved hands to block the punch but he's clearly too weak to defend himself. The blazing-eyed young man who had looked so fresh and handsome as he stood in the ring at the beginning of the fight now flops around drowsily as Fahey rains blow after blow upon him. The knockout punch seems to come from nowhere. Morris falls on his side. The crowd cheers with unrestrained glee. And all the while, beside me, Connor stands transfixed, his hands still balled into fists.

I feel dizzy; a mix of the intense heat, the noise and the unquiet sense of doom that pervades the room. I need to get out of here.

'I'm going to get some air,' I say to Connor, squeezing past him.

'Vanessa, you can't, it's . . .'

His voice is drowned out by shouts of 'Move out of the way, you silly cow!', 'Oy, move it, woman!'

At the end of the row I feel a rush of bodies coming towards me. My way is barred. Panic engulfs me as the crush gets stronger. I can't breathe.

'Are you okay?'

There's a hand on my arm. I look up and see a man in a red baseball cap. He has large blue eyes and a bright-red scar running from his left eye to his mouth. I look at him for a moment, try to speak, but no words will come.

'Vanessa, come on.'

Connor grabs my arm from behind and pulls me through the crowd. When we reach the exit he turns to me and shakes his head.

'Did you really have to do that?' he says angrily. 'The fight was finished. There was no need to make a scene.'

'I'm sorry,' I say, putting my hand to my chest as I attempt to get my breath back. 'It was just so hot . . . and the sight of the blood, it –'

'Come on,' he says, his voice gentle now. 'Let's go and get something to eat.'

The last thing I want to do is eat but Connor is insisting.

'I know a lovely little Spanish place near here,' he says as we take a right off the high street and continue down a small mews. 'Damian took me when I last met up with him. You'll like it. The food's great.'

I try to explain to him that I'm feeling ill, that I can't get rid of the image of that poor young guy being literally torn apart right in front of me, but he won't listen.

'What you need is something to line your stomach,' he says as we approach the glass doors of the restaurant. 'You came here straight from work during rush hour. That's why you're feeling funny.'

He turns to me and flashes a smile. This would usually melt me but this evening, in the light of what I've just witnessed, his smile seems grotesque.

'Okay, but I don't want to stay out late,' I say as we walk up the steps. 'Just eat and then go home. I need to rest.'

'Christ, you sound like an old woman, Ness,' he says as we enter the bar. 'Where's your sense of adventure gone?'

I don't understand what's going on here. Connor's never spoken to me like this before. But then, I realize, I've never really said no to him before.

'Hey, guys. Table for two?'

A tall, olive-skinned woman with striking brown eyes and glossy black bobbed hair greets us at the door. I watch as Connor flashes her the same smile he just used on me a couple of minutes ago as she leads us to a candlelit table by the bar.

'So what can I get you?' she says, talking directly to Connor as though I don't exist. 'Some drinks to start?'

'A menu would be great,' says Connor as she pulls out a chair for him to sit. 'And a bottle of Rioja.'

'Sure,' she says, returning the flirtatious stare as she walks back to the bar.

'A small glass would have been enough for me,' I say, sitting down at the table, opposite him. 'Not a bottle.'

'That's fine,' he says with a sigh. 'I'll drink the rest. Look, Vanessa, what is this?' His voice is loud and brittle.

'What's what?' I say, sweat gathering on my forehead.

'This anger,' he says, leaning forward in his chair. 'You're totally wired, for some reason.'

'Anger?' I repeat, my head feeling hot and heavy. 'I don't know what you're talking about. All I said was that I didn't feel like drinking much.'

'Yes, but you said it in a very aggressive way,' he says.

'No I didn't,' I say, feeling my chest tighten. 'I said it in a normal way, maybe even a tired way, but I didn't say it angrily. You're the one who's raising your voice.'

'You're doing it again,' he says, lowering his voice now.

'Doing what?'

'Projecting,' he says, biting his bottom lip. 'Making out that I'm the one ruining this, that I'm the pissed-off one, when you've spent the entire evening with a face like thunder.'

'Your drinks.'

He looks up at the woman and his face changes in front of me. The dark expression switches to a thousand-kilowatt smile in a matter of seconds.

'Wonderful,' he says as the woman places the glasses on the table and pours a small amount of wine in each.

'And here are the menus,' she says, handing one to Connor while putting mine down on the table. 'Our specials are on the board.'

She gestures to a blackboard on the wall to the right of us.

'Thank you,' says Connor as the woman walks away.

'Well,' he says, lifting his glass. 'Let's start again, shall we? Cheers.'

I don't feel like toasting. I feel like I want to get to the bottom of why he said I was angry, but the truth is I don't have the energy. I feel hot and tired and still shaken up by the sight of that blood. So I let it go and take a sip of wine.

I open the menu, but my appetite has gone.

'I think I'll just have a salad,' I say, closing it.

'You need more than that,' says Connor, craning his neck to look at the board on the far wall. 'Oh, look, they've got Rabo de Toro.'

'What's that?' I ask, dabbing my forehead with a napkin.

'I shouldn't say.'

'Why? What is it?'

'Well, it's a classic Spanish dish,' he says, leaning across and taking my hand. 'Basically, after the bullfight, tradition has it that the bull is slaughtered and the meat fed to the poor. The tail is full of flavour and goodness, and they remove it immediately and make a stew.'

'And that's what's on the specials board?' I say, shaking my head. 'But that's sick.'

'It'll just be oxtail of some sort,' he says, his eyes still on the menu. 'As we don't have bullfighting in this country, they won't be able to serve up the tail of the freshly slaughtered bull. It's just their take on it.'

'It's still sick,' I say, the smell of the blood that filled the room earlier lodged in my nostrils.

'I would have liked to try it but, hey ho, I'll save it for another time,' Connor says, taking a large glug of wine. 'I think I'll go for the octopus salad instead and the patatas bravas. Will you share some with me?'

I nod my head. I don't really feel like eating anything heavy but I don't want to cause another argument.

The woman returns and takes our order. Connor says something to her in Spanish. She looks at me and giggles, then, collecting the menus, walks away, still giggling.

'What did you say to her?' I ask, taking an olive from the dish the woman had put down along with the wine.

'Oh, nothing,' he says with a shrug. 'Just trying out some Spanish I picked up in Barcelona a few years back. I wanted to see if she understood.'

'You said something funny,' I say, removing the olive stone and placing it on the napkin. 'And then she laughed at me.'

'God, Vanessa, what is the matter with you today?' he says, his eyes widening. 'You're in such a bad mood.'

'I just wanted to know what you said to her,' I say. 'And why she laughed at me.'

'She was being friendly,' he says, sighing. 'Smiling and laughing. Christ, is that a crime?'

I don't answer. If I do, it will only make things worse.

We sit in silence for a few moments. Our food arrives and we begin to eat.

'It's delicious,' I say to Connor, doing my best to sound upbeat. 'Particularly the potatoes.'

'You don't have to do that, you know,' he says, smiling. 'Do what?'

'Pretend you're enjoying this,' he says, refilling our glasses with the Rioja. 'It's my fault. I should have gone to the fight alone. Plus, this part of London isn't to everyone's tastes. We should just stick to Chelsea and Clapham and Wimbledon for our evenings out, your comfort zones.'

'No,' I say, feeling genuinely aggrieved. 'I'm not some sort of idiot who can't handle being in the East End. It was just the fight. You told me it was going to be for show. No blood.'

His eyes go cold then and he shakes his head.

'What?' I say, leaning back in my chair as the waitress collects our empty dishes. 'What is it, Connor?'

'Oh, I don't know, Vanessa,' he says, nodding to the waitress as she departs. 'I just feel like I'm the one doing all the giving. I helped you nail the US presentation, I sat up all night helping you come up with straplines for the new lipstick campaign, I helped you draft that tricky email when you had to let the new intern go, and I don't mind giving you a hand, but tonight was just as important to me. I've been working on the branding for UC Boxing for months now and I'd never been to a fight before. It was something I wanted to see, wanted to experience, so I could translate that into the branding. And I'm sorry you didn't enjoy it but there are times we have to do things we don't like because life's not all glitter and powder and lipstick.'

I ignore the dig at my choice of career and let him continue.

'I thought you would be more supportive, that's all,' he says, pausing to take a sip of wine. 'Particularly after all the help I've given you. But you're just like the rest of them.'

'The rest of them?' I say, feeling my cheeks burning.

'Women are wonderful,' he says, smiling. 'I was raised by a single mother. I love them to death but there are just some things they'll never understand. Sam was exactly the same when I took her to a fight.'

He stops then, aware that he's let something slip.

'Who's Sam?' I say, feeling the wine in my bloodstream.

'Oh, just a woman I used to know,' he says, waving his hand dismissively.

'A girlfriend?'

'Girlfriend is a bit generous,' he says with a frown. 'I mean, she was more like a . . . well, it was just a physical thing with Sam. She was a bit of a psycho if truth be told.'

'But I thought you hadn't seen a live fight before,' I say, my body tensing.

'No, I said I hadn't seen a UC fight before,' he says, raising his hand to beckon the waitress. She catches his eye and is by his side in a matter of moments.

'Another, please,' he says, gesturing to the empty Rioja bottle. 'Thanks.'

She smiles and leans across him to take the bottle. When she has gone he sits forward and clasps my hands.

'Listen, let's not waste any more of this evening talking about exes,' he says, squeezing my fingers tightly. 'I know you get paranoid about other women, like the text from Sara the other day, but you have to understand that it's you I love, okay? Now, if you'll excuse me, I'm bursting for a pee.'

He laughs then jumps up from the table and heads across the bar to the loos.

I sit at the table, my heart racing. The way Connor has been talking, he thinks I'm some self-centred, jealous girlfriend. But I do care about his work and it was him who brought up Sam, a woman I didn't know existed until just now, and the fact that they had been to a boxing match together.

'Here we are,' says the waitress, placing the second bottle of Rioja on the table. 'Enjoy.'

She slinks away, clearly disappointed to have missed another opportunity to flirt with Connor. Yet as I think this thought, I ask myself if I am doing what Connor has accused me of: being paranoid. This woman is just being friendly, doing her job, chatting to the customers.

Loosen up, Vanessa, I tell myself as Connor returns to the table. *Show him that you're not being a boring, paranoid sap.*

'Right,' I say, pouring him another glass of wine as Spanish guitar music strikes up. 'Let's start this evening again. I'm sorry I've been a grouch, baby. It's just been a long week and I've missed you.'

'I missed you too,' says Connor, his eyes twinkling in the half-light. 'Let's not waste another second arguing over things that don't matter.'

I smile and take a glug of wine, but it burns all the way down my throat.

15. Now

I walk back to Georgie's house in a daze and I'm trembling so much it takes me three attempts to get the key in the lock. When I finally get the door open I'm greeted by the sight of Jack rushing towards me, his face flushed.

'Oh, it's you,' he says, the colour fading from his cheeks. 'We thought it was . . . quick, come in.'

Georgie appears behind him and puts her hands round his waist.

'Hi, darling,' she says to me, smiling. 'How are you?'

'Make sure the latch is on, Vanessa,' says Jack, looking intently at the door.

He's scaring me now. And after the shock I've just had, this is the last thing I need.

'What's the matter?' I say, the grisly photo of Geoffrey's dead body seared into my mind. 'Is everything okay?'

'Not sure really,' says Jack, smiling unconvincingly. 'It seems there was an intruder spotted in next-door's garden last night. Number 1. Old Mrs Haverleigh's place. Her son came round this morning to let us know. It's probably just kids – or even, dare I say it, Mrs H's mind playing tricks on her. She's almost ninety and gets easily confused. I caught her putting out full milk bottles instead of the empties last week. Still, it wouldn't hurt us to be a bit more vigilant.

Anyway, I need to do some work, I'll be in my study if anyone needs me.'

I glance at my sister as Jack disappears down the passageway. She looks tired.

'Is Jack all right?' I say, putting my own concerns aside for a moment. 'I've never seen him like that.'

'He's fine,' she says, displaying her 'responsible big sister' demeanour: shoulders back, smile fixed. 'He just got a bit unsettled by the . . . by the intruder thing, that's all.'

I take off my jacket and hang it with my bag on the antique metal coat rack. I haven't looked at my phone since I deleted the message and blocked the sender at the station. It now sits, switched off, at the bottom of my bag. I feel that if I don't think about it then the message, the sender, Geoffrey's dead face, cease to exist. Though I know I'm just fooling myself.

'Let me cook tonight, Georgie,' I say, thinking how a few hours' distraction is just what I need. 'Give yourself the night off.'

'Oh, darling, that would be lovely,' she says, her face brightening. 'But let me come and sit with you so we can chat. I get so bored when Jack locks himself in the study.'

In the kitchen I take the pan to the sink and fill it with water. Behind me I hear Georgie opening the French doors. I don't feel safe having them open like that. Though the garden is pretty private, with fencing on both sides, there is a public walkway at the end of it, with only a low hedge between it and the garden. Anyone could climb over that hedge and then . . .

I try not to imagine that scenario. Instead I take the pan to the hob, add olive oil and salt and turn on the gas flame.

'So did Mrs Haverleigh's son say anything else about the intruder?' I say, watching as Georgie takes a bottle of white wine out of the fridge and places it on the counter. 'Did they get a description of him?'

'Only from what Mrs Haverleigh said she saw,' says Georgie, taking two glass goblets from the pale-green French cabinet. 'And as Jack says, she's not the most reliable of witnesses.'

'What did she see?' I ask, taking a packet of pasta from the top shelf.

'She said it was a man, medium build, and wearing some sort of hat,' says Georgie, visibly shuddering as she pours the wine. 'It's a horrible thought, that someone could be prowling around like that. Let's hope it was just a figment of Mrs Haverleigh's imagination.'

She takes a long glug of wine and pulls a dining chair over to the open French doors. I can't help thinking we would all feel safer if she would just close them. As I look at Georgie sitting there, her blue linen skirt billowing slightly in the evening breeze, I get a flashback to Holly Maze House: Geoffrey standing by the open windows, his face almost obscured by the light of the sun.

'I'm making penne arrabbiata for supper,' I say, trying to erase the image, and everything it represents, from my mind. 'I'm just hoping we've got enough basil.'

'Sounds delicious, thanks, Nessa,' says Georgie. 'There should be a bunch of basil in the fridge but if not I can go and pick some from the garden pots.'

A feeling of guilt sweeps through me as I walk over to the fridge. I should be contributing more, paying my way. I make a mental note to place an online grocery order in the morning.

I open the fridge and find two large bunches of basil. I take one, along with an onion, three cloves of garlic and three red chillies, and bring them over to the chopping board.

'More than enough basil,' I say to Georgie as I start chopping onions. 'No need to go out there.'

Behind me I hear her pour another glass of wine.

'I was thinking about Lottie earlier,' she says, coming over to stand by me as I chop. 'Do you think that *was* her you saw in the village?'

'It certainly looked like her,' I say as I press the back of Jack's expensive Kitchen Devil knife down on to a fat clove of garlic. 'Though it probably wasn't. The sun was in my eyes and then that daft guy jumped out at us.'

'Oh yeah, the pantomime horse,' says Georgie, taking a slice of raw onion from the chopping board and popping it in her mouth. 'The things people do for money. It beggars belief. Why don't you give Lottie a call? See if it was her.'

Though Georgie knows that Lottie and I have fallen out, I haven't told her that Lottie went so far as to change her number, and I haven't the energy to tell her now, not with everything that has happened today. Though I must admit it would be nice to see Lottie again, to tell her what's been going on, to have her reassure me that it's all going to be okay.

'Like I said, it probably wasn't her,' I say, taking a frying pan from the hook above the hob and pouring a glug of olive oil into it. 'And if she had come back to the UK for a visit she would have probably gone to Edinburgh to see her mum. There would be no reason for her to be in London.'

I turn to look at Georgie. She has returned to sit by the open French window, sipping wine and fanning herself with a copy of *Wimbledon Life*.

'You're right. Plus, she would have called you if she'd been here. No matter how pissed off she might have been by you moving out of the flat. I'm sure she's got over it by now,' says Georgie. 'God, it's humid tonight. Perhaps we should eat outside.'

'No,' I say, rather too firmly.

She looks at me and raises her eyebrows.

'There were loads of midges out there the other day,' I say, turning back to the hob where the onions are slowly turning golden in the pan. 'You know how I hate them. Anyway, it couldn't have been Lottie because she hates Wimbledon. She only ever came here to see you and even then she used to say it brought back bad memories. You remember that business with Andy, the guy she met in the Crooked Billet?'

'The married man who forgot to tell her about his wife?' says Georgie. 'Yes, that was awful. Men can be such bastards. They really can.'

She gets up and goes to the fridge, taking out a pot of black olives which she tips into a porcelain bowl and places on the counter.

'That sounds ominous,' says Jack, walking into the kitchen. 'Shall I change into my bulletproof vest?'

He looks more relaxed now, the colour has returned to his cheeks.

'Dinner will be about ten minutes,' I say as he goes to the fridge and takes out a bottle of mineral water. 'I just need to set the table.'

'Let me do that,' says Jack. 'It would be nice for this "bastard" to make himself useful.'

Georgie flashes a look at him and I feel the atmosphere cool.

'Thanks, Jack,' I say, handing him the cutlery. 'I'll go and freshen up.'

I walk out of the kitchen. As I pass the coat rack I think about my phone lying in the bottom of my bag and the message I'd received a couple of hours earlier. I know I should just leave it but curiosity gets the better of me and I unzip my bag and take out the phone.

There are sixteen missed calls, all from an unknown number. My legs go numb. What if it's the police? What if they saw me earlier? What if whoever took that photo, the mysterious G, passed it on to them? With shaking hands, I scroll to voicemail but there are no messages.

Keep calm, I tell myself as I put the phone back into my bag and head up the stairs. *It's probably nothing, just sales calls or a wrong number.*

But I know, in my gut, that something is gathering momentum. I am being watched and whoever is watching me knows what I did.

I creep down the stairs and walk along the narrow hallway. The lights are switched off but a thin sliver of moonlight filters through the window, illuminating the framed photo that sits on the sideboard. I see my mum's wide smile, her sparkling green eyes, her tanned arms, and I remember summer 1993, a Spanish beach, my dad holding up the camera: 'Say cheese, Penny!'

I tiptoe towards the living room. The door is closed but I can hear that woman's voice again.

'– off Flushing Lane.'

'But that's just minutes from here, officer.'

'It was instant, Mr Adams. She won't have suffered.'

'My daughters . . . they'll be devastated.'

I run back up the hallway, past my mother's smiling photo. When I reach the safety of my yellow bedroom I flop down on the bed and close my eyes. I'm back in the kitchen. It's morning. Mum is making toast and jam and listening to Terry Wogan. Focus on that, I tell myself, focus on it hard enough and maybe you'll be able to bring her back.

16. Then

May 2018

'The house belonged to Magda Ivanov, the famous Russian artist,' says the estate agent as she opens the door to a vast studio. 'She died last year.'

I stand in the doorway and sniff the air, the smell of oil paint and turps still lingering though the room has been cleared.

The house, a mid-nineteenth-century terrace on Glebe Place, had popped up on the app when I logged on this morning. It had been a while since I'd had my last viewing fix and this house, just a couple of minutes' walk from the office, had piqued my interest. Like all the other ones, it began with a gut feeling. When I saw the photo of this house, with its ivy-clad facade, secret-garden roof terrace and rose-pink door, I knew I had to go and experience it for myself.

'So, you're an art collector, Miss Holmes?'

I smile at the estate agent, a middle-aged, birdlike woman called Melanie, and nod my head.

'I've invested in a few pieces, yes,' I say as she guides me out of the room and into the hallway. 'I'm always on the lookout for early Grimshaw sketches though they're as rare as hen's teeth.'

'I'm afraid I haven't heard of that artist,' says Melanie, consulting her brochure. 'Now, shall we take a look at the kitchen?'

Twenty minutes later, the tour over, I say goodbye to Melanie and watch as she drives away in her silver Audi TT. She has been reassured that Miss Monica Holmes, art collector and hedge-fund manager, will be in touch shortly to confirm whether or not she plans to make an offer.

As I walk back to the office I slip my hand in my pocket and rub the small, wooden doorstop I had taken from the hallway as I waited for Melanie to lock the roof-terrace door. This can take pride of place in the house Connor and I buy, I think to myself, as I walk through the entrance of Luna London and head to the lift. It will be a little good-luck charm, a reminder of what I can achieve if I put my mind to it.

When I get back to my desk I feel invigorated. The house viewings always leave me feeling this way, as though anything is possible. I have a list of emails to deal with but before I get down to work I type out a message to Connor.

> Hi, baby, shall I meet you after work tonight?

He texts back within a few seconds.

> Sorry, flat out here. Going to be another late one. See you when I get back.

The terseness of his message jars. I think back to the heady early days of our relationship, when he would text me numerous times a day, telling me how much he loved me and sending me links to songs that reminded him of me. But ever since the boxing match, something has shifted. Or had it shifted before then, and I just hadn't noticed?

I text back.

No worries. I love you.

I place the phone on my desk and try to read through a press release that Claire, the new marketing assistant, has written but the words blur in front of me. I can't concentrate. All the happiness I had felt after viewing the house has dissipated. I feel wretched and my eyes fill with tears.

'Just popping out for some pastries. Can I get you anything?'

I look up and see Anne standing in the doorway. I quickly dab my eyes and flash her my best 'everything's fine' smile.

'Er, I'm good, thanks, Anne. I had a late lunch.'

'Are you okay, Vanessa?' she says, coming into my office and closing the door behind her. 'You look upset.'

Then, noticing the document on my computer screen, she raises her eyebrows. 'I see you got Claire's press release,' she says, sitting on the arm of the soft chair next to the window. 'I got a copy this morning and couldn't make head nor tail of it. She's got great energy, Claire, but her communication skills require a little more work. Still, not bad enough to reduce you to tears. What is it, Vanessa? You can tell me.'

I look up at her and, to my shame, feel the tears start to stream down my cheeks.

'Hey,' she says, getting up from the chair and coming to me. 'What is it, now? What's made you so upset?'

'You'll think I'm stupid,' I say, pulling out a tissue from the box on my desk and dabbing my eyes with it. 'It's ridiculous, really.'

'Try me,' says Anne, crouching on her haunches, her neat, blue-rimmed glasses perched on the end of her nose.

'It's . . . it's just Connor,' I say, trying to steady my voice.

'Your boyfriend?' says Anne, frowning. 'What's he done?'

'Nothing,' I say, flinching as one of the assistants turns the music up outside. They can't seem to do anything without a soundtrack. 'He's just been working late a lot and we never see each other.' I don't quite know how to put the rest of it into words.

'Ah, but that's perfectly normal,' says Anne. She gets up and walks over to the water cooler. 'I remember when Maurice and I were first married, we barely saw each other. He was commuting to Brussels back then and I was busy setting up the business. You and Connor are both ambitious young people too. But your generation have so much more pressure on you than ours did. There's no such thing as a job for life and you need to sell a kidney to get on the property ladder; I don't envy you. I can see why Connor feels he needs to put the extra hours in but I can assure you that all those sacrifices will be worth it in the end. Maurice and I have just celebrated our thirtieth wedding anniversary and we're as strong as ever. You and Connor, if it's meant to be, will weather any storm.'

She fills a plastic cup with water and brings it over to me. I take a sip then look up as Damian comes to the door.

'Knock, knock,' he says, his hand hovering on the door handle. 'Sorry to interrupt but I wanted to give you these invoices to look over, Anne. I need to get them signed off before three.'

'Oh gosh, yes,' says Anne, taking the papers from him. 'I'm sorry, Vanessa, but I'm going to have to deal with these. Are you sure you're okay?'

'I'm fine, honestly,' I say, feeling rather silly now. 'Thanks so much for the chat.'

'Let's schedule a proper catch-up soon,' she says, heading for the door. 'I'll get Colette to book lunch at the club.'

'That would be lovely, thanks, Anne.'

I return to my screen but as I read I'm aware of a presence. I turn and see that Damian is still standing there.

'Everything okay?' he says, stepping inside.

'It's fine,' I say, taking another sip of water. 'Anne just caught me at a bad moment. I was fed up that Connor and I haven't seen each other much, that's all. Silly really.'

'He's been doing a lot of overtime, yeah,' says Damian. 'He told me last time I saw him.'

'I'm not complaining,' I say. 'It's just tough not seeing him, that's all.'

Damian nods his head. 'He loves you, Vanessa, that much is clear,' he says, taking his glasses off and wiping them with the back of his sleeve. 'And he wants you to have a proper home one day. But for that to happen he has to do what he's doing now. You've heard about the senior position he's going for?'

'Um, I think so,' I say, feeling rather pathetic now. 'What . . . which one?'

'The senior art director role,' says Damian. 'It's going to be up for grabs when the current guy leaves and Connor's putting his heart and soul into this branding job for the sports company so he can be in with a chance of promotion.'

'Oh yes,' I say, taking a sip of water. Why didn't Connor tell me that? 'Of course he is. I feel terrible now.'

'Hey, it's natural to feel that way,' he says, smiling. 'Listen, why don't you organize a date night? Book a table at a nice gaff, that sort of thing. I think the two of you need a break.'

'I might do,' I say as Damian opens the door and the sound of Lewis Capaldi fills the air. 'And thanks for listening, Damian. I really appreciate it.'

'Ach, sure it's nothing,' he says, winking at me as he goes out.

I return my thoughts to the press release but as I'm trying to make sense of it, my stomach knots as I recall something Damian said about the senior role.

'It's going to be up for grabs when the current guy leaves.'

The senior art director is a man. So why, then, did Connor tell me it was a gay woman called Sara who calls everyone 'darling' and whose texts I shouldn't be worried about?

It's 11.30 by the time Connor gets back. I'm sitting on the roof terrace drinking a cup of camomile tea and scrolling, rather half-heartedly, through the Dream Properties app.

'Hey, you,' he says sleepily as he comes out on to the terrace. 'What are you doing up so late?'

'I wanted to see you,' I say, wrapping the blanket round my shoulders. 'It's been a long evening on my own.'

'Well, I do apologize,' he says, sighing heavily. 'If it's any consolation, my dinner consisted of two Rich Tea biscuits and a packet of crisps. Look, Vanessa, you're obviously in one of your moods and I haven't got the energy for it tonight. As if it wasn't enough you embarrassing me at the boxing match.'

'How did I embarrass you?' I cry.

'I'm not doing this, Vanessa,' he says, rubbing his eyes. 'I'm going to bed.'

He walks into the flat, slamming the door behind him.

My chest tightens with a mixture of shock and regret. I hadn't meant my words to come out like that. I'd wanted to be cheerful when he came home, ask him if he wanted a cup of tea, talk about the new job he's going for, but after being by myself all night and staring at page after page of properties, my head feels foggy. That, and the fact that I can't stop thinking about the text from Sara. I had completely dismissed it from my mind once Connor had explained who she was but after hearing that the senior art director is a man, I can't shake this uneasy feeling. Am I just remembering wrong? Or did he lie to me?

I'm leaving the office the following day when I get a text message.

> I'm sorry about last night, baby. I shouldn't have snapped at you but I was just really tired. Things have eased up today so I've left early and I'm having a drink at Rossi's. Fancy joining me?

I smile as I change direction and turn from Sloane Square towards the King's Road. *Don't fuck things up tonight*, I tell myself as I wait at the traffic lights opposite Peter Jones, *no more paranoia*.

Connor is sitting outside when I arrive, a crisp early spring sunlight illuminating his face. When he sees me, he stands up and gives me a long, lingering kiss.

'I'm sorry,' he whispers as he pulls away.

'There's nothing to be sorry about,' I say, taking a seat at the rickety wooden table. 'I was being a grouch. Anyway, let's start again, shall we?'

I realize, as I say those words, that we've been doing a lot of that lately: having arguments and starting again. It's exhausting.

'Okay. Now, Rocco has already been out to inform me that tonight's specials are wild boar tortellini and spaghetti vongole,' he says, pouring me a glass of water from the jug. 'But I told him that we both know Vanessa will just stick to her usual.'

'How rude,' I say, making light of his comment though the meaning behind it – that I'm so predictable – stings. 'In that case, I shall have the vongole.'

'Living dangerously,' says Connor, gesturing to Rocco, the elderly maître d', who has run this restaurant since the 1970s. 'I think I'll have the same.'

After we order, we sit for a moment in silence. There are many things I want to talk to Connor about, but I'm fearful. We've been so out of sync these last few weeks and everything I say comes out the opposite of what I intended.

'So, Damian says you're having a hard time at work,' says Connor, breaking the silence. 'You should have said something.'

'What?' I say, pausing as Rocco arrives with the bread basket, a bottle of Chianti and two glasses.

'You don't have to get defensive,' says Connor once Rocco has gone back inside. 'Damian didn't mean anything bad by it. He's just worried about you.'

My head feels strange, like someone is squeezing it tighter and tighter. I think back to yesterday's conversation with Damian. At no point did I say I was having a hard time at work. I just said I was finding it hard not seeing Connor.

'I didn't tell Damian I was having a hard time at work,' I say, trying my best to keep calm. 'Work's going great. The best it's ever been.'

My voice is strained and I know I sound odd but I'm being accused of saying something I didn't say.

'Look, it's no big deal,' says Connor, taking a piece of bread from the basket and spreading it with butter. 'Damian's a good bloke. He wasn't causing trouble, just looking out for you, that's all.'

I'm about to respond when Rocco appears with the food. He places a huge plate of steaming spaghetti in front of me. I look down at the watery clams and my stomach churns.

'Wow, this looks amazing,' says Connor, tucking in. 'Good choice, Vanessa.'

I take a forkful of spaghetti and put it in my mouth. It tastes of salt and seawater. I immediately regret ordering it though I know I'll have to finish it; if I don't, it will prove to Connor and Rocco that I'm as boring and predictable as they say I am.

'So, how's your work going?' I say, taking a long sip of wine in the hope that it will eliminate the clammy taste in my mouth.

'I thought you'd never ask,' says Connor, raising his eyebrows. 'It's going well though this branding job for UC Boxing is taking longer than we anticipated. Their marketing guy is a nitpicker with no knowledge of branding or design, and he's been a bit of a nightmare to deal with. I think we'll all be glad when it's over.'

'Sounds exhausting,' I say. 'But it will be worth it in the end.'

'Let's hope so,' he says, looking down at his plate. When he looks up, I see his eyes are watering.

'Connor,' I say, putting my fork down and reaching my hand to his. 'What is it? What's the matter?'

'I . . . I just don't want to lose you, Vanessa,' he says, his face crumpling. 'I know it's been hard these last few weeks and we've bickered but . . . the thought of us not being together, it –'

'Who said we're not going to be together?' I say, rubbing his hand gently. 'I love you, Connor.'

'Do you?' he says, leaning forward and clasping my hand in his. 'You're not getting sick of me?'

'No,' I say, thinking back to the first time we made love, the feeling of safety and warmth I'd never had before. 'We've been busy, you're right, and it's been a shock after the early months when we were living in each other's pockets, but that's what being in a relationship is all about. Being patient, understanding each other.'

'I don't deserve you,' he says, taking a napkin and wiping his eyes. 'I really don't.'

'Finished?'

I look up and see Rocco standing in the fading light of the evening sun.

'Yes, thank you,' I say, hoping he doesn't comment on the small pile of uneaten clams wedged at the edge of my plate. 'That was lovely.'

'You like dessert? Coffee, perhaps?'

'Two espressos,' says Connor, collecting himself. 'Thanks, Rocco.'

'I meant what I said,' I say, lightly brushing his leg with my foot. 'I love you. You mean everything to me.'

He smiles and is about to say something when I feel someone standing behind me.

'Hanif,' cries Connor, getting to his feet. 'How's it going, mate?'

I turn to see a young man dressed sharply in a dark-grey suit and sunglasses, who I recognize as one of the men Connor was with at the boxing club.

'Not bad, C,' he says. 'Just meeting some of the others outside the tube. We're off to the Silkscreen Club in Knightsbridge to see Daisy Dangerfield. Everyone's going to be there, including Richard.'

'Oh,' says Connor, looking at me, his smile fading.

I know that Richard is his boss and I know from the expression on Connor's face that he thinks he should go and join his team, show willing.

'You should come along, mate,' says Hanif. 'You too, er – sorry, I didn't catch your name.'

'This is Vanessa,' says Connor, before I get the chance to reply. 'What time are you guys heading down there?'

'Doors open at 7 p.m.,' he says, taking out his phone. 'There's a free bar for the first hour so we'll make the most of that then hang around for the show. Listen, I better go, that's Rach texting to say they're outside the tube. Might see you down there, eh?'

'Yes,' says Connor, glancing at me nervously. 'You might. See you, mate.'

When Hanif is out of earshot he turns to me. 'Look, it's okay. I know you won't want to go,' he says, his mouth turning down at the corners. 'I know what you're like and burlesque won't be your thing, it's just she's this new client, you know. But, like you said, this is our evening and –'

'Shh,' I say, pressing my finger to his mouth. 'I'd like to go. It'll be a laugh.'

'Are you sure?' he says, the thin line of his lips lifting into a tight smile.

'Yes,' I say, reaching under the table for my bag. 'Just give me five minutes to freshen up then we'll head over.'

'Thanks, baby,' he says, kissing my hand. 'Look at you being all adventurous – it's a whole new person!'

Inside the Ladies I feel anything but. I stand looking at my reflection in the mirror and my heart sinks. It's been a long week and it shows in my face. There are dark circles under my eyes and I've got premenstrual spots appearing on my cheeks that no amount of Luna London concealer seems to be able to hide. My hair is in need of a wash and the black trouser suit and white T-shirt I hastily dressed in this morning is not really the right look for an evening in a Knightsbridge burlesque club. *Still,* I think to myself, *it will be dark in there and I owe it to Connor to go along with him after running out of the boxing match like that.* I want to make it up to him. I add some highlighter to my cheeks, apply some of the new Luna London Ripe Red lipstick and scoop my hair into a chignon. *There,* I think, *that will just have to do.*

I walk back through the restaurant, preparing myself mentally for the night ahead, and I'm so lost in thought that I nearly crash into someone coming towards me.

'Ooh,' I exclaim as I stumble.

The man grabs my arm to steady me.

'Sorry, I didn't see you there,' he says, a West Country lilt to his voice. 'Are you okay?'

'Yes, yes, I'm fine,' I say, brushing him off.

He says something as he walks away but my focus is fixed on Connor. He is standing outside the window, his phone pressed to his ear. I hurry out to join him, and as I do he ends the call and stuffs the phone in his pocket.

'Right,' he says, taking my hand in his. 'Let's go and see what this is all about.'

The club is heaving by the time we get there. It's a small space dominated by velvet sofas and gilt mirrors. A speeded-up remix of Madonna's 'Justify My Love' plays out over the speakers and I see that the DJ, standing in her booth, earphones pressed to her face, is an ex-reality TV contestant. It's an odd place. I turn to Connor to point out the famous DJ but he's already making his way over to what looks like the VIP area on the other side of the room. He stops halfway and gestures at me to follow him.

When I reach the velvet rope that cordons off the VIP area from the rest of the club, someone thrusts a glass of champagne into my hands. I've already had three glasses of Chianti and don't normally mix my drinks, but the champagne is ice cold and refreshing, and I take a large glug of it as Connor holds out his hand and leads me inside.

'You made it then?' says Hanif, who is sitting on a red velvet sofa with two women and three men. One of the women, a strikingly attractive blonde with bobbed hair and a tight black dress, jumps to her feet and hugs Connor.

'I'm so glad you came,' she shrieks, almost spilling her champagne.

At this point, I'm expecting Connor to turn to me and make introductions. Instead, he sits down on the sofa next to Hanif, the blonde girl sits on his other side and I'm left standing like a spare part. It will look churlish if I try to squeeze in beside Connor so I sit on the opposite sofa and try to catch his eye. *Stop being paranoid, Vanessa.*

My champagne glass has been refilled for the third time and I'm starting to feel a little light-headed. Hanif and the blonde girl have left the sofa and gone to mingle while Connor has been joined by a tall, elegant man with white hair and tanned skin, who I assume, from Connor's body language, is Richard, his boss. They talk for a few minutes, then Richard gets up and leaves. Taking this as my cue, I go over to where Connor is sitting. He looks up and smiles.

'Hey, sorry about that,' he says, patting the spot that Richard has just vacated. 'Work stuff.'

I don't know whether it's because I've drunk too much champagne but Connor's voice sounds odd, manic almost. I try to engage him in conversation but the music is so loud we can barely hear each other. Then he leans towards me and bellows in my ear, 'Wait here a sec. Just going for a pee.'

I watch as he crosses the VIP area, pausing to speak to the blonde woman. Her cheek presses against his as she leans in to whisper something in his ear, her hand clutching his arm.

'All right?'

Hanif flops down on the sofa next to me, looking rather dishevelled.

'Yes, thanks,' I say, my throat hurting from having to raise my voice.

A woman appears in front of us with a tray of champagne. I shake my head but Hanif takes two glasses and hands me one.

'Go on,' he says, thrusting it into my hand. 'You have to make the most of a free bar.'

I smile politely, then scan the room for Connor. There's no sign of him. I see the blonde woman standing at the bar, chatting animatedly. Something about her unsettles me though I can't put my finger on it.

'Who's that?' I say to Hanif, my lips loosened by the drink. 'The blonde woman by the bar.'

'Oh, that's Sara,' he says, his voice coming in and out of range. 'She works in accounts.'

My body judders.

'I thought Sara was the art director,' I holler into Hanif's ear. 'Is that her girlfriend she's talking to?'

He gives me a strange look.

'Nah,' he says, shaking his head. 'The art director's a bloke called Ian. And that's Jess, Richard's wife. Sara doesn't have a *girlfriend*.'

I go to speak but as I do there's an explosion of light and colour and music.

'Here we go,' says Hanif, pulling me to my feet. 'Show-time.'

He drags me out of the VIP area towards the stage. I can see movement up there but it's just a blur of reds and golds and pinks. The music grows louder, there's a stamping of feet and then I feel someone's hands on my waist.

I turn round and see Connor.

'This is great, isn't it?' he says, pressing his face into my neck.

I nod my head, try to focus on what is happening on the stage, but I'm so tired I can barely stand up. I hear a high-pitched female voice and a thudding bass beat.

The room fragments into neon pieces. I feel my legs buckle and I reach out to hold on to something solid. A man asks me if I'm okay. I look up at him but his features melt into the background. The music grows louder; my head feels like it will burst. Someone's hand is on my back, pushing me forward.

Next thing I know I feel a blast of cold air. I hear Connor's voice though it sounds like it's coming at me from a great distance. I see the lights of a taxi. It stops and I'm bundled inside. I turn to see Connor get in beside me. The taxi moves off and I can see the lights of Sloane Square up ahead, but my eyes are heavy, my head thick with drink. I put my head on Connor's shoulder, close my eyes and fall into a deep, dreamless sleep.

17. Now

'There you are,' says Georgie as I return to the kitchen. 'I was getting worried.'

In my absence, she has warmed up and served the pasta and has also made a large green salad. Jack is grating Parmesan into a dish and looks up at me wearily.

'Everything okay?'

'Yes, I . . . er, I just got a bit distracted,' I say, sitting down at the table. 'This salad looks lovely. Oh, now I feel really bad. You were supposed to have tonight off.'

'Don't be silly. It's just a bag of rocket with a bit of olive oil drizzled over,' says Georgie, her words slurring. 'This pasta is delicious, darling. Well done.'

Beside me, I notice Jack raise his eyebrow though I'm not sure if the expression is aimed at my tardiness or Georgie's tipsiness. It's clear she's had a couple more glasses of wine while I've been upstairs.

'Cheese?' says Jack, offering me the dish.

'Thanks,' I say, taking it and sprinkling a teaspoonful over my pasta.

The food is comforting though all I can think of is the missed calls.

Oblivious, Georgie and Jack discuss the intruder.

'It just means we tighten our security, that's all,' says Jack, after Georgie says she'll find it hard to sleep tonight. 'Starting with closing doors.'

He gets up from the table and, to my relief, closes and locks the French doors.

'Oh, bloody hell,' says Georgie, grabbing her glass and taking a long draw of wine. 'That's madness, Jack. It's a summer's evening and we're sitting right next to it. These hot flushes have been getting worse and I need the fresh air.'

'Well, maybe if you didn't knock back so much plonk the flushes would ease up,' says Jack, gesturing to the wine.

'Oh, so now you're a gynaecologist, are you?' says Georgie, stumbling over the word. 'The hot flushes are down to my being perimenopausal and have nothing at all to do with having a glass or two of wine.'

'And the rest,' says Jack, though he mutters this under his breath so only I, sitting so close to him, can hear. 'Anyway, we were talking about tightening our security. Vanessa, may I ask you to close your windows at night and lock the door behind you when you come back to the house?'

'Yes, of course,' I say, feeling rather unsettled by the serious tone he has taken. 'I'll be extra vigilant.'

'Good girl,' he says, with a brisk nod.

'She's not a girl, Jack,' says Georgie, her eyes glazing. 'She's thirty-two years old.'

'Apologies, Vanessa,' says Jack, turning to me with a sheepish look. 'You know what I meant. It's funny but you'll always be a little girl to me.'

'Little Nessa,' says Georgie.

She's reaching the maudlin, nostalgic stage of drunkenness now. It's making me feel even more on edge.

'I'll clear these,' I say, getting up and taking the empty dishes over to the sink.

'Thanks, darling, that was lovely,' says Georgie, draining her glass. 'See, I always said you could cook.'

I'm about to reply when there's a loud hammering on the front door.

Georgie's eyes widen and she jumps to her feet. She looks at Jack.

'Who can that be?' she says, her voice catching.

'It's okay, I'll get it,' says Jack. 'Don't look so worried, my dear. Burglars don't tend to knock.'

He laughs nervously, then heads out into the hallway. We stand in silence, listening as Jack opens the door, closes it with a thud, then clatters back up the Yorkshire stone hallway.

'It was just a delivery,' he says as he re-enters the room, his face visibly relieved. 'Another parcel for you, Vanessa.'

He places the brown paper-wrapped package on the table.

'Right,' he says, taking his glass of water from the table. 'I'll be in my study if anyone needs me.'

'Surprise, surprise,' says Georgie, rolling her eyes. 'I think I'll have an early night. You don't mind, do you, Ness?'

'Not at all,' I say, though I'm not really listening to her. I'm too busy staring at the parcel in front of me.

When Georgie and Jack have left the room I pick it up and give it a shake. Something rattles inside.

I hear Georgie's feet thudding up the stairs and Jack's study door close, then I take the parcel up to my bedroom. It's time I faced up to what's happening.

Placing the parcel on the floor, I slowly slide the other three from under the bed.

The first contains the remains of the dress Connor picked out for me before the US presentation. It arrived a few days after I moved in with Georgie, ripped into tiny little pieces. The second was sent a couple of days later. I remember almost cutting my fingers as I put my hand into the box, where I found the silver-framed photo of me and Connor that used to sit on the mantelpiece in the bedroom, the glass smashed into little shards. The third parcel contains my childhood letters. I can barely remember writing them though I do recall how comforting I'd found the character of Angus. I must have written the letters as a kind of therapy then shoved them into a drawer and forgotten about them. When the parcel arrived I'd thought perhaps Dad had found them amongst the boxed-up stuff in the loft and sent them to me, but now I think Connor must've got hold of them somehow. The lack of a note, the neat wrapping, it all smacks of him. Which means, I realize, he isn't giving up. And, what's more, he has proof of my obsession with Geoffrey Rivers. What might he do with it? I dread to think.

Now here is another one. Taking a deep breath, I rip open the paper. A chill slithers right through me. The parcel has been wrapped in pages torn from a book, which I immediately recognize as the first few pages of *The Spirits of Holly Maze House*. I scrabble, panicking, through the pages and find his signature. It's the signed edition I'd left at the stones. How did he find it?

Inside is another box, plain, white, again sealed tightly with tape. I think of the message, the photo of Geoffrey's dead body, and I know that I should take this parcel and throw it in the nearest wheelie bin. Yet something compels me to open it.

With trembling hands, I tear off the sellotape from each corner.

What I see makes me want to throw up.

There, covered in dead leaves and soil, is the glass blackbird. I lift it out and hold it in my hands; its blue eyes, dulled with grit and dirt, stare back at me, accusingly. Then, looking down, I see there is something else in the box. A note. I take it out carefully and read, almost dropping the bird as I do.

I know now for certain. Connor is stalking me. And he's not going to give up until I'm behind bars.

For there in red-inked capital letters are five words that chill my blood.

I KNOW WHAT YOU DID

18. Then

I wake drenched in sweat. Beside me, Connor snores gently. I have a vague memory of leaving the burlesque club, the taxi, then falling asleep with my head on Connor's shoulder, but everything else is a blur.

I take my phone from the bedside table and check the time. It's 6.30. Still early, but I'm wide awake now. I gently pull the covers back and make my way to the bathroom.

The sight that greets me in the mirror makes me gasp. My hair is knotted and sticking to one side of my face. My eyes are red and yesterday's make-up is smudged across my face like a painting that's been left out in the rain. I stand there feeling hollow, hoping that I didn't spend the entire evening walking around the club looking like this. And then I feel it, a sticky fluid running down my legs. I look and with a sick feeling of dread run my hand along my inner thigh, praying that it's just sweat. But as I hold it to my nose and recognize the sharp, salty scent, the scent of Connor, I feel my legs buckle.

I grab a towel and quickly wipe it away then hurry back to the bedroom and scour the floor, the table, the end of the bed, for a telltale wrapper. But there's nothing. This is a nightmare. I have no recollection of having sex, let alone using protection. I run back into the bathroom and turn on the shower. Stepping underneath the hot stream of water, I scrub at my skin and my crotch, almost using up the whole bottle of shower gel. *This can't be happening*, I tell myself as I step, red raw and burning hot, on to the cool tiled floor.

I need to think straight. What should I do? My first instinct is to call Lottie but that's not an option. Okay, what would Lottie tell me to do? Go to Boots and get the morning-after pill. It had happened a couple of times before with other boyfriends when we'd got carried away in the heat of the moment and not used a condom; another time, the condom had slipped off. I'd tried going on the pill in my early twenties but it gave me such terrible migraines I had to come off it. I reasoned that condoms would be enough though I still had some accidents. But on all those occasions, I had a clear memory of having sex. I had . . . consented.

I'll go to the chemist, I think as I shakily dry myself off, trying to block out the terrifying word that is rolling around my head. I'll go to the chemist and ask for the morning-after pill. I'll slip out before Connor wakes up and then, when I get back, we can talk about what happened.

I tiptoe back into the bedroom but as I'm pulling out the drawer to retrieve a T-shirt and leggings, I hear Connor stir behind me.

'Morning, baby,' he says sleepily. 'What are you doing? It's Saturday. Come back to bed.'

'I was . . . er,' I begin, not quite knowing how to put it. 'Connor, what happened last night? When we got back from the club?'

'You mean, you don't remember?' he says, smiling. 'You seemed to be enjoying it.'

'Was I?'

'What are you talking about, Ness?' he says. 'You mean you really don't remember?'

I shake my head.

'It was amazing,' he says, reaching out and stroking my cheek. 'Hotter than we've ever been before. I think it must have been the burlesque. You kept telling me how much it had turned you on.'

All I can recall of the burlesque is a blur of colours and noise.

'By the time we got home you were . . . well, I've never seen you like that before,' he says, propping himself up on the pillows.

'Connor, listen,' I say, sitting down on the edge of the bed. 'Did we . . . did we use anything?'

'Ness, this is crazy,' he says, leaning back in exasperation. 'Are you having a laugh here?'

'No,' I say, my stomach twisting. 'It's just . . . well, I woke up and there was . . . you know, *you* on my legs and . . . I genuinely can't remember having sex.'

The colour drains from his face and he sits up straight.

'You said "Don't stop",' he says, his voice shaking. 'We were both so into it. I asked you if I should get a condom and you said not to. You told me to carry on.'

'So I was . . . I was awake?' I say, my hands trembling now. 'I was conscious?'

'What the fuck are you saying, Ness?' he says, his eyes glaring. 'Are you accusing me of –?'

'No,' I say, my heart thudding. 'Of course not, I just . . . well, I've had a few accidents in the past and now I never take chances.'

'Well, you did last night,' says Connor, his neck reddening.

'Okay,' I say, trying to calm things. 'We need to sort this out. I'll head up to Boots and get the morning-after pill. Just to be on the safe side.'

'There's no need to do that,' he says, sighing. 'There's no risk.'

'What are you talking about?' I say incredulously. 'Of course there is.'

'Once I realized how drunk you were I stopped,' he says, turning to me with a wounded expression. 'Christ, what do you take me for?'

'But . . . but what about the . . . what was that on my legs then?'

'I have no idea. Sweat? Jesus, Vanessa, this is insane.'

He shakes his head, then, jumping out of the bed, pulls on his dressing gown and storms out of the room.

I find him sitting on the sofa, his legs pulled up to his chest.

'Connor,' I say gently, sitting down next to him. 'Connor, I'm sorry. I didn't mean to . . . it's just I have no memory of it and –'

'You've got to stop this, Vanessa,' he says, turning to me, his eyes red and swollen. 'I love you but I can't take much more of this.'

'What?' I say, panic gripping my chest. 'What are you talking about?'

173

'The drinking,' he says, his voice trembling. 'Every night I come home from work and you're half-cut. The recycling bin is a bloody embarrassment. Then there's the paranoia, checking my phone, the emotional outbursts. But this, this is just the very worst. How can you sit there and accuse me of – God, I can't even say it . . .'

I think back to the previous evening: the three glasses of Chianti, glass after glass of champagne at the club.

'You were so wasted. And what you said to Richard . . .'

'What did I say to Richard?'

'Oh Christ,' says Connor, his eyes widening. 'You're telling me you don't remember telling my boss he was very attractive for an older man?'

I shake my head, and a horrid feeling of guilt rips through me. I've done it again. I've fucked up, again.

'Bloody hell, Vanessa.'

It's all too much. I feel my bottom lip quiver.

'I'm sorry,' I say, my head throbbing. 'I don't remember. I would never usually say something like that. I don't know what's happening to me.'

'Hey,' says Connor, shuffling closer to me. 'Baby, it's okay. Everything's going to be okay. I'm going to help you.'

'Connor, listen to me,' I say, taking his arm. 'I am so sorry but I swear to you I'm going to sort this. I'll stop drinking. I know I've been knocking it back a lot recently and this is my wake-up call. I promise you.'

'And the other stuff,' he says, wiping his eyes with his dressing-gown sleeve. 'The checking up on me? The outbursts?'

'All of it,' I say, putting my hand to his face. 'I'll stop. I can't lose you, Connor. Tell me you won't leave me.'

It's my turn to cry then and as I feel him pull me to his chest, feel the warmth of his skin, I tell myself that I will be true to my word. I've already lost my mum and Lottie. I can't lose Connor too.

'I don't know what to do, Connor,' I say. 'I've never blacked out like that before.'

'We're going to get through this, Vanessa,' he says, lifting my face to his. 'Do you hear me? I'm not giving up on you. I love you.'

'I don't deserve you,' I say. 'I really don't.'

'Everything's going to be okay,' he repeats. 'Trust me.'

He kisses the top of my head, and as I sink into his arms, I feel wretched for ever doubting him.

19. Now

When the first light of morning arrives, filling the bedroom with a pale, silvery glow, I pick up my phone from the floor and check the time. It's 6.45. I get out of bed and go to the window.

The common is already dotted with people, despite the early hour. I see the landlady from the Crooked Billet pub putting out deckchairs for the sun-seeking drinkers who will descend on the pub at lunchtime. A group of men and women, clad in workout gear, are practising yoga up by the copse. A big collie dog bounds in between them, almost knocking one of the women, an impossibly svelte redhead, off her feet.

As I stand there I scan the figures, the faces, the hidden corners, the shadows, searching for Connor. He could be out there now, waiting to make his next move.

I think of his words – 'I know what you did' – and I shiver.

Then, like a photograph that hasn't fully developed, the outline of Geoffrey's body flashes in front of my eyes again. I'm standing in the hallway of Holly Maze House and he's lying at my feet, blood pooling beneath his head.

Stop it, I tell myself. *Stop torturing yourself.*

My legs feel weak as I leave the bedroom and walk down the stairs. I take deep breaths, recalling the advice from Anne's mindfulness class. *Be in the present. Keep calm.*

If I just focus on the next hour or so, then I can keep the panic at bay, clear my head, and then, afterwards, try to work out what to do.

But as I walk into the kitchen, still focusing on my breathing, my legs almost give way. For there, in front of me, as large as life, is Geoffrey Rivers.

NEW LEAD IN CHILDREN'S AUTHOR MURDER CASE

The headline appears across the TV screen, temporarily obscuring Geoffrey's photo. Georgie and Jack's large flat-screen TV that hangs on the wall in the snug off the kitchen is a hangover from the days when Imogen and Harry would huddle up in here to watch movies with their friends. Nowadays, it's rarely used, yet today someone has turned on the news channel and set the volume to loud. I hunt around for the remote control amongst the cushions and as I do so the sharp voice of the female newsreader drills into my skull:

'*Police investigating the murder of Mr Rivers who, in his day, sold over sixty million books worldwide, are now exploring a link between his death and the sale of his lavish Hampstead home. It is thought that Mr Rivers had opted to show potential buyers round the property himself rather than handing over the task to the estate agent. We spoke to Viv Shackleton from the National Association of Estate Agents who said that, after the Suzy Lamplugh case, tighter rules were brought in to ensure the safety of estate agents and vendors. However . . .*'

I grab the remote control and switch off the TV. My body feels like ice as I sit down at the table, my back to the French doors, and try to make sense of what I have just heard. I'm the new lead, that's what that report was saying. Though I may have gone to the police station voluntarily, the police have not given up. They're closing in on me. And, even worse, Connor has photographic evidence of me returning to the scene and placing the stolen items next to the gravestones.

He was never going to let me go without a fight. But how could he have known I would be at those stones then? Has he been following me? Was he with me every step of that journey? And how would he know how much I loved those books? I don't think I ever spoke about them to him. As far as I was concerned, I had left Geoffrey and Angus and the little spirits back in the nineties along with my mother's death. Yet Connor had a way of finding things out about me without me realizing.

I'm lost in my thoughts when the French windows suddenly burst open and Jack walks in. I jump from the table in fright and the phone I've been clutching in my hands clatters to the floor.

'Jesus!' I cry, my heart in my mouth.

'Oh gosh, Vanessa. I didn't mean to scare you,' says Jack, closing the doors behind him.

'Jack,' I say, slowly regaining my composure. 'What are you doing out there at this time of the morning?'

'I've been for a jog,' he says, helping himself to a bottle of water from the fridge and taking a long glug. 'I've decided to get healthy. More exercise, less booze.'

I look at him as he leans against the sink, clutching the water bottle. He's not exactly dressed for jogging, in his jeans and loose, linen shirt, but I decide not to ask questions. Not after the frosty atmosphere between him and Georgie last night. Still, he doesn't look okay. He seems jumpy and agitated. His hands shake as he lifts the bottle to take another sip. I think back to my sister's behaviour, the multiple glasses of wine with dinner, the sharp way she had spoken to Jack. *They've had an argument,* I reason. Jack slept in the guest room then got up early and went for a walk to clear his head. The 'jog' lie would be to spare having to worry me. That will be it.

Anyway, despite my fright, I'm actually glad Jack is up and about. I feel less vulnerable with him here. I've always felt that way. There is something solid and immoveable about my brother-in-law, the man who first came into our lives when we were destroyed by grief. His is a reassuring presence.

'Well, that all sounds very healthy,' I say, walking across to the kettle. 'Now, would you like a coffee or are you off that too?'

'Oh God, no, I need my caffeine,' he says.

I fill the kettle then go to the fridge to get the milk. There's only a drop left.

'Is black okay for you, Jack?' I say. 'We're out of milk.'

'Ah, damn, I forgot to pick it up yesterday,' he says, rubbing his eyes. 'I better go and get some. Your sister gets tetchy if she doesn't have her cup of builder's tea and I'm guessing she'll have quite the headache this morning.'

I watch as he grabs his wallet and keys from the kitchen table and heads out of the door.

Suddenly alone, I feel vulnerable. I look out of the window at the tangle of garden with its hidden corners and twisty pathways. Anyone could be hiding out there. I go to the French windows, make sure Jack locked them properly. He did. Of course he did. Stop worrying. But then I hear something outside. Rustling. Is someone there or is it just the breeze whistling through the trees? I can't be sure, but what I do know is that I feel unsafe here, exposed.

I decide to go upstairs and get dressed, distract myself. After my shower I carefully apply some make-up and take my favourite blue sundress out of the wardrobe. I always feel happy when I wear it.

I open the curtains and look out at the common. There's a golden haze hanging above it, another beautiful summer's day. I see old Mr Allen walking his dog, a mother and child sitting on a yellow picnic blanket patterned with bright-red stars, and a man in a suit, striding across the overgrown path, head bowed over his phone. Beyond them, I see joggers and commuters, nannies with their charges. The day is breaking open.

But as I stand here looking out at all those people going about their business I feel an overwhelming sense of sadness. I had been like them once, happy, busy, focused, planning my future with the man I loved. And then it was all ripped away from me, in a heartbeat.

Hearing Jack's key in the lock, I step away from the window, but as I do so my phone bleeps. I pick it up. It's a text message from a number I don't recognize. I hear

Jack's footsteps on the stone floor downstairs as I open the message and read the words.

> You looked beautiful just now. Blue has always been the perfect colour for you.

My body goes cold despite the heat of the day.

Without thinking, I click on the number and wait for it to ring but it's a dead line.

If this is Connor, has he set up another new number? And if so, why is the line dead?

My brain fizzes with fear and confusion.

One thing is certain: whoever sent this can see up to my window and they're out there right now.

Watching.

20. Then

July 2018

It is six weeks since the night of the burlesque club and I still haven't had a period. There must be some explanation for it, I think to myself as I sit at my desk trying to focus on the presentation I'm preparing. I press save on the document, pick up my phone and search 'missed period not pregnant'. There is a list of possible reasons, from stress to sudden weight loss to polycystic ovary syndrome. I search the latter. It can't be that because I don't have any symptoms. I haven't lost weight either. Stress? Well, the last few weeks have been a bit fraught, though I wouldn't say I've been so stressed as to cause my periods to stop. The only plausible reason would be pregnancy but that is impossible because Connor told me he'd stopped when he realized I was so drunk.

I miss Lottie more than ever now. She's the only person I could be completely open with. Though I know Georgie would want to know, I still feel a bit like she's my mum – like she'd be disappointed in me somehow. I try to imagine what Lottie would say. She'd probably suggest I get a pregnancy test to rule it out. That would be the sensible thing.

I close down my computer, grab my bag and jacket and head out to the King's Road. When I get to Boots, I take a quick look round to check that there's no one from the office milling about. I know some of the younger staff still buy their cosmetics from here despite their 10 per cent discount on Luna London products. Thankfully, the shop is quiet. I quickly grab a testing kit, take it to the counter and pay. When I get out into the fresh air I feel light-headed. I take deep breaths as I slowly make my way back to the office.

The test stays in my bag for the rest of the morning. I'm aware of its presence as one would be of an unexploded bomb. Finally, as most of the staff troop out for lunch, I grab my bag and head for the disabled toilet at the far end of the first floor.

With shaking hands I rip off the foil wrapper and follow the instructions. As I wait, a heavy feeling descends on my shoulders. My periods have been as regular as clockwork since the age of thirteen. A no-show like this can mean only one thing. But still, when the two minutes are up and the word 'pregnant' appears on the digital screen my heart feels like it has been ripped from my chest.

I'm terrified, not just because I'm pregnant but because now I know for certain that Connor lied to me.

When I was a little girl I used to imagine what it would be like when I had children of my own. Losing Mum at the age of ten had made me determined to recreate the magical time we had spent together in those early years. In my imagination, the moment of conception would have been planned for and it would feel momentous and fated. Finding out the news would be a shared experience – the father and I would sit together, excitedly, as we waited for the result to appear. Then we would embrace, perhaps jump up and down with glee, before starting to make plans.

Doctor's appointments would be made, names chosen, nurseries decorated.

This reality bears no resemblance to what I'd imagined. Sitting in a disabled loo, holding a stick and trying to remember the actual act that led to this had not been part of the plan. I feel removed from it all, a ghost floating through a story I have not written.

But I know one thing for certain. I can't tell Connor. I have to deal with this myself and I know, under the circumstances, that there can be only one outcome.

The appointment was relatively straightforward to make. When you already feel disconnected from yourself, answering a few personal, probing questions to a disembodied voice on the phone doesn't matter like it would have in the past. A date and time was confirmed, and now I find myself, five days after taking the test, sitting in a clinic, listening to a nurse called Helena describe what will happen to me over the next forty-eight hours.

It all sounds so simple. I will take one tablet – named mifepristone – at the clinic and this will stop the pregnancy by blocking the progesterone hormone. I will then be given the second medicine – misoprostol – which I will take twenty-four hours later at home and that will make my womb contract and expel the baby.

Moments ago I had lain on the examining table while Helena rubbed a clear jelly-like substance on my tummy then rubbed over it with a probe. It was a moment I had imagined for years. The moment I finally saw my baby. Never in a million years had I thought it would be like this.

'Do you want to see the screen?' Helena had asked. 'It's okay not to. Most women don't.'

I had shaken my head and Helena had turned the screen away from me. Whatever was on it, whatever existed in my womb at that point, had no right to be there.

I blink away the memory as Helena outlines possible side effects — nausea, cramping, dizziness — and gives me the instructions for taking the second pill. Then she hands me the first pill and a glass of water. I stare at them, suddenly unable to move. Helena had already asked me if I was completely certain a few minutes earlier as she gave me the consent form, and I had nodded my head in a kind of daze and signed it. However, the sight of the pill, the finality and enormity of what I am about to do, makes me suddenly question myself. This is a baby, a life I have created. Two days ago I had stupidly looked up the dates on a pregnancy app and saw that at seven weeks, as the baby now was, it was forming its brain and hands and limbs. As I sit here looking at the small white pill, itself no bigger than the baby in my womb, I feel wretched, like a woman about to jump off a cliff. Then Helena asks me if I'm okay, if I want to proceed, and I'm hauled back into the moment. This is not a baby, I tell myself, this is the result of something I cannot remember. And it's my body, my choice. I put the pill in my mouth and swallow it down.

I can't go back to the flat until this is all over. I can't go to Lottie's as she's no longer there and I don't want to tell Georgie and Jack, so I end up booking myself into a cheap hotel on Putney Bridge. It isn't luxurious, but it is clean and private, somewhere I can lock myself away, undisturbed, for a couple of days. I told Connor that I was going to Edinburgh for a series of meetings with retailers. On the way to the hotel I go into the Waitrose Local in Putney and buy a couple of tubs of pasta salad, some fruit and two large bottles of water. I also buy a hot-water bottle, which Helena had recommended for the pain, and settle myself in to my new home for the next two days, telling myself that this square, neutral room is a little haven, a place to clear my head and rest.

The next day, at 3 p.m., I administer the second pill and wait. At first, nothing happens. I turn on the TV and, as the opening credits of *Bargain Hunt* begin, start to feel a dull ache in my stomach. I take the painkillers that Helena gave me and get into bed. The pain gradually increases but it's bearable. What isn't bearable is the voice inside my head, telling me that I am a bad person, that I am killing my own flesh and blood, that I don't deserve to ever be happy again, that by doing this I have brought bad luck down on myself for ever. I put my hands over my ears to try and block the voice out, but it gets louder and more insistent. When, finally, the pain reaches a crescendo and I run to the loo just in time to feel the baby leave me, the voice is screaming.

It's still screaming as I slump back to bed and sleep a dead, dreamless sleep and it's still there when I wake up at 7 a.m., dress and make my way back to the flat.

I reach into my bag to retrieve my keys and as I do I bring out the leaflets Helena gave me at the clinic. 'How to cope after an abortion.' 'Contraception advice.' 'Having sex again after an abortion.' I feel sick as I read the words. I don't want any reminders of what I've just done. Scrunching the leaflets into a ball, I throw them, and my appointment card, into the wheelie bin outside the flat then make my way inside.

Thankfully, Connor is not there and I dump my coat and bag in the hallway and head into the living room where I curl up on the sofa with a blanket pulled over me, still bleeding but no longer in pain.

I wake to someone vigorously shaking my arms. At first I think I'm dreaming but as I come to I see Connor standing by the sofa. His face is red and his mouth puckered. He looks furious. I blink my eyes and panic floods through my body. He is holding the appointment card from the clinic and the follow-on leaflets Helena gave me. How has he got them? I know I threw them away.

He puts his face to mine and hisses in my ear.

'What the hell have you done, Vanessa?'

21. Now

'Fancy a bit of brunch in the village?'

I look up from my phone and see Georgie standing in the kitchen doorway. She looks much better this morning. Her face is clear and bright, and she has washed and blow-dried her hair.

'No worries if you're busy, though,' she says, gesturing to the phone.

I'd deleted the message, after trying to call the number and making a note of it, then blocked the sender. *That was the right thing to do, wasn't it?* I ask myself, watching as Georgie tries the handle of the French doors. I feel wary of leaving the house. What if Connor is still out there? Waiting for me. Still, better to be with Georgie than stay in the house. He can't do anything to me if I'm with others, outside.

'No, I'd like to come,' I say, popping my phone into my jeans pocket.

I'd changed out of the blue dress after getting the message. I'd almost ripped it off in my haste. 'I could do with some fresh air.'

'Did you see Jack this morning?' says Georgie, scooping up her door keys from the kitchen counter.

'Yes,' I reply, checking, despite Georgie already doing so, that the French windows are locked. 'He was up and about early, said he's on a fitness kick.'

'Hmm,' says Georgie, a frown darkening her face.

'He came back then went to get some milk,' I say, getting my sandals from the rack in the hallway. 'I think he's in his study.'

'Nessa and I are off for brunch and shopping,' Georgie calls down the hallway. 'We'll be back around three.'

'Righty-ho,' calls Jack, his voice muffled. 'Have fun.'

'Come on then,' says Georgie, taking my arm. 'I'm starving.'

She opens the front door and we step out into bright sunshine.

'Gosh, it's only 10.30 and it's scorching,' says Georgie as she locks the door. 'I'm glad I remembered to put my sunblock on.'

She strides down the path while I check that the door is locked. Despite watching Georgie do it just moments earlier I feel I have to double-check, just to be certain. I think back to that message and shiver in spite of the heat.

As Georgie and I cross the common I turn my head from left to right, scrutinizing everyone we see, scanning the crowds for his face.

Chloe's Deli is situated on the edge of the common on a little side road that leads into the village. Georgie points to one of the outside tables, which looks very inviting, but I can't risk sitting in such a prominent spot. Anyone could see me there, photograph me . . . I shudder at the thought.

'Can we sit inside?' I ask. 'That sun's rather fierce and I don't want to burn.'

Georgie is understanding and we take a table by the counter where she spends the first five minutes chatting to the owner, Chloe, about sourdough recipes, before the woman is pulled away to serve another customer.

When the food arrives we sit in silence. Georgie dips hunks of bread into her shakshuka, while I nibble at my toast and strawberry jam. Then Georgie leans back in her chair, sips her coffee and tries to initiate small talk, asking me about my job applications and whether I've contacted that friend of hers who works in recruitment.

I answer her questions as best I can, but it's hard to focus on what she is saying as every time the door opens I flinch.

Once we've finished our coffee and cleared our plates I catch Chloe's eye and ask for the bill. I need to get out of here now. It's filling up and the rush of bodies is making me nervous.

'Are you sure you don't want another coffee, darling?' says Georgie softly. 'We're not in any rush and it's nice to spend a bit of time with you.'

'I'm sure,' I say, trying to suppress the dread that is rising through me. 'It's so hot in here. We should go and have a walk, get some fresh air.'

'But you said it was too hot to sit outside,' says Georgie, laughing. 'Honestly, you're just like Jack sometimes. Never able to make your mind up. I'll get this.'

She grabs the bill from the silver dish that Chloe has just placed on the table before I have the chance to look at it.

'Do let me pay, Georgie,' I say, the familiar guilt emerging. 'You're always paying for things. I feel bad.'

'Don't be silly,' she says, taking her bank card out of her pocket and placing it on the tray. 'It was my suggestion to come for brunch and, besides, you made that delicious supper last night.'

She winks at me and smiles so warmly I feel overcome with emotion. Perhaps now is the right time to tell her everything, to finally get it off my chest. And I mean everything – Lottie, Connor, the parcels, Geoffrey . . . But before I can speak, Chloe arrives at the table with the card machine and the moment is lost.

We spend the rest of the morning looking round the shops in the village. A new cosmetics store called Village Visage has opened up in the spot where the florist had been. I take a look at it then go to walk on, not able to face another reminder of my old life, but Georgie grabs my arm and drags me in.

The old me would have been intrigued by this shop. She would have been checking out the stock, asking questions, making notes on anything unusual or interesting that she could take back to Luna London. But the new Vanessa, the scared, broken person standing by the lipstick shelves as myriad colours blur into one, grotesque shapes in front of her eyes, just wants to get out of here as fast as she can.

'Hi there,' says the assistant, a bright-eyed young woman with shiny red hair and perfectly contoured make-up. 'Would you be interested in a Colour Match Makeover? We're offering ten per cent off every session this week to celebrate the store launch.'

'No thank you,' I say, smiling politely as I head to the door. 'I was just browsing.'

'Oh, go on, Nessa,' says Georgie, taking my arm and leading me back into the store. 'It will do you good to have a little pamper.'

I look around me. The store is quiet and, to be honest, I would love to have a bit of a spruce. I've been feeling so grubby lately. So I relent and the assistant, who introduces herself as Verity, guides me to a tall stool upholstered in green velvet. While she gathers her products I sit there looking at myself in the spotlit mirror. What I see makes me inwardly gasp.

There are purple half-moons under my eyes, my skin is grey and dull, my hair lank. I seem to have aged ten years in the last few weeks.

But I try to relax, to put all negative thoughts out of my head as Verity sets to work cleansing my face with a Vitamin C-packed foam, applying micro fine moisturizer, then a matte primer. She gives me the name of each product, its ingredients and benefits. As someone who has spent the last five years working in the cosmetics industry this should feel like a bit of a busman's holiday, but Verity is clearly passionate and informed about her products and I'm drawn in. 'This foundation, Silk Sheen, is so light that it just looks like you've got great skin rather than wearing a mask of make-up,' she says as she sponges a heavenly scented lotion on to my face. 'And it blends so well, see?'

I lean forward towards the mirror and nod my head. She's right. This is an excellent product. I must make a note of its ingredients to pass on to Anne. Then I remember I don't work at Luna London any more.

Georgie was right, though. This has been just what I needed. The sound of Verity's voice as she enthuses about the products, the smell of her perfume, the hum of the radio in the background, make me feel safe. No one can get to me here. I close my eyes as Verity applies a soft grey eyeshadow to my eyelids and I recall those nights when I would watch my mum get ready to go out. The smell of Penhaligon's Violetta and M&S Magnolia talcum powder mingling in the air, the lotions and potions lined up on her dressing table, the way she opened her mouth into an 'o' shape as she applied mascara to her lashes.

'Gosh, that Dove Letter eyeshadow looks great on you!' says Verity, after applying blush and a gorgeously glossy lip tint called Rose Cream. 'There we are. You're all done.'

She stands back and I look into the mirror. What I see almost makes me cry. It's the old Vanessa. She looks back at me and smiles: this groomed, perfectly made-up woman. And I tell myself that, no matter what it takes, I have to get her back.

I get down from the chair and go to the counter where Verity is standing at the till.

'Oh, it's okay, it's already been paid for,' she says as I offer my bank card.

Georgie is waiting outside the shop when I emerge.

'Oh, wow, you look beautiful, darling,' she says, her eyes welling up. 'Just perfect.'

'Thanks, Georgie,' I say, hugging her. 'Though you really shouldn't have paid for it. Brunch was more than enough.'

'I didn't pay for it,' says Georgie, looking confused. 'I went for a walk up to the bookshop while you were in there. I wanted to see if they had the new Kate Atkinson.'

'But the woman . . . Verity . . . she said it had been paid for,' I say, glancing back at the shop, panic fluttering through me. 'I need to go back and ask her who paid for it.'

'Oh, I wouldn't bother,' says Georgie, taking my arm. 'It looks like she's given you a freebie. I did mention when we first went in, on the quiet, that you'd worked for Luna London. She probably wanted to secure you as a contact. Now, come on, let's go for that walk.'

We arrive back at the house at 1 p.m. As Georgie puts the key in the lock the door opens. Jack is standing there.

'Oh,' he says, looking surprised. 'I wasn't expecting you two back for another couple of hours.'

'Well, we're early,' says Georgie, squeezing past him. 'Honestly, Jack, this is my house too. Surely I can come and go as I please.'

I can sense the rumblings of a row so I excuse myself and head upstairs. After a couple of minutes, I hear the door slam. I look out of the window and see Jack storming off across the common. I flop down on the bed, the happiness of the morning dissolving. I know that the tension between Jack and Georgie is all down to me. They were always so loved up, so close, but since I turned up my sister is drinking every night and Jack can't bear to be in the house.

I look at my phone. There are three notifications in my email inbox. Two are from recruitment sites, but the most

recent one has no subject line and has been sent by someone called G@LOSTSOUL.COM

My stomach twists as I open the email and read:

> My, don't you look pretty. Back to your old self again.
> And doesn't Dove Letter bring out the blue of your eyes.
> Perfect.

22. Then

July 2018

The sun is already blazing though it's barely 7 a.m. As I sit here on the roof terrace I look out across the sparkling rooftops of South London and try to clear my head.

Today is my first day back at work since the abortion, the first step back into ordinary life. Though it's been ten days since the procedure I still feel delicate, like I've lost a vital part of myself. Maybe I have.

'So, you're definitely going back then?'

I look up and see Connor standing in the doorway. His hair is wet and he's holding a mug of coffee.

'Yes,' I say, trying to sound upbeat. 'I couldn't keep putting it off. Besides, the team needs me.'

'Your baby needed you,' he says, his voice barely audible.

'Please, Connor, don't do this,' I say, getting up from the bench. 'I really don't want an argument on my first day back.'

'I'm not starting an argument,' he says, standing aside to let me pass. 'I'm simply stating a fact. I know you feel guilty about what you did, Vanessa, but I told you I forgive you.'

'What I did?' I cry, my cheeks reddening. 'I think you played a part too. You told me you'd stopped.'

'And I did,' he says, placing his mug on the draining board. 'But we'd had sex countless times that month, before that night. One of the condoms must have split. That's the only explanation.'

I look down at the floor, a familiar panic engulfing me. If only I could remember that night, but I still have no recollection of it. The one image that returns to me again and again is that of Connor guiding me into a taxi on Sloane Street, then nothing else. But maybe he's right, maybe I got pregnant before that night. Maybe a condom ripped without us realizing it.

'Look, you took matters into your own hands without even consulting me,' says Connor, following me through the living room as I go to get my bag and coat from the hook. 'What kind of person does that? Just sneaks off without letting their partner know. If I hadn't found those leaflets on the doorstep I'd still be none the wiser.'

'I was scared,' I cry, my head tightening. The morning I returned to the house I'd been sure I'd thrown those leaflets in the bin, but I was so woozy and exhausted I must have dropped them. I try to imagine how Connor must have felt, seeing them on the doorstep like that.

'Scared?' he shouts, his face beetroot red. 'Yeah, well I bet our baby was scared when you murdered it.'

His words fall into the space between us like bullets. I stand, unable to speak, unable to move. We've been having a version of this argument every day since I woke to find him clutching those leaflets. So many times, that I'm starting to feel like I'm losing my mind.

'Look, let's just stop this,' says Connor, his voice softening. 'I've told you I forgive you but it's going to take some time for things to get back to normal.'

And every time I think it's getting too much, he says something like that, and I give in.

The morning passes in a blur. When I first arrived the girls had huddled around me, asking me if I felt better after the horrible flu that had laid me low, filling me in on snippets of office gossip, letting me know how the campaign for the new Spring Shimmer eyeshadow was going. Eventually, it all got too much and I had to excuse myself.

Now, as I sit here at Anne's weekly 11 a.m. meeting, my brain feels slow and sticky. I try my best to focus on what Anne is saying but all I can think of are Connor's words: *I bet our baby was scared when you murdered it.*

'What do you think, Vanessa?'

I look up. Damian, sitting on the opposite side of the table, is speaking to me.

'I . . . er . . .'

I suddenly feel very hot. White spots appear in front of my eyes. It's like the feeling you get when you stand up too quickly.

'Vanessa?'

'I'm sorry,' I say, scrambling to my feet. 'I'm not feeling too . . . I need some water.'

Outside, in the open-plan office space, the air is full of voices, music, the click-clack of keyboards. I hurry to my office, closing the door firmly behind me.

I sit on the armchair and put my head in my hands, try to remember the breathing exercises Anne is always urging us to do. As I sit here, there's a knock at the door. I look up and see Anne.

'Vanessa, is everything okay?' she says, her eyes full of concern as she brings a chair over to where I'm sitting. 'You look terribly pale.'

'I'm fine,' I say, summoning a smile. 'I just got a bit overheated. Give me a few minutes and I'll be able to rejoin the meeting.'

'You said it was flu,' says Anne, getting up and fetching me a beaker of water from the cooler.

'Yes,' I say, taking the water from her. 'It was a particularly bad bout.'

I feel terrible for lying to her but I have no choice.

'Hmm,' she says, regarding me through her smart acetate spectacles. 'It looks to me like you're post-viral. You know these viruses can take a good few weeks to clear up. I think you need to rest today, Vanessa. Don't worry about the meeting. I can email you anything you've missed.'

'Honestly, Anne,' I say, taking a long sip of water, 'I'll be fine in a few minutes, really.'

'Vanessa, this isn't a suggestion, it's an order,' she says, taking my jacket and bag from the back of the chair and handing them to me. 'You still look ill to me and I wouldn't be a responsible employer if I let you stay here in this state. Would you like me to book you a taxi?'

'No thank you,' I say, slipping my arms shakily into my jacket. 'The fresh air will do me good.'

'If you're sure, darling,' says Anne gently. 'But do text me when you get back just to put my mind at rest.'

I nod my head and smile.

'I know,' says Anne as she guides me to the lift, 'I'm a fussy old thing, but that's what happens when you're a mother. You just want to keep all your babies safe and well.'

Her words stay with me as I enter the lift and a sharp, razor-like feeling of guilt slices through me. Connor was right. I am the worst possible person.

The fresh air does seem to do me some good and by the time I arrive back at the flat my head feels a little clearer. I put the key in the lock but as I open it I hear something, the sound of muffled voices coming from inside.

My skin prickles as I stand at the door, not daring to go inside. Then I look up and see Connor standing at the top of the stairs with a towel wrapped round his middle.

'Vanessa, what are you doing here?' he says as I walk slowly up the stairs.

'Anne sent me home,' I say, pausing to hang my bag and jacket on the hook. 'I wasn't feeling very well. Who's up there? I heard voices.'

'Just the radio,' he says, fussing with the cushions as I slump on to the sofa. 'God, Vanessa, I told you it was too soon to go back.'

The air smells stale, like cigarette smoke. It catches in my throat.

'What's that smell?' I say, curling into a ball, my hand clasping the fluffy cushion. 'Have you been smoking?'

'Don't be so ridiculous,' he says, hurrying into the kitchen where I hear him slam the roof-terrace door shut. 'It's the new people next door,' he says, returning to the living room. 'They smoke out on their balcony and the smell wafts over here.'

My eyes feel heavy though I know if I try to sleep the nightmares will come.

'Anyway, what are you doing here?' I say, stretching out my legs.

'I had a client meeting in Chelsea,' he says, readjusting his towel. 'It finished earlier than I expected. There was no point going all the way back east so I've been doing some work here.'

I look at him. His eyes look strange and there's a manic edge to his voice.

'Anyway, I'm glad you're here,' he says jumpily, 'because I've got a surprise for you. I was going to give it to you this evening but . . . give me a minute.'

My eyes grow heavier and as I hear his footsteps disappear down the corridor I close them and feel myself start to drift.

'Vanessa.'

I look up. Connor is now dressed in jeans and a black T-shirt. He's holding something in his hands, a small velvet box. He sits down next to me on the sofa and opens the box. Inside is a pear-shaped diamond ring.

'Connor, I really don't think . . .' I begin, my head foggy with sleep.

'Shh, it's okay,' he says, his voice less manic now. 'This ring belonged to my grandmother. I loved her very much and when she died she left me this ring with a note telling me to give it to the woman I wanted to marry.'

My chest tightens. I don't understand. Only this morning he was telling me I'd murdered our child and now he's asking me to marry him.

'You're probably feeling overwhelmed,' he says, taking the ring out of its box. 'I just would love you to wear it. It can be our little way of healing, I guess. After everything we've been through these last couple of weeks I think we need something to look forward to, some good news to outweigh the bad.'

I have no words. I'm dog-tired and the cramps have started up again. They are not as painful as they were but sharp enough to make me feel rather queasy. I look down at the ring and laugh. It's a nervous laugh but Connor seems to interpret it as acceptance.

'I knew you'd love it,' he says, slipping the ring on to my finger. 'Now we can move on properly, really plan our life together.'

I look down at the ring and I feel nauseous suddenly.

'I know,' says Connor, jumping to his feet. 'Let's go for a drink to celebrate.'

'Connor, no,' I say, rubbing my head. 'I still don't feel too good.'

'We won't go far,' he says, grabbing my jacket and bag and handing them to me. 'Just up to Lavender Hill. And we can have sparkling water.'

To be honest, the thought of staying in this flat on such a warm day is not an appealing one. At least in the open air I can clear my head.

Connor rushes me down the stairs, grabbing his bag from the vestibule by the door. The sun is blazing and I realize that I don't need my coat. I tell Connor I'll just take it back to the flat quickly but he grabs it and says that he will carry it for me.

He takes my hand. As we turn on to Queenstown Road, the cramping intensifies and I clutch his arm, inhaling his familiar peppery scent. This used to be the most appealing and reassuring of smells but today it seems to stick in the back of my throat.

'We should try that new little place up by the library,' says Connor as we take a right on to Lavender Hill. 'Some of the guys at work went there at the weekend and said the food was amazing and . . .'

His words fall away as the pain gets stronger. I still haven't fully recovered from the abortion. I should be resting. But I can't say that to him and risk another fight. We go a little further and as we do I feel myself heating up, then my heart starts to thud violently. I can feel myself falling but there's nothing to hold on to. With a crack, I hit the pavement. The last thing I hear as I lose consciousness is Connor's voice.

23. Now

I am thankful that Georgie and Jack have decided to have a TV supper rather than a roast this evening. I feel so twitchy and nervous I don't think I could have sat still had we gathered round the table, and then Georgie would have fretted and asked me what was the matter. At least, this way, all eyes are on the TV screen instead of on me. Not that tonight's viewing is doing much to calm the hostilities between Jack and Georgie.

'The bloody *Antiques Roadshow*,' sighs Georgie, her plate of homemade chicken pie and greens balanced on her knee. 'Is there nothing else on? Really, Jack, I don't know why you insist on watching it.'

Sundays. Even as a child I hated them. When Mum was alive she would alleviate the dread by making the day truly fun-packed. She'd take me out for a big walk up to Caversham Park pond to feed the ducks and we'd have hot chocolate with marshmallows at the cafe. Home in time for Sunday roast with all the trimmings, including cauliflower cheese, my absolute favourite, then a warm bubbly bath before bed, tired and happy. So very happy. But Sundays after she died were never the same. That was when the Sunday-night feeling intensified and the smell of roast beef and Yorkshire puddings no longer made my mouth water. Monday mornings loomed with the incessant questions from pupils and teachers alike as to how I was coping and did I miss my mum. Then home time, where I would have to navigate a sea of mothers before escaping into Georgie's battered old VW Beetle. She still lived in Reading in those days and would leave work early to come and collect me from school then wait until Dad got back from the office at 6 p.m. And though she would try hard to do the things Mum had done – making me snacks, checking if I had homework to do, asking about my day – it just wasn't the same. I was ten years old and I needed my mum. Georgie was twenty-three and needed to concentrate on her own life. We were at opposite ends of the spectrum, with Dad, grief-stricken and bewildered, floating somewhere in between.

Now here I am again, running back to her like a needy child.

'The *Antiques Roadshow* is comforting,' says Jack, turning up the volume. 'The televisual equivalent of chicken pie.'

Georgie glances at me and raises her eyebrows.

'What would you like to watch, Vanessa?' she says, taking a sip from the glass of Chablis that she has balanced on the slim side table. 'There must be something a bit more interesting on. How about we try Netflix?'

'This is fine,' I say, taking a bite of pie. The pastry sticks in my throat. 'Like Jack says, it's comforting.'

'Well, what a pair of old biddies you are,' says Georgie, putting her plate on the table and tucking her feet underneath her. 'It's been going for donkey's years this programme. Mum used to love it. Remember how she used to go and raid the loft and the cabinets, Vanessa, to see if she had any priceless antiques hidden away?'

I nod my head. Not only do I remember but I had been Mum's accomplice on those explorations. I can see her now, dressed in Sunday casuals – loose linen trousers and her favourite blue-and-white Breton top – climbing up the rickety ladder into the loft. Once up there she would reach her hands down and haul me up to join her. 'Now, Nessa, let's see if we can find anything interesting, shall we?' she'd say as she hunted through the dusty boxes. 'It's amazing what treasures are hidden in the home.' I would invariably find an old *Judy* annual of Georgie's or a sparkling bit of costume jewellery that I would insist on bringing downstairs. Mum would watch as I made my way unsteadily down the ladder then she would stay up there for the rest of the evening, hunting for treasure. She never found any though, no matter how hard she looked.

'Look at this guy,' says Jack, leaning back in his armchair. 'Bought this contraption for ten quid in a charity shop in Thirsk and it's just been valued at six grand.'

He points to the screen where a ginger-haired man is standing next to what looks like a rusty scythe.

'Good grief,' says Georgie, shaking her head. 'Still, I've seen worse in certain art galleries.'

'That fella looks like the grim reaper, clutching that thing,' says Jack, chuckling.

I look at the screen and the ginger man suddenly transforms into Geoffrey. His eyes bulge and he starts to wheeze as he squeezes the scythe tighter in his hands. 'It was you,' he hisses at me through the screen. 'You did it.'

Just then my phone rings in my pocket and I almost drop my plate in fright.

'He's right,' says Jack, oblivious to my distress. 'She did do it. It was his wife who convinced him to buy it.'

'Is that your phone, Ness?' says Georgie, glancing at me.

I nod my head as I take the phone out of my pocket.

'Unknown number' is displayed on the screen. My throat goes dry. I had blocked the email earlier but it's no use. I remember Connor telling me at the beginning of our relationship how he devised his branding campaigns: 'You attack them from all sides, become part of their consciousness, until they're left wondering how they ever lived without you.'

'I'll just take this,' I say, getting up and walking out into the hallway.

I take a deep breath then press accept. This has to stop and only I can make that happen.

'Enough, Connor,' I hiss into the phone, hearing the laboured breath at the other end. 'You have to stop this now. Do you hear me? Just leave me alone.'

'Miss Adams?' says an unfamiliar male voice.

Startled, I almost drop the phone.

'Er, yes,' I say. 'Who is this? What do you want?'

'This is DS Collins from West Hampstead police station.'

The voice is deep and resonant, with the faintest trace of a West Country accent.

'I'm calling to ask you to attend the station tomorrow.'

'What's this about?' I say, my throat tightening. 'What do you want?'

'We'll explain everything tomorrow, Miss Adams,' he says calmly. 'If you report to reception at 1 p.m. and ask for me we'll take it from there. Good evening.'

I hear a click on the other end. I stand there motionless, the phone clasped in my hand, the trill of the *Antiques Roadshow* theme music filtering through the living-room door.

This is it, I tell myself as I make my way upstairs. *I'm going to be arrested.*

And I deserve to be. Because they've got it right. I killed Geoffrey Rivers.

PART TWO

24.

Wimbledon Magistrates Court
25 February 2019

The first thing I see as I am led into the courtroom is a large picture hanging on the wall, to the right of the public gallery. It's a charcoal drawing, post-impressionist in style, of a street puppet dancing, its strings being pulled and manipulated by a faceless man. The puppet smiles manically, though its eyes are dead, while the man controlling it blends into the background. It's a disturbing picture and I turn my face away from it as the court usher leads me to my place, try to focus on what I have to say.

In front of me, the barristers look down at their papers. All except one. My adversary. He adjusts his gold cufflinks then sits, poker straight, and fixes me with a cold, unblinking stare. A shiver flutters through me as I consider this man's power. With a few words he can destroy me. I have to keep calm, have to have faith in my story, stick to it and pray that the jury will believe me.

I take my seat and look up to the public gallery. Georgie and Jack are sitting in the front row. My sister smiles reassuringly, just as she had done at Mum's funeral and my graduation and all those other times when I needed to know someone had my back. I return her smile then turn away. I need to focus, need to keep my emotions in check or else it will all unravel.

But as I sit I feel another pair of eyes upon me. I lift my head and see him. Connor. His hair has been cropped short and he's lost weight. The stress of the last few months is etched across his face. He looks back at me with thinly disguised disgust. He hates me for what I've done. That much is clear. His mother sits with her hands clutching the rail of the public gallery. As my eyes meet hers she shakes her head and scowls. Like her son, she wants to see me destroyed today, to get my punishment.

Alongside me, I hear a commotion. I turn to see the judge entering. My heart sinks as I regard him. A man in his early seventies, small beady eyes, a mouth curled naturally into a sneer. The last person I would expect to show mercy to me. As I watch him glide to his seat, the black robes billowing in his wake, I think of Iris, resplendent in her blue velvet cape.

And then I'm back there, walking up the gravelled driveway, hearing the buzz of traffic from the high street grow fainter, feeling weightless, as though the real world has ceased to exist and all that matters is the story I'm entering.

I recall the tall, stone griffins standing guard either side of the solid oak door, their bared teeth chipped, their wings eroded by the weather. I recall the date engraved in the centre of the door arch and the feeling of exhilaration that fizzed up my spine as I whispered the numbers into the stagnant summer air.

1647.
The year of wonder.

I recall the sensation of falling under that spell again.

I recall Geoffrey's face as he opened the door, the beaming smile belying the sad eyes. And I realize that my decision to go to that house led me directly to this courtroom.

As the judge begins to speak I steady myself and return to the present. All I have to do is tell my story, calmly and concisely, and hope that they believe it.

25. Then

August 2018

'Vanessa, this is ridiculous.'

I had got up extra early, hoping to sneak out of the house before Connor woke, but now he is here, standing at the top of the stairs while I put on my coat.

'You can't go into work today,' he says, running down the stairs in just his boxer shorts. 'Not after what happened last week. You collapsed in the street, for God's sake.'

'I'm feeling much better this morning,' I say, putting my phone and keys into my bag. 'Last week was just a blip. I got overheated.'

'Look, even Anne is expressing concern at your behaviour,' he says, sitting down on the middle step. 'We're all worried.'

'Anne wasn't expressing concern at my behaviour,' I say, feeling irritated now. 'She was concerned at my being physically unwell.'

'Like I said, we're all concerned,' says Connor gravely. 'Your behaviour these last few months has been erratic to say the least. I was already worried about your drinking, and you promised me you'd stop, then the abortion.'

'I told you, Connor, there was no other choice.'

I can't do this again.

I yank open the door, gulping in the fresh air. As I step out I hear him running down the final few stairs.

'How dare you?' he hisses, grabbing my arms and twisting me round to face him. 'What about my choice? What about our baby's choice?'

'Connor, stop,' I say, releasing myself from his grasp. 'I have to go.'

'Well, I think you're making a mistake,' he says, shaking his head. 'You're in no fit state to work at the moment. You should take some time out to get better.'

'What are you saying?'

'I'm saying that right now you're unwell,' he says, his eyes boring into me. 'And you should seriously consider taking time out.'

'Quit my job, you mean?'

'If that's what it takes to get you better then maybe, yes.'

'But I love my job,' I say, not quite believing what I'm hearing. 'You know that.'

'Look, Vanessa,' he says, his voice softening, 'one of my friends had a breakdown a few years back. We were all so worried about her. I recognize the warning signs. I can see you heading for a full-on breakdown if you don't slow down and get help.'

I look at him for a moment, try to imagine myself through his eyes. Yes, I have been drinking more than usual and, yes, I did get an abortion without telling him, but I had no choice. The pregnancy was not planned. I blink away the thought of that lost night.

'I'm not giving up my job, Connor, and that's final.'

Then I step outside into the August sunshine, closing the door firmly behind me.

When I get to the office a party is in full swing. The open-plan area has been decked with lemon and silver balloons, there's a table groaning with glasses of champagne and breakfast pastries, and 'September' by Earth, Wind & Fire is blasting out from the speakers. The marketing team, led by Claire, is huddled round Claire's phone doing a live Instagram chat. As I approach, I hear her say, 'We're so excited to reveal our exclusive new palette: Shades of Autumn.'

The other women whoop excitedly and my heart sinks. Today is launch day for Shades of Autumn, the new cosmetics line for the upcoming season we've spent the last five months working on. There will be a full day of publicity ahead, calls to beauty editors, Instagram chats with bloggers and influencers, calls to the major stores that stock Luna London as well as online meetings with the US suppliers as Anne decided a joint UK/US launch would create a big buzz. With a sick feeling I remember the missed calls from Anne these last few days, the emails piled up in my inbox that I chose to ignore in favour of curling up in the foetal position. I thought Anne had been calling to check how I was. It was rare for me to call in sick so I just assumed she was concerned. How could I have forgotten about the launch? As I stand with my hand poised on my office door handle, I hear someone call my name. I see Claire rushing towards me, holding a glass of champagne.

'We're so glad to have you back,' she says, handing me the champagne. I politely refuse. 'There's been such an amazing response already. Ruby Tiller has just put up an Insta story showing herself wearing the complete range. That is a fucking brilliant endorsement. Anne is over the moon.'

'That's great,' I say, remembering that it was me who had connected with Ruby Tiller, a London actress starring in a big US Netflix series, and sent her the full Shades of Autumn range. 'Where is Anne now?'

'On the phone to New York,' says Claire, her eyes gleaming. She's only been here a few months but she's extremely ambitious. I should see her as a threat but I just feel numb.

'Okay,' I say, pushing my office door open. 'I'll catch up with her in a moment.'

'Are you not going to join the party?' says Claire, looking at me expectantly. 'Damian's loosened his purse strings and bought us pastries from Daylesford. You must come and have one.'

'I will,' I say. 'Just give me a few minutes and I'll be right out.'

'Awesome,' she says, smiling a smile that doesn't reach her eyes.

I close the door, take off my jacket and sit down at my desk. This is one of the biggest days in the Luna London calendar and it had completely slipped my mind. I should be out there rallying my team, getting stuck in, promoting this product I've put my heart and soul into, but I can't move. I feel empty, devoid of any emotion, whether good or bad. What is happening to me? Then a cold shiver courses through my body. Is Connor right? Am I falling apart?

I need to pull myself together, need to snap out of this fog. I look at my inbox. I should at least attempt to tackle that before I see Anne but then my phone bleeps on the desk. I look down and see a notification from the Dream Properties app. 'Three new properties waiting for you,' it reads. I click on the app, feeling a familiar sense of exhilaration rise up inside me. As the images load on the screen I breathe a sigh of relief. It's been too long.

Amy, the estate agent, is waiting for me on the river path when I arrive. She is young, in her early twenties, with a soft, trusting face, and she rushes towards me as I approach.

'You must be Imogen,' she cries, extending a tanned hand with French-polished fingernails. 'It's so good to meet you. Shall we go take a look?'

It was so easy I can barely believe it. I made an online booking using the name of my niece. I felt it might be a good omen to take on her persona for a couple of hours, and I was right. I can leave everything behind.

'I'm afraid you're going to have to be patient with me as I'm not familiar with this property,' says Amy, turning to me with a beaming white smile as we head down the drive. 'It's my colleague, Jenny, who deals with these kinds of properties but her son's sick so I had to step in at the last minute. I hope you don't mind?'

'Not at all,' I say, looking up at the ivy-clad, red-brick facade. The house is a waterside pile in Goring, worth in the tens of millions.

'So this, obviously, is the main entrance,' says Amy as she juggles the bulky set of keys with one hand while keeping a firm grip on her hot-pink handbag with the other.

'Right,' she says, gasping as she unlocks the door. 'Let's go and have a look, Imogen.'

The name makes me smile and I feel a burst of energy as we enter the house. The entire entrance hall is filled with bookshelves, rising all the way up to the ceiling.

'Oh, wow,' exclaims Amy. 'Someone likes their books. I've never seen so many.'

'It's extraordinary,' I whisper. 'Like a secret library.'

'It really is,' says Amy. 'But, God, I wouldn't like the job of dusting them all.'

She laughs and the sound reverberates around the room.

We spend the next ten minutes strolling from room to room with Amy pointing out the stunning views. The living room, which looks out on to the river, is spectacular, with polished wood flooring, plush velvet sofas and tasteful dove-grey painted walls.

'Right, shall we go and see the kitchen?' she says, consulting her phone, on which I can see a vast floorplan on the screen. 'Do you like to cook, Imogen?'

I pause before replying, my eyes still fixed on the bookshelves. Did Imogen like cooking? I'm not sure. I think back to when she was a young teenager and got rather obsessed with *The Great British Bake Off*. Every time I visited, there would be an aroma of slightly burnt sponge cake hanging in the air and a flour-spattered kitchen. Georgie used to roll her eyes at it. How could a feminist Oxford graduate like my sister have produced a daughter who just wanted to bake cakes? I had found it all rather comical though I could see the relief in Georgie's face when Imogen eventually tired of baking and returned to her books, finally gaining a place at Oxford herself.

'Er, I like to bake from time to time,' I say, following Amy down a narrow, dimly lit, wood-panelled corridor.

'Ooh, lovely,' says Amy, her voice growing fainter ahead of me. 'My mum loves baking too, though I have to be careful as I can put on half a stone just looking at a cake.'

Though the living room had been light and modern, the rest of the house is in need of updating. Amy had pointed out earlier that the property belonged to an elderly couple and this is evident as we enter the kitchen. There's a bottle-green Aga, an ancient-looking white fridge and a counter with chipped orange tiles. All very much in vogue circa 1982. 'Oh,' says Amy, unable to hide the disgust from her face. 'It's a little dated but then I always find clients want to put their own stamp on a kitchen. It could be fabulous, once all this clutter is removed.'

I walk across to the kitchen counter, a strange feeling rising inside me. I run my hands along the orange tiles that I last saw in my childhood home in Caversham and suddenly realize why I'm feeling so spellbound. Unlike all the other houses I have visited, this one feels like a home. Like I could actually live here. Not Imogen or Tabitha or any of the other personas I've adopted, but me: Vanessa Adams. All that is missing is Radio 2. And Mum.

Just then Amy's phone rings. The sound makes me jump.

She looks at the screen, smiles then turns to me, holding the phone in the air.

'I'm really sorry, but I'm going to have to take this,' she says, her eyes twinkling so much I seriously doubt it's a work call. 'Can I leave you to have a look round the kitchen? I won't be a sec.'

'Of course,' I say, trying to hide my delight. 'Take your time.'

'Thanks, Imogen,' she says, beaming as she answers the call and hurries out of the room.

I stand listening as her footsteps disappear down the corridor then make my way over to the oak dresser. There are four sturdy-looking drawers midway down it. I pull open the first one and look inside. Whoever lives here is obviously a bit of a hoarder. There are scraps of paper, a ball of elastic bands, old packets of seeds and some soiled gardening gloves. I close the drawer with a shove then open the next one along. This one is full of old perfume bottles, most of them empty. The contents, like the kitchen, look like a freeze frame of the early 1980s. There's Chanel Number 5, Le Jardin, Poison by Dior and, to my amazement, Penhaligon's Violetta, the perfume my mother wore. The bottle is almost empty. I lift the stopper off and inhale, and as I do, I'm back in my mother's arms, nuzzling into her neck. It smells of happiness and safety. It smells of Mum.

I hear Amy's footsteps coming back up the corridor so I shove the drawer closed then hurriedly place the bottle into my bag.

'Sorry about that,' says Amy, bounding into the room. 'Now, shall we go and see the garden?'

'Actually, Amy,' I reply, the bottle a reassuring bulk in my bag, 'I don't think this is the house for me after all.'

My mood is so much better when I get back to the flat that I barely register the coat. A camel-coloured coat hanging on the hook in the hallway. A woman's coat. There's a murmur of voices coming from the living room: Connor's and another. A woman's.

I stand in the doorway and look into the room. Connor is sitting on the sofa. A woman with shoulder-length dyed auburn hair and a Bardot-style cream top sits next to him, her arm wrapped round his shoulder. She is holding something in her hand. Her hands are wrinkled, the skin paper thin with bulging blue veins, old woman's hands that belie the highlighted auburn hair and youthful clothes. It's then I realize this is Connor's mother. I recognize her from the photo he keeps on the bookshelf. I have never met her, though I've asked Connor enough times if I could. He has always said she was busy or working away. As I step closer I see what she's holding. It's my appointment card from the abortion clinic.

I clear my throat and they look up at me. Up close, Connor's mother resembles a piece of jagged driftwood: brittle and tawny.

'Vanessa,' says Connor, jumping to his feet and smiling nervously. 'You're home. Come in. We need to talk.'

'That is my personal property,' I say, my voice shaking, gesturing to the appointment card. 'What are you doing with it?'

'Mum's come to talk to you,' says Connor. 'She knows we're going through a tough time and she wants to help.'

His mother nods her head then fixes her eyes on me. It feels odd to finally be in the same room as the elusive Jackie. I've been with her son for almost a year and have never once been invited to her house in Harrogate; nor has she ever come to see us at the flat, at least not while I was home. Now, here she is poring over my private documents. She might as well have seen me naked.

'My son is very upset,' she says. Her voice is sharp with a strong northern accent. 'He's been calling me almost every night in tears. Do you have anything to say? Any explanation?'

'This is a private matter between me and Connor,' I say, walking further into the room. 'I don't think it's appropriate that he has brought you into it.'

'I'm his mother,' she cries, her nostrils flaring. 'And he's been going through hell for the last few months. He needs my support. Which is why I've travelled hundreds of miles to come and sort this out.'

'And I appreciate that, Mum,' says Connor, smiling meekly. 'I really do.'

'It's not only what you did. It's the secrecy,' she says angrily, my appointment card gripped in her hand. 'Just going off and doing it without telling Connor. It's obscene.'

'Mum, calm down,' says Connor, placing his hand on her shoulder. 'I've told you, this hasn't been easy for either of us. Vanessa has suffered too.'

'And so she should,' says Jackie. 'She killed your child. My grandchild.'

'Mum, please,' says Connor. 'You have to understand, Vanessa's been struggling, even before the abortion.'

He looks up at me.

'Haven't you, Vanessa? Be honest.'

'This is insane,' I say, my head pounding. 'You have completely violated my privacy and now you're trying to tell me how I feel?'

'You know you haven't been yourself for a long time,' he says, his voice a sickening simper. 'The drinking, the anger, the meltdowns.'

'Meltdowns?' I cry. 'What are you talking about?'

'Well, it looks like you're just about to have another one,' says Jackie.

She clicks her tongue and, with that, the anger I have spent the last few minutes holding in comes tumbling forth.

'Why don't you tell her the truth?' I cry, rushing at Connor. 'Why don't you tell her what really happened?'

His eyes flash angrily and he grabs my wrists.

'You're talking nonsense, Vanessa,' he cries. 'Now calm down.'

As I free myself from his grip I hear his mother's voice somewhere on the periphery of my consciousness, but it's dulled by the rage boiling inside my head. How dare he try and make out like there's something wrong with me? The anger twists and thickens in my stomach then rises, like fire, through my body until it reaches my temples and I hear a deafening scream. My own.

I lunge at Jackie and snatch the card from her hands.

'Vanessa,' cries Connor. 'Stop this.'

He holds my arms and shakes me so hard the card falls to the floor. I look at his face, which is just inches from mine. His brown eyes are full of something I have never seen there before: hatred.

'Just pull yourself together, can't you?' he says, squeezing tighter.

As I stand there like a limp rag doll, unable to move, I get a flashback. Connor lying on top of me, his face as angry and twisted as it is now. Me, crying in pain and begging him to stop. Truth shines through the mire of my brain and galvanizes me. I feel the stored-up anger taking over.

'No, I won't pull myself together,' I cry, yanking my arms from his grip. 'You did this to me. You are the one hurting me.'

'Oh, for Christ's sake,' he says, shaking his head. 'You need help, Vanessa, you really do.'

At those words something inside me snaps and I throw myself at him with such force he falls backwards on to the sofa.

'Enough,' yells Jackie, grabbing me by the shoulders. 'I will not have you abuse my son like this.'

'Get off me,' I cry, pulling my arm away. 'This is none of your business.'

Then I hear a scream. Connor leaps up from the sofa.

I turn round. Jackie is holding her hand to her face. When she takes it away I see a pink patch on her cheek.

'Mum?' cries Connor, rushing to her side. 'Oh God, she's bleeding.'

He turns to me, his face red and sweating.

'Look what you've done,' he says. 'You fucking psycho.'

26. Now

August 2018

It's 9 a.m. I have lain here in bed for the last hour, staring at the ceiling, wondering if this is my last morning of freedom. I try to imagine what prison will be like – the noise, the smell, the thud of the cell door as it closes behind me.

Enough, I tell myself as I climb out of bed. I will need to keep a cool head today. So I start to focus on the practicalities.

I have to be at West Hampstead police station at 1 p.m. It's a thirty-minute walk from here to Wimbledon station then just under an hour to get to West Hampstead on the overland train. The thought of travelling on public transport makes me feel ill. I will be visible, exposed. Connor could be on that train with me, watching me, following me, and I would never know.

The best solution is to get a taxi. Sitting on the edge of the bed, I scroll through my phone for the Uber app that I haven't used in months. Memories of Lottie and me, tipsily clambering into shared Uber rides, come flooding back. Lottie, merrily chatting away to the other passengers: 'Hi, I'm Lottie and this is Nessa. What are your names? Are you going far?'

I smile, then a surge of sadness overcomes me. I miss her so much. I didn't realize how much I needed her until it was too late.

I book the taxi and, leaving the phone charging in the socket by the bed, head across the landing to the bathroom. After a cool shower I feel almost human again. I wrap a large fluffy towel around me then head back to the bedroom. But as I reach the door I hear voices coming from Jack and Georgie's room.

'I don't want to hear it, Jack.'

'Well, you should. You're part of this too.'

'I'm part of it? You're the one who's behaving strangely.'

'Says the woman who is now self-medicating because she's worried about her sister. Christ, give me strength.'

I hear his footsteps thudding towards the door and I dart into my room, closing the door behind me.

I mull over their words in my head as I dry my hair, the familiar pang of guilt settling in my stomach. Jack sounded so angry, so fierce, not at all like the Jack I've known since I was a little girl, the calm, solid Jack we all depend upon.

This is my fault. I have brought all this to their doorstep and I'm ripping them apart. I had been tempted, when I got the call last night, to tell them what was happening, get them to contact Frank Solomon. But now, after hearing the argument, I am even more determined to do this alone. It's not fair to drag Jack and Georgie in even further.

I finish off my hair as best I can, then hurriedly get dressed. It's getting close to 10.15 now. The taxi will be here in five minutes. I dress soberly in black trousers, a cream linen blouse and flat, black loafers. I need to make a good impression, to appear responsible, professional and calm, which is difficult when I feel like I'm about to fall apart at any minute.

I hear the front door slam and I look out of the window. Georgie and Jack are walking down the path. Georgie heads toward the common – she'll be going to the station then on to Mayfair – while Jack gets into his black Saab. Part of me wishes I had asked to walk to the station with my sister. I would have felt a little safer. But then we would have had to get different trains – she, the Piccadilly Line to Green Park; me, the Thameslink to West Hampstead, where anyone could have got on and followed me. No, I think to myself as I step away from the window and unplug my phone, best to get a taxi.

I'm halfway down the stairs when I hear the letterbox clatter. I hurry down the last of the steps and see, lying on the doormat, a postcard.

I creep gingerly towards it, my skin prickling. When I see what it is I almost throw up. The picture on the front is a pencil drawing of Holly Maze House, complete with stone griffins and topiary animals.

I bend down to pick it up and as I turn the card over my body goes cold. There is no stamp, no postmark, just my name and six words, written in capitals.

ISN'T IT JUST TO DIE FOR?

There's a loud knock on the door and I leap backwards, almost dropping the card.

This is it. He's here. Connor. He's come for me and I'm alone. What do I do?

My whole body begins to shake. Then my phone bleeps in my trouser pocket. I take it out. It's a text from Uber. My taxi has arrived.

It's okay, I tell myself. It's just the taxi driver. Everything is okay.

I slip the postcard into my bag and open the front door.

The driver, a hawkish man with cropped black hair and narrow grey eyes, looks at me curiously as I climb into the back seat of the car.

'West Hampstead police station, yeah?' he says.

'Yes, please,' I say, shakily pulling the seat belt across me. I look at my watch – 10.20. I'll be in West Hampstead in just under half an hour. It's ridiculously early for my appointment but I figure I'd rather get out of the house than wait around and stew. I'll find a coffee shop nearby where I can sit and gather my thoughts.

The driver nods his head but as the car pulls away I'm suddenly frozen with fear.

What if he is part of this? The car had arrived at the same time as the postcard came through the letterbox. What if he's taking me somewhere else? What if . . .

I try to calm myself as we drive through the village and all the familiar landmarks flash by – the independent bookshop, the Italian restaurant where we celebrated Jack and Georgie's twentieth wedding anniversary, the dog groomers where Mr Allen takes his fat retriever, the florist – but my heart is pounding so much it feels like I might pass out. When we reach Wimbledon station I take off my seat belt and sit forward.

'I've changed my mind,' I say, my voice trembling. 'Drop me here.'

'But this is not what you booked,' he says, shaking his head. 'This is not West Hampstead.'

'I know, but I don't feel very well,' I say, scrambling for the door.

'Don't be sick in my car,' he cries, pressing a button that releases the door. 'I charge extra for soiled seats.'

I jump out of the taxi, aware that I will have been billed for the entire trip to West Hampstead, but I don't care. I felt so scared being in that enclosed space. At least on the train, I tell myself, there is safety in numbers.

I hurry towards the station entrance, my forehead soaked with sweat, and as I walk through the ticket barrier my phone bleeps.

I dare not look at it. What if it's him? What if he's here, watching me? But then it could be something important, I tell myself. The police. Or Georgie. I look down at the screen. There's a number I don't recognize but the message underneath makes my heart soar.

Hello, stranger. Long time no see. Listen, I'm back in the UK and this is my new number. I'm staying with some friends in Maida Vale and would love to catch up. I know it's short notice but are you free this morning? If so, how about we meet for coffee. There's a lovely little cafe on Formosa Street near Warwick Avenue tube. We could meet there. I'll be there from 11.00. I know there's lots we need to talk about.

I don't have to be at the police station until 1 p.m. I won't have much time but I'll be able to have a quick coffee with Lottie then jump in a cab. It will be worth it, just to see her. I quickly text back.

I'm free. See you there x

I put my phone into my pocket, relief flooding through me at the thought of seeing my best friend again. It's like she knew exactly when I needed her most. I don't care what has happened in the past, I need her. And she was right about Connor in the end. I just hope she can help get me out of this mess.

27. Then

I sit on the edge of the sofa, my eyes swollen and raw from crying. The sun has just come up and I can hear Connor in the kitchen. As I sit here I try to piece together the events of the previous evening: Jackie holding my appointment card, the anger that rose up inside me when Connor told me I needed help. It had felt like they were coming at me from all sides, pressing down on me until I couldn't breathe. And the flashback? It had been so clear, so real, but now I'm not sure whether it was just my mind playing tricks on me. In the cold light of day I can see that Connor was right. I haven't been myself these last few months. It's like I'm spiralling into some terrible abyss with no chance of salvation.

'You're awake then?'

I look up and see Connor standing at the living-room door. He looks terrible. His face is pale and drawn and there are dark circles under his eyes. He comes into the room tentatively and perches on the edge of the armchair, keeping plenty of distance between himself and me.

'I'm so sorry, Connor,' I say, trying to stop myself from crying. 'I really am. But you have to believe me, it was an accident. I didn't see your mum standing behind me and then . . .'

'That's just it, Vanessa,' he says, clasping his hands together. 'You don't see, do you? You didn't see how terribly you behaved at the boxing night and you didn't see how appalling it was that you accused me of having sex without your consent or that you went behind my back and had an abortion. I've put up with your behaviour all this time and I've tried to help you but, fucking hell, hitting my mother is something else.'

I shudder, recalling the blood that had dripped down her cheek from where my engagement ring had cut her. So much blood, down her smart top, spotting the carpet.

'How is she?' I ask, recalling how Jackie and Connor had fled the house while I was still raging. 'Did she get the train okay?'

'Yes, she got the train,' says Connor. 'It's a three-hour journey back home and she had to do that with a gash across her face. Christ, Vanessa, she'd travelled all that way to help us.'

I nod my head. I feel sick with guilt. I have never hit anyone in my life.

'She has every right to press charges,' says Connor, his eyes blazing. 'But Mum's a good woman. She can see you're troubled and, like me, she just wants you to get some help. Proper help.'

'I will, Connor,' I say, the tears I've been trying to hold back rushing forth. 'I promise you I will.'

'I don't need your promises,' says Connor. 'You keep on promising me you'll change but it doesn't happen. It just gets worse. What we need is solid action.'

'What do you mean?'

'Well,' he says, taking a deep breath, 'we start by acknowledging that you are seriously ill. I've been doing my research, and you're displaying all the symptoms of a breakdown.'

I nod my head. Before last night I would have disagreed with him but the incident with Jackie was so out of character it had scared me. I am ill. I know that now.

'You also need to inform work,' says Connor, his tone brisk and businesslike. 'I know you love your job but you're not in any fit state to be working at the moment.'

I think back to yesterday, how I had completely forgotten about the Shades of Autumn launch, the feeling of disconnect I got every time I walked into the office. Maybe a break will be good. Then I can clear my head.

'Okay,' I say, wiping my eyes with the back of my hand. 'I'll do it. I'll hand in my notice.'

'Good girl,' says Connor, getting up and coming to sit beside me. 'And then we will go to the GP together and get some help. You're going to get better, Vanessa. It'll take some time but I'll be with you every step of the way. Okay?'

I nod my head. He pulls me towards him and as I sink into his arms I feel like I'm falling.

I arrive at my office with five minutes to spare. As I walk in all is as it should be – the wide reception desk flanked by two glass columns, the pink velvet sofa with rose-gold cushions, the gold-rimmed glass coffee table on which are piled design books and magazines next to a tall vase with pale-pink peonies poking out. All familiar and reassuring features I have barely noticed as I walked through each day for the last five years. This time, however, I note every detail and, though they haven't changed, I have. What is more, I know as I walk towards my office that this will be the last time.

I see Anne before she sees me. She and the HR manager – a tall, pale, auburn-haired woman called Heidi Wilson – are standing in Anne's glass-fronted office, their backs to the door.

I feel a pang of sadness as I knock on the glass and enter, remembering how Anne had taken a chance on me – a green, inexperienced young woman with only enthusiasm and half-formed ideas to offer – all those years ago. Now here I am, about to throw it all away. Still, I only have myself to blame.

The fifteen minutes after I hand in my resignation pass in a blur. Where Anne is incredibly sympathetic, though bewildered at my lack of an explanation, Heidi Wilson is steely-eyed and professional. Both of them want answers but I'm reluctant to give any, save to say, vaguely, that I have some personal issues I need to deal with.

I sit in the comfy chair opposite Anne, as I have done so many times, and she looks at me like a mother would look at a daughter who has transformed, seemingly overnight, from a positive, eloquent, happy child to a surly teenager. I can see she is desperately trying to reach out to me but I refuse to meet her eye, knowing that if I do I will crumble. I can't allow myself to do that.

Heidi Wilson is impatient and pressing for a reason but I remain vague.

'Vanessa, the company has recently introduced the Luna London Living scheme, which I'm sure you're aware of,' she says, glancing down at her notebook.

I am well aware of the scheme. In fact, I helped devise it with Anne at the end of last year. I had seen a lot of the team, particularly the younger members, struggle with city living over the years and both Anne and I felt we should do something to help. The scheme offered therapy, counselling, mindfulness and yoga sessions, and was available to all employees.

'I am aware of it, yes,' I say, trying not to look at Anne, imagining her bemused expression. 'But I don't feel it's relevant to my situation.'

'Vanessa, please talk to me,' says Anne, reaching her hand out to touch my arm, her voice trembling with emotion. 'I don't know what has happened but you know that I am here for you twenty-four/seven. You're my right-hand woman, Vanessa. I . . . I can't imagine Luna London without you.'

She stares at me intently, as though willing me to share whatever it is that is going on in my head. 'We just need you to be open with us, Vanessa,' she says pleadingly. 'Whatever it is that's troubling you, we can sort it out.'

As she says those words I make the mistake of meeting her eye. When I do I remember those endless Sunday lunches round her kitchen table, the joy on her face when I cut my first deal; then, in a blink, I see crumpled sheets, two bloodied boxers staring each other down, the nurse asking me if I am quite sure, Connor's mother clutching her face, my own blood smeared on hotel towels, and my eyes fill with tears.

I can't do this, can't carry on being Vanessa, the levelheaded professional. She, and the life she had enjoyed, are gone for ever. This is the new reality: trembling hands, heart palpitations, anger and fear. In the course of a few weeks I have turned into a wreck. I have to get out of here. I have to not be around people because I can't keep my anger in check and that is what scares me more than anything.

'I'm sorry, Anne,' I say, getting unsteadily to my feet. 'I just can't do this. And I don't want to cause you and the team any more inconvenience. You don't deserve that. I can't work here any more. I'm sorry.'

It's like a stranger has invaded my body and is speaking on my behalf. This place, this job, the pretty art deco building overlooking Sloane Square, has been my life, my dream. The elation I felt, five years ago, when Anne offered me the position, was like nothing I'd ever experienced before. I had become an adult. My life had begun.

'Vanessa,' cries Anne as I head for the door. 'Please think about this. Let us help you. You're obviously going through something stressful, that's clear to see, but it's not insurmountable. Talk to us, Vanessa, before you do something you'll regret.'

I turn then and look at her. Anne, my mentor and confidante, the woman who took a chance on me, who cared for me and nurtured me, had filled a mother-shaped gap like Georgie had – and Lottie too, I suddenly realize. How can I treat her like this? I owe Anne so much more.

But the pain inside me is so great it outweighs any sense of loyalty or duty. All I know is that I have to get out of here. I have to do as Connor says.

'I'm sorry, Anne,' I say, wiping my eyes. 'But this is my final decision.'

*

'You did the right thing,' whispers Connor as we lie in bed that evening. 'I'm proud of you, baby.'

I'm curled up in my usual foetal position. Connor pulls me towards him and kisses me deeply. At first it's nice but then as I feel him growing hard I remember the gnawing pain as the baby came away, the blood on the sheets, the towels.

'No, Connor,' I say, pushing him off gently. 'I'm not feeling too good.'

'That makes sense,' says Connor, a sharp edge to his voice. 'I read that frigidity is another symptom of nervous breakdowns.'

He kisses my forehead.

'But don't worry,' he says, turning away from me. 'We'll get you well again.'

After a few moments I hear him start to snore. I lie here looking up at the ceiling, street lights casting strange shapes. I feel exhausted but sleep won't come, so, taking my phone from the side table, I climb out of bed and go into the living room.

Sitting in what has become my usual spot in the corner of the sofa, I click open the Dream Properties app and allow myself to fall away. Most of the period properties I have seen before so I type 'new build' into the search engine. I don't particularly like new-build houses but tonight I feel so on edge I need to have something to look at.

The first couple of houses are depressingly ugly and ostentatious, the sort of thing a footballer might buy, but then halfway down the page I see something that makes me pause.

It's described as 'An eco house with spectacular sea views located in the heart of fashionable Whitstable.' I click through the images. The decor is sparse, all white and silver and rounded edges. Its clean lines are so at odds with the dirt and mess my life has been reduced to. Maybe if I go to see it I will feel a bit better. *Maybe some of its purity will rub off on me*, I think to myself as I click on the 'Book an appointment' box.

And then, seemingly unbidden, a name pops into my head. Eleanor Hawkins. I have no idea who Eleanor is or what she wants from me but I know that if I become her for a few hours then I'll be able to escape the crushing sadness that is pressing into my chest.

I type the name and as I do I feel something lighten. The magic is happening again. I'm about to become someone else.

28. Now

When I get to Warwick Avenue there is a queue to get through the turnstiles and I quickly scan the crowd. There's a woman with a rucksack, a teenage boy wearing headphones, a mother with a baby strapped to her chest and two men in suits who look like they're on their way to a work meeting. All of them are focused on getting out of the station and heading to their respective destinations. No one seems in the least bit interested in the anxious young woman following them through the turnstiles. It seems, for now, I'm safe.

As the crowd disperses I make my way out on to Warwick Avenue. It's a bright morning and the sun beats down on the stucco buildings, making sugar houses of them. To the left of me the Little Venice canal shimmers snake-like as it passes under the bridge. It's a perfect summer's day and as I cross the road and head to Formosa Street I almost forget the looming appointment at the police station. It feels like old times, when Lottie and I would spend a summer's day drinking iced coffee on the King's Road, people watching and putting the world to rights as the hours rolled by.

When I reach the corner of Formosa Street I get a flutter of nerves. Last time I had seen Lottie she was shaking with rage. What will she say when she finds out what I've done?

A sharp ray of sunshine hits the street, temporarily blinding me, and I nearly walk straight into a startled passer-by. I should have brought my sunglasses to hide behind, but I left the house in such a hurry. I glance around, looking to see if anyone is following me.

As I approach the coffee shop, which sits in the middle of the curved street, the sun dips and I blink as white dots bounce in front of my eyes. Then I hear it. A familiar voice: animated and warm. A voice I haven't heard in months. Lottie.

I look ahead and see her. She's sitting at one of the tables outside the coffee shop, deep in conversation with a man. The man has his back to me but I recognize the dark-brown curls, the straight back, the blue-and-white Adidas Gazelle trainers.

It's Connor.

29. Then

Sitting on the 10.30 from Victoria to Whitstable, I look down at the loose-fitting cotton harem pants and linen shirt I'm wearing and breathe a sigh of relief. For the next few hours I will be Zen-like Eleanor Hawkins, floating off on a cloud of patchouli oil and loose linen clothing to view her future home.

As the train hurtles through open countryside, the Kentish oast houses rising like wicker men from the scorched earth, I practise the mid-Atlantic accent I'd ascribed to Eleanor when I first saw the pictures of the house on the app. My initial attempt was a bit hammy, like Madonna's voice when she married Guy Ritchie, yet the more I talk, the more Eleanor emerges. A teenager dressed in tracksuit top, jeans and trainers smirks at me from the seat opposite. He probably thinks I'm mad but I don't care. I'm on a roll now as more pieces of Eleanor's backstory come together. Her upbringing in New York, the only child of Rosa and Anthony, two high-achieving college professors who placed more importance on academic excellence than spiritual well-being. Eleanor growing up feeling pressured and out of place, not helped by the fact that she was dyslexic and therefore found the books her parents thrust under her nose almost impossible to decipher. Words, to

Eleanor, were a great mystery, a puzzle she had no chance of solving. Her parents threw money at her 'condition' as they called it and sent her to the best schools but she still ended up flunking out of high school with a set of grades that made her mother cry. Lost and in need of some kind of direction, Eleanor found herself answering an online advert in the *New York Times* to attend something called a Transcendental Meditation class. Though she was unsure of what to expect, what happened next changed the course of her life. Meditation became the key to discovering the happiness and peace she had spent her young life searching for and she became a true devotee. Trips to retreats in India and the Himalayas followed, which culminated in Eleanor becoming a yoga and meditation practitioner and setting up a highly successful YouTube channel while based in LA. With a cult following and six million subscribers, Eleanor soon became a financial as well as spiritual success. Now, she has one goal left. To set up a wellness clinic in her favourite part of the world: the south-east coast of England.

So absorbed am I in Eleanor and her story that, before I know it, the train is trundling into Whitstable station. As I step off the train, I run over what the estate agent had told me on the phone. We have arranged to meet at the property, which is accessed via a private lane called Toad's Hatch. The name made me think of Tolkien and I smiled, remembering my mother reading *The Hobbit* to me each night before bed.

Best not to think of that, I tell myself as I type the post-code into Google maps and take a left out of the station car park, best to focus, because for the next few hours all that exists is Eleanor Hawkins and her quest to find the perfect home.

When I see the sign for Toad's Hatch, I take my compact out of my handbag and have a look at myself. I've kept my make-up dewy and understated, with a liberal use of highlighter on my cheekbones to give the impression of inner wellness. My hair is swept back in a loose bun tied together with a wooden clip. All good.

As I set off down the broad driveway I practise my opening greeting, taking care to stick to the flat vowels of New York-born Eleanor. There's a silver car parked up outside the house. As I draw level with it the door opens and a sharp-faced woman with cropped red hair steps out.

'Ros Coverley,' she says brusquely, extending her hand. 'You must be Mrs Hawkins?'

I open my mouth to reply that it's actually *Ms* Hawkins but before I can get the words out Ros Coverley is striding ahead of me towards the house.

The squat, white building looks as though it has sprung out of the ground. It's nothing like the photos on the app. As I draw closer my heart sinks. It looks more like a prison than a potential wellness centre.

When we reach the glass front door, Ros Coverley takes a square fob out of her pocket and points it at the alarm panel. A green light flashes and the glass door opens.

'So, Mrs Hawkins,' she says as we step into a vast hexagonal space that appears to be made solely of glass and metal, 'you didn't say what your position is. Are you chain free?'

'Er . . . yes,' I say, scrambling for the New York accent I had perfected on the train. 'I'm a . . . a cash buyer.'

She frowns, her eyes locking on me.

'A cash buyer?' she says incredulously. 'I see.'

I gulp down my nerves as she leads me across the nuclear wasteland that is the entrance hall towards another set of glass doors that open automatically as we approach. It feels wrong, all of it.

'Through here to the living area.'

I follow her through the doors and into what looks like the inside of a spaceship. The walls are white and sparse, and everywhere I look there are panels with flashing lights, like the alarm at the front door. It feels as if I've stepped into some kind of interrogation centre. Beside me, Ros Coverley does little to dispel this feeling.

'You're from New York?' she says as we step from the soulless living space into a kitchen that has all the warmth of an industrial refrigerator. 'My partner's a New Yorker. Whereabouts are you from?'

I take a breath to buy some time, try to remember the bio I'd put together for Eleanor Hawkins so effortlessly, but my mind is blank.

'I . . . er . . . grew up in . . . Manhattan,' I say, almost swallowing the word back down.

'Oh, really?' she replies, her eyes flashing. 'What district?'

I search my mind for an answer but all I can think of is toads. Toad's Hatch. Hatching eggs. *Think, Vanessa*, I tell myself. Think of a district of Manhattan. But it's no use. My head is full of nonsense.

'I . . . er . . . perhaps you can show me the bedrooms?' I say, my cheeks reddening. 'The description on the website said they have amazing sea views.'

'Sure,' says Ros, her eyes narrowing. 'The master bedroom is on the first floor. This way, please.'

She leads me up a flight of stairs that are so polished I have to grip the metal banister to stop myself from slipping. At the top there is a vast landing with floor-to-ceiling windows. I follow Ros through a doorway and step into what looks like a padded cell. The walls have been decorated with a strange, textured paper, there's a stone floor and a metal bed with pale-blue, prison-style bedding.

'Here you are,' says Ros, striding towards the window. 'You can see all the way to Margate from here.'

'Wonderful,' I say, but I'm not looking at the view. Instead, my eye has been drawn to a tiny picture hanging to the left of the window. I step aside to take a closer look and see that it's by Grimshaw, my mother's favourite artist. It depicts a mother and child walking down a moonlit path and looks so out of place in this white mausoleum I feel I have to liberate it.

'Over here is the en suite,' says Ros, walking over to a metal door at the far side of the room. 'Again with sea views.'

I watch as she opens the door and steps inside. I quickly lift the picture from its hook and I'm about to slide it into my bag when she puts her head round the door.

'What the hell are you doing?' she says, striding towards me and grabbing the picture from my hands.

'I . . . I was just taking a closer look,' I say, my heart flipping in my chest. 'My, er . . . mom loved this artist and I wanted to see if it was him.'

'You were about to put it in your bag,' she cries, her eyes blazing. 'Now come on, get the hell out of here.'

She grabs my arm and escorts me down the stairs.

'I'm sorry,' I say, my voice trembling, my accent slip-ping. 'I've been having a bad time lately. I don't know what came over me. Please don't call the police, I beg you.'

She pauses by the front door and looks at me, her face softening slightly.

'Just get out of here, okay?' she says, pointing the fob at the front door, which opens with a whooshing noise. 'I'm not going to call the police this time but I am going to put the word out among my agency colleagues across the county and if I ever catch you trying to do this again I will call the police, do you understand?'

I nod my head then stumble out of the house, taking gulps of cold air as I hurry down the driveway. When I reach the gate I take a cursory look back and see Ros Coverley standing in the doorway, her phone pressed to her ear. Watching me.

I run all the way back to the station. Luckily, there's a London-bound train waiting at the platform. I jump on and find a window seat. As the train pulls away I press my face to the glass, a sick feeling in my stomach.

By the time I get back to the flat I am mentally and phys-ically exhausted. Even the walk up the stairs feels like an enormous effort. When I get to the top I hear voices com-ing from the living room and my heart sinks. Please don't let Connor's mother be here. I can't face another grilling from her, not after the day I've had.

I hang my coat on the hook in the corridor then push the living-room door open, bracing myself for the wrath of Jackie. But it's not Connor's mother I see, it's something much worse.

'Vanessa,' cries Connor, leaping up from the naked woman lying beneath him. 'What the hell are you doing?'

I'm in such shock I don't register the ridiculousness of my naked, cheating boyfriend asking me what the hell *I'm* doing when he's on top of another woman. Instead, I stand in the doorway, shock freezing my bones, while the woman places a cushion over her breasts. It's then that I recognize her. The blonde bobbed hair, the flawless skin, the violet eyes. It's Sara, the woman I last saw in the burlesque club.

'I can explain,' cries Connor as I finally find my feet and run out of the room and back down the stairs, grabbing my bag from the hook. 'You've been so difficult lately, Vanessa. I had no choice.'

Those are the last words I hear as I slam the front door behind me and run down the street.

30. Now

Before I can turn and run, Lottie sees me. She gestures to Connor. I have to get out of here.

I can hear Connor's footsteps gaining on me as I hurry up the street. I can't make sense of what I have just seen. Why were Connor and Lottie together? They have always hated each other.

I hear someone call my name and I run across the zebra crossing, the red-and-blue tube sign of Warwick Avenue station looming ahead of me.

When I get to the other side I have to weave my way through a procession of schoolkids clutching clipboards and following their teacher.

'Excuse me,' I cry, pushing them aside in my agitation. 'Please, I have to get past.'

I hear the teacher say something about bad manners as I finally extricate myself and hurry towards the station.

The sun is blazing into my eyes as I pause to cross another side road, the white stucco houses rising ominously in front of me. I put my hand up to shield my eyes and as I do someone grabs me from behind.

I try to scream but they put their hand over my mouth.

My eyes fix on a tabby cat lolling on the ground. I hear the grumble of the trains beneath my feet as I'm pushed towards the cat. The hand presses tighter. I can smell something, a sharp chemical scent, and then all is black.

31. Then

I stand on Georgie's doorstep hammering the door with my fist, the image of Connor and Sara lying naked in each other's arms imprinted on my mind.

'Georgie, it's me,' I cry, tears obliterating my vision. 'Open the door.'

I ring the doorbell again, keeping my finger pressed down on it. A light goes on in the hallway then I see the tall outline of Jack walking towards me.

'Good grief, Vanessa!' Jack says in his clipped public-school voice as he opens the door. 'Whatever's the matter?'

He's dressed in a pair of navy-and-cream striped pyjamas, his salt-and-pepper cropped hair sticking up on the top of his head. I have no idea what time it is as I've spent most of the evening walking around Clapham in a daze, but I guess I've woken them up.

'I need to see Georgie,' I whimper, my lip trembling. 'Can I come in?'

'Of course,' says Jack, ushering me inside. 'She's sleeping but I'll go and wake her. Why don't you go into the living room and get yourself comfortable. I won't be a moment.'

I watch as he stumbles up the stairs, his hand gripping the sleek banister, then I head to the living room.

I step inside and look around, as if for the first time. The soft, squishy sofas draped with thick cashmere throws, the delicate glass lamps pouring soft light on to the rug-strewn wooden floor, the reassuring warmth of home. Only, it's not my home.

I cross the room and stand in front of the large stone fireplace. Above it is the picture Mum left to Georgie. It's a print by an artist named John Atkinson Grimshaw and depicts a cobbled street bathed in moonlight. It's winter, the trees are bare, the street deserted save for one solitary walker. The only light comes from the moon, peeking through the trees, and from the windows of a beautiful house on the edge of the picture. The house, partly hidden behind the trees, has tall brick chimneys with wisps of smoke rising out and narrow windows behind which glows a warm and golden light. Mum used to say the painting, titled *A Moonlit Road*, should have been called *Coming Home* because that's how it always made her feel.

I stand for a moment and look up at the painting, my eyes drawn to the figure on the pavement. I'd barely noticed the picture when I was a child, though I knew Mum loved it. She had hung it in her bedroom, on the wall opposite the bed. She liked to look at it before going to sleep, said it soothed her.

I think back to that terrible moment in the eco house when the estate agent caught me trying to steal an original Grimshaw painting, which would have been worth hundreds of thousands of pounds, and I cringe inwardly. Yet, as I stand here, I realize I have become the figure in the painting, cast out on the street, looking longingly at a warm and inviting home that will never be mine. I thought Connor was my home. I thought that he loved me. I see that image again, Sara's hands clutching his back, the noises they were making, and it hurts so much I almost lose my breath.

'Nessa, what is it? What's happened?'

I turn to see Georgie standing in the doorway. Her black hair is scooped back into a messy ponytail and she's wearing Jack's blue dressing gown, which is at least three sizes too big for her. My sister has always borne more resemblance to my dad, yet tonight the expression on Georgie's face is so like Mum I start to cry.

'Oh, darling, what is it?' she says, rushing towards me and pulling me to her chest. 'What's the matter?'

I want to tell her about Connor and Sara, about his mother and the abortion, about the night of the burlesque, those lost hours. I want to take all my fear and panic and pain and pour it out at the feet of my older, wiser sister, but I don't have the words to even begin. She'll be so disappointed in me for not telling her. For letting it get to this.

'Is it Connor?' she says. 'Have you two had an argument?'

'It's over,' I say, crying so heavily my voice is barely audible. 'Connor and me, we're . . . oh God, Georgie, I don't know what to do.'

'Shh,' says Georgie, stroking the back of my head just like my mum used to. 'It's okay, darling. You're here now.'

'Can I stay for a bit?' I say, easing myself from her embrace. 'Just until I get myself sorted?'

'Of course you can,' she says, wiping a tear from my face. 'You can stay as long as you like.'

'I . . . I need to get back on my feet,' I say, trying to steady my voice. 'I haven't told you, but I quit my job.'

'What?' says Georgie, her eyes widening. 'But why? What happened?'

'It's a long story,' I say, trying not to think about the pain of the last few days. 'I've been a bit stressed and . . .'

'Come on, darling,' says Georgie, taking my arm. 'You need a good rest. We can talk about it in the morning.'

She leads me upstairs to Imogen's room where she hands me a pair of freshly laundered pyjamas and settles me into bed. As I get under the covers I think of clever, funny Imogen, who is doing great things at Oxford, blissfully unaware that her sad, washed-up aunt is taking up residence in her neat, pretty bedroom.

'Try to get some sleep now,' says Georgie as she turns out the light. 'Whatever it is, we can sort it out, Nessa.'

She stands for a moment in the doorway, the light from the landing illuminating her strong, solid figure. So unlike mine, which is so small, so insubstantial, I sometimes wonder why I haven't floated away.

'Thanks, Georgie,' I whisper. 'Night, night.'

'Night, night, my darling,' she says as she closes the door.

I lie for a moment looking at the shadows on the ceiling and try to make sense of what has happened. I think back to the text message from Sara, her flirtatious behaviour at the burlesque club, and I realize with sickening certainty that this must have been going on for a long time. I recall the day I came home early from work and found Connor dressed only in a towel. I'd heard voices as I came up the stairs and smelt cigarette smoke but, as always, he convinced me it was nothing. I think about the abortion, Connor's mother lecturing me on morality. All the time he was sleeping with someone else behind my back.

Across the landing I hear Georgie and Jack's muffled voices. She will be telling him what has happened. They are so close; they tell each other everything. That's what I wanted, what I thought I'd found in Connor, but it was all an illusion. As I lie here in a borrowed bed I feel like the last person on earth. Georgie has Jack and the kids, my dad has Lynda, Connor has Sara, Lottie is hundreds of miles away. The only person who could make me feel better is dead. Maybe that's it, I think to myself, shivering despite the heat of the evening, maybe I need to go find Mum, maybe that's the only way I will stop this hurt.

My eyes fill with tears. Never, even in the terrible days and months after her death, did I ever think I wanted to die. I've always loved life and I wanted to bring my mother back to it, not end mine to join her. But now I look at my life and just see a series of fuck-ups. I have no boyfriend, no job, no home. There is nothing worth living for.

My phone bleeps from inside my jeans, which are lying on the floor. It will likely be Connor, I think to myself as I get out of bed and take the phone from my pocket. He'd called me six times as I sat on the train from Clapham Junction to Wimbledon. I'd ignored all of his calls. There was nothing to say. I'd seen his deceit with my own eyes.

I look at the screen. Sure enough, there are five more missed calls and a text.

> Please pick up the phone, Vanessa, I can explain every-
> thing. You can't just throw it all away like this.

My chest tightens with a mix of anger and grief. After all he has done, he's still blaming me, telling me that I am throwing it all away. But behind my anger, even now, there's a small part of me that agrees with him. That wants to do what he says.

There are two more notifications on the screen. One is a text from my mobile provider, the other from the Dream Properties app: 'One new property for you to see.' After the disastrous eco-house viewing I know I should delete the app but I'm too upset to sleep. I need a distraction to stop me from doing something stupid.

I click on the notification and as the image fills the screen I almost drop my phone in shock.

There it is, displayed in thirty-seven high-res photos: a place I haven't seen since childhood, the house depicted in the book my mother bought me just hours before she died.

'It can't be,' I whisper as I scroll through the pictures. 'It's impossible.'

But there it is, in bold lettering at the top of the page. Three words. The name of my life raft.

HOLLY MAZE HOUSE.

And I realize as I make a note of the viewing instructions that Mum has done it again, she has reached out just when I needed her most.

32. Now

I open my eyes to thick, velvet darkness. My head is throbbing and the ground beneath me is hard and cold.

Blinking, I press my hands against the floor, try to haul myself up, but my body feels like lead. The events of the morning come back to me in fractured images: white stucco houses rising up around me, a tabby cat lolling in the sun, Lottie's text message and Connor running after me down the street.

He's taken me somewhere, though in this half-light I can see only the outline of the room. Tall shapes rise up like distorted sea monsters, the air smells stale and fetid. I have to get to my feet, have to try to find my way out of here. I press down on the heels of my hand but my arms won't carry my weight and I sink back down on to the hard floor. My heart palpitates with the exertion. I try to breathe slowly, try to calm the panic that is twisting up my insides.

I'm on my second deep inhalation when I hear something, footsteps coming towards me. I crouch into a ball, a defensive posture that I realize is pointless. I hear the sound of curtains being pulled back then a sharp strand of light cuts across the floor.

I feel a presence bearing down on me, the sound of shallow breathing. I pull my hands over my head and pray to my mum to keep me safe.

'Come on,' he says, his voice muffled. 'You don't have to be scared of me.'

I feel a hand on the scruff of my neck then he slowly pulls me up. I instinctively look down at the ground, but he takes my chin and lifts my face to his.

I scream.

'Shh,' he says, putting his hand over my mouth. 'I told you. There's no need to be scared.'

He is dressed all in black – a long-sleeved T-shirt, jeans and a balaclava with holes for his eyes and mouth.

'Why are you doing this?' I ask when he takes his hand away from my mouth. 'What do you want from me?'

'We're going to have a little adventure, just the two of us,' he says, his voice muffled. 'A little explore. You see, I know your secrets. The ones you tried to hide from everyone. The fact that you like looking at houses, other people's houses that you can't afford. Nosy little so-and-so, aren't you?'

At this, he grabs my shoulders and spins me round to face the room. My legs almost give way as I see the sweeping wooden staircase, the grand stone flooring covered in faded tapestry rugs, the moss-green velvet drapes, the outline of the stone griffins outside the window, and I realize with utter dread that I am in the hallway of Holly Maze House.

33. Then

The following day I make my way to Hampstead. The estate agent is a small boutique one, tucked away in a little square behind the high street. Its mullioned bay window and sage-green door with heavy brass knocker bring to mind Scrooge's counting house in *A Christmas Carol*. It's rather a fitting place to be marketing a property with such an illustrious literary heritage as Holly Maze House. I catch sight of my reflection in the window. I have borrowed Georgie's pale-pink suede Stella McCartney shift dress. It's a few seasons old but it gives the right impression: stylish, understated, wealthy.

A bell rings as I step inside and a young man, thin and wiry with John Lennon glasses and a mop of curly black hair, looks up from his desk by the window.

'Good afternoon,' he says, getting to his feet. 'How can I help you?'

I take a deep breath to steady myself, before explaining that I have come to enquire about viewing Holly Maze House.

The man raises an eyebrow, then invites me to sit down on the rickety wooden chair opposite his desk, introducing himself as Ed. Behind us, a young woman with inky-black cropped hair is answering calls.

'Good afternoon, Price Burrows, how may I help you?' she trills as Ed gets the details up.

'This is a very special property,' he says, his eyes brightening. 'I don't know whether you're aware, but the house was the setting for a famous series of books.'

'Really?' I reply, not wanting to let him into my secret. 'How fascinating.'

I smile as Ed gives me a quick summary of *The Spirits of Holly Maze House*, revealing himself, in the telling, to be utterly ignorant of the nature of both the books and their author.

'Yes, it's about, er . . . ghosts who haunt this house and . . . there's a bird who, er, gets involved . . . and . . . well, the author, apparently has, er . . . lived in Hampstead all his life.'

I nod my head, recalling Geoffrey's countless interviews where he told the story of his West Country childhood, his early marriage, the teaching career he'd had to let go for the stories that were burning inside him.

I grimace slightly. Ed must notice because he starts to backtrack.

'Not that this house is haunted or anything like that,' he says, his face reddening. 'Not in the slightest. It's just, the owner was inspired to write the story there. It's a lovely place. Not a hint of any darkness at all.'

'Oh, don't worry,' I say, relaxing in the wake of Ed's nervousness. 'I'm not scared of ghosts. In fact, I'd find them rather reassuring. It's the living we have to worry about more than the dead, don't you think?'

He regards me for a moment then, assuming I'm making a joke, bursts into uneasy laughter.

'Yes,' he says, straightening his tie. 'I must say I'm far more scared of my mother than any poltergeist. Now, where were we? Right, I just need to get a few details from you before we proceed. If we could start with your name.'

I freeze. For the first time I have quite forgotten to create a persona.

'Iris,' I say, letting the name fall from my lips like a delicate butterfly.

'That's great,' says Ed, his head bowed over the computer. 'And your surname?'

I look up at the enlarged street map on the wall behind Ed's desk. The first name I see is Lawson Industrial Park.

'Lawson,' I reply, hardly missing a beat. 'Iris Lawson.'

'Excellent,' says Ed. 'And I'm going to need a contact telephone number and address.'

Shit. I hadn't thought about that. I can't give a fake address as Ed will quickly suss me out. I decide to give Georgie's. It's a suitably impressive postcode and it's highly unlikely Ed or his colleagues will follow it up.

'Okay,' he says, once he's entered the details into his computer. 'Now, may I ask a little more about your situation? Are you a cash buyer? Chain?'

'Cash buyer,' I say, thinking on my feet. 'I've been left an inheritance.'

'Lucky for some,' he says, grinning awkwardly. 'Now, taking a look at the appointment schedule, we could get you in to view the property on Friday if that works for you.'

My chest tightens. It can't wait until Friday. It has to be today.

'I don't suppose you could do it this afternoon?' I say, putting my head to one side, coquettishly. 'You see, it's rather important I see it as soon as I can. It's a matter of urgency. Er, what I mean is, I really think this is the house for me.'

I stop, angry at myself for blurting out that it was a matter of urgency, but my passion seems to have an effect on Ed and, with a hefty commission in sight, he picks up the phone.

'Let me see what I can do,' he says, typing in a number. 'We may just be able to sort something.'

I listen as he speaks to the person on the other end of the phone.

'Yes,' he says, nodding. 'This afternoon, if possible. You can? Oh, that's splendid. I'll send her along. Thanks so much. Goodbye.'

'We're in luck,' he says, putting the receiver down then looking up at me with a broad smile. 'Mr Rivers is free to show you the property at 1.30. Does that work for you?'

'Mr Rivers?' I try to disguise my shock. 'You mean –'

'That's right,' says Ed. 'The vendor.'

'Geoffrey Rivers is going to show me round the house?' I say slowly, still unable to grasp the sudden turn of events.

'Er, yes,' says Ed, his smile fading slightly. 'At 1.30 this afternoon. Is that okay with you? I mean, I know it's not usual but –'

'It's great,' I say, fixing him with my widest smile. '1.30 is perfect.'

'Wonderful,' he says, the brightness returning to his face. 'Now let's just give you the details you need.'

I watch as Ed scribbles down directions on a piece of paper and hands it to me.

'It's very easy to find,' he says. 'From the high street head north, then take a right on to Flask Lane, then . . .'

His voice dissolves into a kind of aural soup as I sit there, staring into space.

This is it. I'm going to Holly Maze House.

Twenty minutes later I'm walking up the cobbled driveway. My heart lifts as I pass the rows of topiary animals that line the path. The cockerel, the squirrel, the frog and the rabbit; they are real after all.

I stand at the door, which is flanked by two stone griffins – *when the dead walk the earth the griffins shall rise* – and look up at the crest above, the year 1647 carved in stone.

This is it, I tell myself as I lift the brass knocker, *there is no going back*.

I wait a few moments, then hear footsteps behind the door. It swings open and an old man with thinning white hair, rheumy eyes and a stout belly stands in front of me. He looks startlingly different from the dapper figure with dark curls and piercing blue eyes who had been a regular on the chat-show circuit in the nineties, yet when he speaks there is no doubt that this is the person who enchanted a generation of children with his ghostly tales.

'You must be Iris!' he says, his voice low and honey rich. 'I'm Geoffrey. Do come in, dear.'

I follow him inside and, as I step into the grand entrance hall, the years fall away and I'm ten years old again. Like the driveway, everything in this hallway is just as it had been described in the books. The heavy tapestries hanging on the stone walls with their carefully embroidered winged angels and lean deerhounds, the suit of armour, polished to perfection, standing guard in the centre of the room, the black iron candelabra chandelier on the ceiling with real candles wedged into its spikes. It is comforting and disconcerting in equal measure.

Behind me, I hear Geoffrey clear his throat then he begins to tell me the history of the house. I turn and give him my full attention.

'This part of the house, and the bedrooms just above where we're standing, date back to 1647,' he says briskly. 'Later additions were made by previous owners at the turn of the last century and then again in the 1960s, though thankfully the older parts were listed and therefore had to be preserved.'

'It's a magical house,' I say.

'Yes, it is,' says Geoffrey. 'Or at least it was, anyway. I don't know whether you're aware but the house was the inspiration for some books I wrote.'

He smiles modestly.

'Oh yes,' I say. 'I am aware. In fact, I'm a huge admirer of your work.'

He nods his head briskly and his smile fades a little.

I instantly regret my outburst. I will have to be careful or else Geoffrey will think I'm some silly fan girl, a time-waster. I have to think of something to prolong the visit.

'When I say that,' I tell him, regaining my composure, 'I mean that it was this house and your amazing storytelling that, er, inspired me to write my own books.'

He nods wearily at this. He has obviously heard all this before and probably thinks I'm some wannabe hoping for a hand up the ladder. I move on hastily.

'In fact,' I continue, 'my books are the reason I'm able to afford this house.'

Geoffrey smiles politely, though he seems completely disinterested.

'Well done, you,' he says, glancing nervously at the staircase. 'Though I must say, I don't envy anyone getting involved in the publishing industry. It's a rotten business. Still, a young woman like you shouldn't find it too difficult to get on. That's what publishers are looking for nowadays. I'm afraid I'm one of those old, male dinosaurs they want nothing to do with. Now, come this way and I'll show you the living area.'

He looks worried all of a sudden and the warmth he had greeted me with at first has faded. In fact, there's a distinct chill about him as he leads me from room to room, politely pointing out the various features.

I'm surprised to find that the inner rooms, later additions, as Geoffrey informs me, are pretty dull and nothing like as magical as the main hallway or the rooms in the book. There is a rather dated, nineties-style kitchen with pine cupboards and stained, beige tiles, a living room with faded floral wallpaper, a dado rail and well-worn, soft leather sofas. It's all so ordinary I might as well be in Dad and Lynda's new-build bungalow in Reading.

As we stand at the living-room window, Geoffrey turns to me and asks if I have any children.

I am rather taken aback by the question and at first I don't know what to say.

'I only ask because this house has a beautiful garden,' he says, his voice softening. 'Perfect for children to play in.'

I look out of the window and see the dream world I had first discovered in the books. There are the purple, speckled foxgloves lined up against the stone wall. Beyond them the other set of topiary animals: the fox, the hare and the badger. And there, right at the back, the tall holly maze that leads to the graveyard.

'Er, no, I don't have children,' I say, my voice catching.

'Are you all right, dear?' says Geoffrey, placing his hand on my arm. 'You look rather upset.'

'I'm fine. Just a bit of hay fever,' I say, wiping my eye.

'Oh gosh, we better avoid the garden then,' says Geoffrey, grimacing.

The sight of the garden brings the story back to me in such vivid detail, my thoughts turn to the boy protagonist.

'I always felt sorry for Angus,' I say. 'He seemed so lonely.'

'Lonely? Gosh, no,' says Geoffrey, shaking his head. 'How could he be lonely when he had his special friends?'

'But they weren't real,' I say. 'They were ghosts.'

'They were real to him,' replies Geoffrey softly. 'And that is all that matters.'

'I bet your son enjoyed growing up here,' I say.

'Son?' he says, frowning. 'I'm afraid you must be mistaken. I don't have a son. My readers and those funny little ghosts out there were my only children.'

'Oh,' I say, taken aback.

I'm sure he had mentioned a son in an interview years back, but then everything about those years after Mum's death is rather foggy. There had definitely been a wife, I remember that, but there was talk of some family tragedy in the papers that was never fully explained. Maybe she died. Poor Geoffrey.

'It must be hard to leave somewhere as special as this,' I say.

'The time is right,' he replies, his eyes glistening. 'And I want to spend my retirement travelling. Seeing the world has suddenly become a priority to this old home bird. There's a sense of time running out for me.'

I nod my head. That much is true.

'It's all right for a young person like you,' he says wistfully. 'You have plenty of years ahead, but . . . well, let's just say I won't be sad to start afresh. Now, I suppose I ought to show you around upstairs.'

He gestures to the door but as we make our way out we hear a loud thud. Geoffrey looks startled. He glances at the door then turns on his heels and guides me back into the living room.

'I'm awfully sorry,' he says, regaining his composure, 'but will you excuse me?'

He walks out of the room. I hear his footsteps on the stone floor, the slow, laboured gait. I wander into the hallway and see a large walnut sideboard to the left of me. Then something catches my eye. It's the glass bird, sitting on top of the sideboard. I step towards it, a shiver running through me as I recall how this special talisman, the black glass bird with the yellow bill that the boy, Angus, had to take in his hands to gain entry to the past, has haunted my dreams since I was a little girl.

As I draw closer to it, the bird's eyes seem to flash and I feel my skin prickle.

'I don't think he needs you any more,' I whisper, taking the bird and slipping it into my bag. 'Best you come with me.'

I return to the living room and sit down on the edge of the soft armchair, feeling light-headed suddenly. Seeing the bird has brought it all back: the horror of my mother's death, those long lonely hours sitting in my room lost in the story of this house and its ghosts.

Where can Geoffrey have got to?

I stand up and walk into the hallway and, as I do, a peculiar thing happens: with each step I take I feel myself being drawn further into the story. I'm no longer Vanessa Adams, I am Angus, the lonely, sleepless boy. I gaze at the tapestry. The bloodied deerhounds seem to spring to life. I hear them barking, feel the crunch of leaves under my feet, smell the crisp, winter air. I'm falling under the spell of this house, sinking deeper into its folds.

Time freezes as I follow the hounds through the woods. I hear shouts and screams, a loud bang echoing through the air. Then, suddenly, I'm crouched at the bottom of the stairs.

Geoffrey is lying on the floor at my feet. He's sprawled at a terrible angle and a pool of blood is gathering at the back of his head. My hand is on his neck.

I leap backwards, my heart lurching inside my chest. What have I done?

The room starts to spin, the deerhounds snarl at me from the tapestry. I feel like I'm going to pass out. I reach out to grab something to steady myself but there's just empty space.

The next thing I know, I'm running down Hampstead High Street, gasping for breath, the glass bird hidden in my bag, Geoffrey's blood on my hands.

34. Now

'I thought I'd give you a little private tour. Isn't that exciting?'

He bundles me inside the living room. It has been transformed since I was last here. The furniture is covered in plastic sheets, there is yellow-and-black tape stuck to the floor and a layer of what looks like chalk dust clings to every surface.

'As you can see, the police have had a little refurb,' he says, his hand pressed to my back. 'What brutes they are, ruining such a literary landmark as this.'

His voice sounds odd, like he's deliberately changing it.

'Connor, why are you doing this?' I say as he takes my arm. 'How did you even get in here?'

'I thought it would be fun,' he says, gripping my arm tighter. 'A little game of make-believe. After all, you like pretending, don't you?'

He laughs and it sounds so menacing I shrink into myself. Please don't let him hurt me.

We walk out of the living room, back to where we started.

'Here we have the grand hallway,' he says, sweeping his arms out like some deranged estate agent. 'Or, as we like to think of it, the gateway to Holly Maze House. The late owner liked to claim that this part of the house dated back to 1647 but that was just bullshit to fool a load of gullible children. The truth is that this house was actually built in 1930, so the chances of it being haunted by a load of seventeenth-century, plague-addled ghost kids are pretty slim. But, hey, never let the truth get in the way of a good story. And you'd know all about that, wouldn't you?'

He pauses then and as he stares at me I catch a whiff of cologne. It smells sharp and citrusy and it sticks in my throat.

'Now, this stupendous piece of trash is, if our esteemed late author friend is to be believed, a rare Jacobean walnut sideboard,' he says, still gripping my arm. 'Though only for the purposes of flogging books and houses. It's actually a great big fake, like everything else in this house. You know he actually shipped that maze here from a garden centre? Ha! And the gravestones? He commissioned them from a stonemason and got him to carve the names of the characters on them. Then he told the press he'd "stumbled on them" when out for a walk and the discovery had inspired the books. The truth was he'd written the first book before he even moved here. It was all just a marketing ploy, the lot of it. What a fucking joke. Oh, look though, something's missing.'

He pushes me towards the sideboard, holding his hand firmly on the small of my back.

'What's missing?' he says, his voice gruffer now. 'Can you tell me?'

I shake my head, tears springing to my eyes.

'You don't know?' he says mockingly. 'Oh, I think you're fibbing. You know very well what's missing because you came in here and took it, didn't you? The day old Mr Holly Maze was bumped off.'

I feel a chill when he says that. How does Connor know about the bird? Did he follow me that day? Did he see what happened?

He pulls me away from the sideboard and heads for the stairs. I flinch as I recall Geoffrey lying in a heap at the foot of them, the blood on my hands.

'You do realize that all of this is a story?' he says, pulling me to him. 'That, like the maze and the gravestones, none of it is real?'

I am shaking uncontrollably now, fear coursing through me like an electric current.

'The glass bird is nothing more than a cheap ornament,' he says, his voice getting more muffled the angrier he becomes. 'It can't speak. It can't open up time portals. It's a fucking inanimate object. Do you understand?'

He presses his face into mine so hard I can hardly breathe. Ever since the day I left him, one memory has been growing stronger, clearer and more vivid; playing itself over and over in my head. For weeks, when I close my eyes, all I can see is Connor holding me down on that bed, forcing me, subduing me. Just as he is now.

'Right,' he says, keeping his eyes fixed on me as he mounts the staircase. 'I think we should go and see the bedrooms now.'

And I realize, with sickening dread, that the nightmare has just begun.

35. Now

'No,' I scream as he hustles me out of the hallway and up the dark, wooden staircase. 'Please, Connor. Don't do this. I beg you.'

He laughs mockingly.

'I guess you remember this bit from your favourite story,' he says, gripping me tighter as we reach the landing. 'The hidden rooms.'

I look ahead of me at the passageway. A shaft of light illuminates the tapestries on the wall, depicting blood-stained deer and men with swords, and I am filled with terror.

'Connor, please,' I say as he drags me along the passageway. 'Just stop this. I don't want to be here. I want to go home.'

'But, Iris,' he says, pausing outside the door at the end of the passageway. 'This is your home.'

'What did you just call me?' I say.

'You always wanted to be part of this story, didn't you?' he says, pushing the door open with his gloved hand. 'And now, thanks to me, you can be.'

He shoves me into the room, which appears to be a boy's bedroom. The bed has a Star Wars quilt cover, the shelves are lined with books and action figures. The desk, under the window, is covered with bits of cardboard, pots of paint, glue and scissors. Then I see, sitting on the windowsill, its wings now torn, its paint faded: a model aeroplane.

All Angus wanted to do was make planes.

'Whose bedroom is this?' I say, turning to Connor. He is standing by the door, his hands on the frame, blocking my exit.

'A young boy's,' he says, staring straight at me. 'Isn't that what buyers want to see? A family house, somewhere that's been lived in, enjoyed. Not some mausoleum.'

'How did you get in here?' I say, looking around incredulously. 'How come you know so much?'

'You mean you don't remember?' he says, closing the door and coming towards me.

'Remember what?' I say, my chest tightening as I think of the night of the burlesque, his arms pinning me to the bed. He grabs me and presses his face to mine. 'Connor, please don't do this, please, I beg you.'

'Why do you keep calling me Connor, Iris?' he says, letting go of me. 'Surely you know who I am? How quickly people forget. One minute you're a famous author with people falling in adoration at your feet, the next you're yesterday's man, forgotten, washed up.'

It's then I hear the West Country burr, the sing-song cadence to his voice.

'Geoffrey?' I whisper, my throat tightening. 'It . . . it can't be?'

'Oh, Iris,' he laughs, shaking his head. 'You are so funny. What are we going to do with you?'

'Who –' I say, gulping down my fear. 'Who are you then?'

'You really don't remember?'

I shake my head. He comes right up to me again, his face inches from mine. Then he takes the balaclava off.

'Still don't remember?'

I shake my head, fear pinching at my skin. The man is in his late thirties with a shaved head, piercing blue eyes and an angry red scar running across the left side of his face. There's something familiar about him, like I've seen him somewhere before, though I don't know where or how.

He gazes into the space beyond my shoulder, his brow furrowed.

'All those letters,' he says, his eyes hardening. 'You above everybody else seemed to understand me.'

'I don't know who you are,' I cry, my throat tightening. 'I'm so sorry but I don't.'

'He always took away the people I loved most,' he says, his lip curling. 'He always had to be in control.'

'Who did?' I say. 'Who are you talking about?'

'Him,' he says, almost spitting out the word. 'Our beloved Geoffrey Rivers. My dear old dad.'

36. Now

'But Geoffrey didn't have a son,' I say, trying my best to keep calm. 'He told me himself. He seemed sad about it, regretful.'

'Sad that his little cash cow had dried up,' says the man, sitting down on the bed.

'What do you mean?' I say, glancing at the door. I should make a run for it now, get out of here as fast as I can, yet something is stopping me. It's a memory of candy-floss stalls and men on stilts breathing fire.

'He told you he didn't have a son because I was no longer any use to him,' he says, staring at the floor. 'But the truth is I ceased to exist a long time ago. I stopped being his son the day he decided to replace me with Angus.'

'The boy in the book?' I say, trying not to think of his hands gripping my arms. Every sane part of me is yelling 'get out', but my feet are fixed to the floor.

'Yes,' he says, looking up at me. 'Angus, the hero of Holly Maze House. You see, my father based that boy on me. And he got the idea of the ghosts and the gravestones and the bird from my life. I had lost someone I loved dearly. Mrs Perkins was her name. She was our next-door neighbour. Her husband gave me that glass bird when she died and when we went to visit her grave I told her that I would never forget her, that I would think of her always and that if she ever needed to contact me she could do so through the bird. It would be our messenger. It was kids' talk. I was only six years old and trying to make sense of things. But he was there the whole time, good old Dad, he was there listening, watching, jotting it down. Never actually talking to me, never helping me with it all. He didn't even like Mrs Perkins, thought she was common. No, all he wanted was to write something that would make him rich and famous – he took my life and sold it for cash.'

He puts his head in his hands and as I stand looking at him I'm overcome with a mixture of pity and guilt. I had been one of the kids who fell for Geoffrey's stories, who believed in them, and in doing so had helped make him rich and famous. And all the while he had been taking advantage of his own child.

'Why did you bring me here?' I beg, collapsing on to the floor as the adrenaline seeps out of me. 'What do you want from me?'

He looks up and smiles.

'You haven't changed,' he says, his voice softening. 'You're still the same nervous little girl I met at the party.'

'The party?'

'Surely you remember it? Go on, look out there.' He gestures at the window.

'But –'

'Go on,' he hisses.

Shakily, I stand up and go to the window where I can see the garden fully. I see the maze in the distance, the topiary animals, and then all of a sudden I'm back there, weaving in and out of groups of children dressed in seventeenth-century costume. There's a tap on my shoulder. I look up and see a young boy with dark hair and cornflower-blue eyes.

'Those parties,' he says with a sigh. 'My father liked to remind himself of his own importance by throwing the doors open to his child readers. Every year, the Geoffrey Rivers fan club would hold a competition where children had to answer an easy question from the book. The correct answers would be put into a hat and then the names of twenty lucky kids would be drawn and they'd be invited for an evening of "wonder beyond their wildest dreams". It was bullshit, really. All of it. Just a ruse to make him look like a magnanimous philanthropist, to keep his face in the papers and the books selling.'

'I . . . I hadn't thought it was real. I thought I was remembering the book,' I say, stepping away from the window.

But I'm starting to remember now. My mum had died and I was in a really bad state. Had I entered a competition?

He looks at me, his face expressionless.

'On the morning of the party I got hold of the guest list,' he says. 'I wanted to see what kind of people would be stupid enough to fall for this crap. But then I saw your name and beside it there was a note: *Vanessa has recently lost her mother and may be feeling sensitive. If she is at all uneasy during the party, call her dad on the following number.* And when I saw that I knew I had to meet you. I had lost my mother too, but I didn't have anyone to look after me with Dad gallivanting around with any other kid but me. I wanted to see if you would understand.'

As I listen to him, my eyes fill with tears as I imagine that little girl going along to the party, trying to be brave when inside she was falling apart.

'I found you by the candy-floss stall,' he says, smiling. 'I heard one of the helpers call you Vanessa, so I knew it was you. You were dressed in a little blue smock dress and lace-up hobnail boots. You looked so thin and fragile, like you might break apart at the slightest touch. I tapped you on the shoulder and you flinched like you'd been hit.'

I nod my head, remembering how nervous I had been in those days.

'I asked you which character you had come as,' he says, his eyes softening, 'and you said "Iris". I remember your voice trembling when you spoke.'

It's incredible how much of those months following Mum's death have been lost. So raw was my grief, I had blocked out entire days and weeks.

'We chatted for a little while,' he continues. 'You were nervous but kind. I could tell that about you. After a while you opened up a bit and told me what you enjoyed most about the book. You said it was the glass bird, that you wished you could have a bird like that. When I heard this I felt like you truly were a kindred spirit so I told you about Mrs Perkins and Mallison Street, how I'd been left the glass bird by her when she died. You listened to me so attentively it made my heart hurt. I offered to get you some candy floss but you said you didn't want any. Then the firework display began and I noticed it was making you jump. I asked if you were okay and you said you wanted to go home.'

I sit in silence, trying to recall the events he is describing, an old sadness tugging at my heart.

'I went to find the party planner and asked her to call your dad,' he says. 'As she led you away, you turned back and waved at me. You were the saddest person I had ever met. But in a strange way, I liked your sadness because it made mine seem less terrible.'

He looks at me. The scar on his cheek is illuminated by the light coming through the window and I see now that it's an old burn.

'When you left, I felt empty,' he says, 'like all the lights had been dimmed. I knew I had to see you again, to speak to you properly away from everyone. So imagine my surprise when you wrote to me. Well, I say me, you actually addressed the letters to Angus, though I didn't mind.'

'My God,' I say, a chill rippling through me as I recall the box of letters that had arrived at Georgie's house the other day. 'You . . . you were . . .'

I try to speak but my throat is dry. I can't quite believe what I'm hearing.

'It was amazing,' he says, his eyes shining. 'You had such sweet handwriting. You told me about school, how you weren't really enjoying it as the kids kept asking about your mum. You told me a lot about her, how she liked gardening and dancing and how, when she smiled, it made you feel warm and loved.'

My heart feels like it's being ripped from my chest as I listen to him. How isolated I must have been to have felt that the only person I could confide in was a fictional character.

'After that first letter you wrote to me almost every week,' he says. 'I couldn't write back to you as you didn't include your address but I didn't mind. I thought that if I wrote back you'd be disappointed. I didn't inherit my father's way with words so any letter you got from me would have been deathly dull. Best to let you do the writing and believe that the person you were talking to was Angus. But I used to look forward to seeing those little yellow envelopes landing on the doormat. It seemed I'd finally found someone who understood me.'

I see myself sitting at the little wooden desk in my bedroom, writing carefully on the pale-lemon notepaper Mum had bought me for my last birthday.

'I treasured those letters,' he says, his voice piercing my memory. 'But then my father found them and told me I had to get rid of them. Said it was inappropriate because I was fourteen and you were just a kid. But it wasn't inappropriate, was it, Iris? It was beautiful. Anyway, I ignored the old goat and kept the letters. Once I found out where you were living I decided to send them to you, see if you would remember.'

I look up and suddenly the fog of twenty years begins to lift.

'It wasn't a story,' I say, my voice trembling. 'You were real.'

'I guess so,' says the man with a shrug. 'Though I've always felt like a half-person, like if I ever showed anyone the real me, I would be a huge disappointment.'

He stands up and goes to the window.

'My father robbed me of my childhood,' he says, scratching his finger along the pane of glass. 'He stole my identity and sold my life to the world as a dream when in reality it was hell.'

I glance at the open door. I should make a run for it but something holds me back. Is it that I feel sorry for this lost and lonely man?

'After you left the night of the party, I came back up here and tried to get on with my work,' he says, his eyes fixed on the window. 'I was making a model aeroplane. That was one of the things that helped to calm me – focusing on the details helped keep the bad stuff out of my head. But there was so much noise coming from the garden, the fireworks display, the shouting and shrieking from the kids. Finally, after messing up the paint on the body of the plane, I decided enough was enough. I hammered on the window and yelled at them to shut up, but I didn't realize how fragile the glass was and my fist went straight through. My hand never really healed.'

He turns and shows me his right hand. There's a crescent-shaped scar running from the knuckle of his thumb to the wrist.

'My father heard the noise and told the kids the party was over,' he spits out bitterly, returning to the window. 'When they had left I went to look for him. The house was deathly quiet but the garden door was open. Outside, the torches were still lit, the stalls still up and the cushions still strewn about the lawn. And then I saw him, sitting with his back to me, huddled in the light of one of the torches. He looked up and, when he saw me, his face grew dark. He ordered me to explain my behaviour, why I had thought it necessary to smash the window and cause a scene. I pleaded with him, explained that I'd just got fed up with the noise, that the broken window had been an accident. But that wasn't good enough for my father, nothing ever was.'

I sit here trying to reconcile the jovial Geoffrey, chat-show favourite and children's hero, with the person his son is describing.

'He told me that I shouldn't have been in my bedroom,' he continues. 'That my job was to stay at the party and play the role of Angus. But I was sick of having to pretend. I wasn't bloody Angus. He got angry then and told me to mind my language. And then I really lost it. I told him how ludicrous it was to hear that from the man who valued all my thoughts, all my experiences, enough to trap them inside a story, but in real life couldn't stand me. Who wouldn't come near me no matter if I yelled or cried. And yet he felt the real crime was a bit of bad language. He screamed back that I ought to be honoured to be his muse, that most boys would be thrilled to be the subject of a bestselling book series.'

He shakes his head and pauses. When he resumes the story his voice cracks with emotion.

'I...I told him I didn't want to be his muse, I wanted to be his son. And you know what he said? He said that whether I liked it or not, I was his son, and a spoilt son at that. That he had given me everything I could have ever wanted: a beautiful home, money, holidays, more than most boys would have in a lifetime. But that wasn't what I wanted, that wasn't what she wanted, my mum. All she wanted was to stay in our tiny house in Mallison Street where he had written the first book, which sold so well he could afford to buy this place. Mum hated it here. Neither of us wanted what he gave us. And you know what he said then?'

He turns to me and raises his eyebrows. I shake my head, bile rising in my throat. I sense that his story is nearly over and fear for what will come then.

'He said that what happened to Mum was my fault. I couldn't believe what I was hearing. My mum had killed herself because of depression, not because of me. If anyone pushed her to it, it was him – he was the one who took her from everything she loved. And my father, the man beloved by kids across the world, leaned across and hissed that he didn't blame her for feeling low with me as her son. That I clearly wasn't right in the head either. Then . . .'

He pauses and wipes his eyes.

'He said that he wished I could be the son I was supposed to be, but that I was incapable. That I was such a disappointment he'd had to invent another boy to replace me.'

'I'm so sorry,' I say, my mind whirring with images of Geoffrey, of his poor dead wife and lonely son.

'That was the final straw,' he says, pressing his fist to the glass. 'I ran at him then, but I lost my footing and fell on the open flame of the torch. As you can see, the scars have never healed.'

He steps away from the window and suddenly the atmosphere shifts. His face darkens and he walks towards me.

'I'm what our society would refer to as a loser, Vanessa. I've never had a proper job or a proper relationship, never bought a house or started a family. And it all stems from what happened that night; he baited me and I was marked for ever as the failure I am. I lost the use of my hand for a while and needed extensive skin grafts on my face. I was traumatized and needed help but my father's solution was to hide me away, pretend I didn't exist. He never mentioned me to the world again. So I set up home in the rooms along this corridor and we left each other alone. But then this year he announced he was selling up and using the proceeds to travel the world. The old bastard had landed on his feet yet again, no matter what the cost to anyone else, even those he was supposed to love. And he has never been punished for what he did to my mother or for what he did to me. For ruining both our lives, first with those books and then by doing this.'

He grabs my hand and runs it along the mottled scar.

'Who would ever love me looking like this, who would employ me?' he says, his eyes blazing. 'He'd trapped me in the house, inside the bloody fairy story, and now he was going to throw me out on to the street. I don't think so. That's why I don't feel a shred of guilt for killing him,' he says. 'Yes, that's right, Iris. It was me who finished him off.'

My heart leaps to my throat. I realize with sickening dread just how much danger I'm in. His face is so close to mine I can feel the warmth of his breath. I daren't move, daren't speak.

'In the end it was you who drove me to action,' he says, stroking my face. 'I'd found you again and I was enjoying watching you going about your business. I followed you from the estate agent that afternoon and then, while the old bastard was showing you round, I hid in the hallway and listened. When I heard him say he didn't have a son, I knew the time had come to kill him. So I came upstairs and pushed the table over, knowing it would make a noise and he'd come running. Always keen to preserve his little secret.'

My body freezes as I recall Geoffrey's startled expression as he made his excuses and went upstairs.

'In the end it was easier than I thought,' he says in a cold, flat voice. 'I waited at the top of the stairs and when he drew level I reached forward and pushed him down.'

Nausea wells up inside me as I remember Geoffrey lying there, blood pooling underneath his head. I'd put my hand on his neck to check for a pulse and I'd been so traumatized that was the only memory I'd retained, it was all I could see. No wonder I was sure that I'd killed him.

'It was perfect,' he says, still stroking my face. 'That old bastard was dead and you, my lovely Iris, had finally come home.'

Then his face hardens and he moves his hand to my throat, gripping it tightly.

'But then you ruined it all by running away,' he whispers.

'What?' I gurgle, my throat closing under his grip.

'I came down the stairs and saw you,' he says, his mouth just inches from mine. 'You looked like an angel crouched there in your beautiful pink dress. He was lying at your feet. God, Iris, it was perfect, like a scene from a painting. I tapped your shoulder and you turned and screamed. I tried to talk to you, tried to tell you that everything was okay, that we could be together, but you wouldn't listen.'

He presses tighter and as I struggle to breathe I'm transported back to that day. I remember now. I heard footsteps on the stairs then a hand on my shoulder. I'd tried to block it out, to erase the image from my mind: the man with the piercing blue eyes who had appeared from nowhere, like a monster in a dream.

'You ran away,' he hisses. 'When all I wanted to do was talk to you. I thought you were different, Iris, I thought you cared.'

37. Now

His face crumples and his grip on my throat loosens. Seizing the opportunity, I push him in the chest, fumble with the door and run out of the room.

'Iris, what are you doing?' he cries, appearing in front of me in the corridor. 'Surely you remember that Angus's room has two exits?'

I step backwards, my heart hammering madly.

'Please,' I say, trying to keep my voice calm though my whole body is trembling. 'Please just let me go home. I won't tell anyone what happened here, I promise you.'

'But you are home,' he says, frowning. 'You know that as well as I do. When I heard you say your name was Iris when you arrived for the viewing I knew you were giving me a sign, that you remembered me, that you wanted us to be together, that what we have is special. This is why I brought you here – now that Geoffrey has gone, we can live here together. You were in shock last time, that's why you ran away. This is your second chance. Oh, Iris, we can be so happy. It would be the fairy tale you've always dreamed about. It's what you've always wanted. I know that. I know everything about you.'

He grabs my arms and pulls me down to the floor. His grip is more forceful this time and I have no chance of breaking free. I need to keep him talking, stall for my chance.

'How do you know everything about me?' I say breathlessly, his arms tightening round my chest.

'It wasn't hard,' he says, fixing me with those strange eyes. 'After all, in this modern world, everyone puts their lives on display for all to see, don't they? I eventually found you on one of those fan pages for the book. "The Holly Mazers", I think it was called.'

I feel sick as I recall joining that group on Facebook one drunken, idle evening years earlier. I hadn't given it a second thought, hadn't imagined that by doing so I was making myself visible, vulnerable.

'It took no time to find you on there, as there weren't very many members,' he says. 'Once Harry Potter came along, people forgot all about poor old Geoffrey and his ghostly friends.'

'But how did you recognize me?' I say, thinking of my polished Facebook profile photo, taken by Anne for the Luna London website. She'd filtered it so much I barely even recognized myself when I first saw it. 'You hadn't seen me since I was a kid.'

'I knew it was you the moment I saw your photo,' he says, smiling to himself. 'You had the same kind eyes. Eyes tell you everything you need to know about a person and yours were the loveliest ones I've ever seen. They haven't changed.'

'Why didn't you just send me a message?' I say. 'Once you'd found me.'

'I was scared,' he says, exhaling deeply. 'I'm not the most social of people. After what happened to me that night, I hid away from the world.'

'The night of the party?'

'Yes,' he says angrily. 'My father destroyed my life that night.'

My head starts to throb. I try to wriggle free of his arms but this only makes him pull me tighter towards him.

'Finding you was the best thing that ever happened to me,' he says, his voice softening. 'After all that longing, all that searching, I'd finally found you. My Iris.'

He's not well, I think to myself. *I need to use this, convince him to stop.*

'All those pages you were on,' he says, his voice getting louder suddenly. 'They were like little chapters all contributing to the bigger story. They told me everything I needed to know about you. Facebook told me who your friends were, what music you liked, the restaurants you rated. It told me where you lived, what hotels you'd checked in to, the name of your boyfriend.' He pauses when he says this and his face darkens.

'World building,' he says, nodding his head. 'That's how Geoffrey used to describe the writing process. Creating a world from the things that make up a character. I was able to build a picture of you and your world from the information you'd put out there yourself. It was like magic. Twitter was very much your work and business life. It was there I found out all about Luna London. Wow, that seemed like the perfect place for little Iris to work. All that glitter and sparkle, helping people become the best versions of themselves – you said that yourself in one of your tweets. It was wonderful. Your boss, Anne, seemed perfect for you too. I liked her profile picture – the one where she's holding up the pot of powder over one eye so she looks like some glamorous pirate. She has kind eyes too. I wanted to poke them out.'

As he speaks, my body goes rigid with fear. All pity flees.

'But it was Instagram where I found the real you,' he says, looking into my eyes and smiling. 'Gosh, there was just so much. I was spoiled for choice. There were all those photos of your holidays – mostly with that friend of yours, the tall woman with the lovely red hair. All those places you visited. I was so envious. I was stuck here, too scared to leave the house, and there you were, little Iris travelling the world. I loved that photo of you in Prague, all buttoned up in your black winter coat, your eyes shining against the twinkly lights of the Charles Bridge. Now, all authentic characters have to eat, don't they? And those photos of your meals were just amazing, so well lit they looked like they'd been taken by a professional. You loved that Italian restaurant on the King's Road, didn't you? Rossi's. Though I notice you don't go there any more. I liked it too, particularly that evening when I got to watch my little Iris enjoying her Chianti, though you weren't keen on that vongole, were you? I didn't think much of that bloke of yours. He likes telling you what to do, doesn't he? It hurt me to see you with someone else, Iris. Particularly someone as horrible as him. It should have been us sitting at that table. I would have made sure you had the food you really wanted. I would give you anything.'

I think back to that evening, sitting outside with Connor, the night everything changed. I'd got so drunk I have little memory of it, but this man had been there, he had been watching.

'And the boxing match,' he says, shaking his head. 'I could tell my lovely little Iris wouldn't want to see such violence but that man wouldn't listen, would he? It got so bad you had to run out. That's when I knew I needed to step in and ask you if you were okay. Poor little lamb, you were so pale and your hands were shaking when I touched you.'

I go cold as I recall the man in the red baseball cap, the scar across his face. I had thought he was a beaten-up boxing fan but it was this man and he had followed me there. I feel sick with fear and disgust.

'But best of all were your stories,' he says, his voice light as though addressing a child. 'Isn't that just the best thing about social media? The fact that we don't need books and stupid authors any more because now we can make up our own stories, and we're in control, not them. Yours were just wonderful. But the one I liked the best was the one of you and your sister going for a walk on Wimbledon Common. You both looked so happy. It was like something from a dream. That's how I found the lovely house you live in with your sister, the one you fled to when it all went wrong with your boyfriend. I helped you along the way, of course . . .'

'What . . . what are you talking about?'

'Those abortion pamphlets you threw in the bin outside your flat,' he says manically. 'I felt that boyfriend of yours needed to know what pain he'd put you through and, hopefully, you'd break up. So I fished them out and put them on the doorstep.'

My body goes cold. This man has followed me everywhere. I think back to that afternoon when I woke to find Connor standing over me, the appointment card in his hand.

'But even then, after all of my work, you still couldn't see me,' he says, an edge to his voice now. 'In fact, you looked right through me every time our paths crossed. That's when I realized I was nothing more than a story in a book.'

'No,' I whimper as he presses tighter on my neck. 'That's not true. You're a real person, a good person who had bad things happen to him. You don't have to do this. You can stop it now and go on to have a normal life, be happy.'

He loosens his grip. I try to get up but his hand is still pressed into the base of my back.

'What do you mean?' he says, his voice cracking. 'You mean, we could . . . we could make a life together? You and me?'

He pulls my face towards him and for one horrible moment I think he's going to kiss me, but then the sound of a siren fills the corridor and he freezes.

'No, Iris,' he hisses, his eyes blazing. 'Tell me you haven't been so stupid?'

38. Now

I try to scream but his hand is pressed over my mouth as he drags me down the stairs. The sirens stop and I hear the thud of car doors slamming and heavy boots on the gravel drive.

The police are here. Only seconds away. But now he's dragging me into the garden and his arm is around my neck so I can't shout.

I have to escape and to do that I must summon every bit of strength I have left. He falters a little as we enter the tall, ragged maze and I take advantage of this and bite down hard on his hand. He yelps and releases his grip.

I run on ahead, disorientated and scared. Behind me I can hear him shouting, his voice ringing out into the air.

'Iris, don't do this,' he cries. 'Stay with me. I'll look after you. I'm the only person who can protect you.'

I take a left turn but go tumbling into a wall of sharp holly, a dead end. Pain shoots up my leg as the spikes puncture my skin. It's my recurring nightmare made real. I turn round, my breath catching in my throat, desperate to find a way out.

Then, miraculously, the sun comes out from behind a towering black cloud. It illuminates my way and I take a right, then a left, then right again. I'm almost there. I can sense it. But as I stumble forward I feel a thump on the back of my head then a weight pressing down on me, pinning me to the ground.

'Look what you've done, Iris,' he whispers in my ear. 'You've ruined the story.'

He pulls my head back and points west. I see plumes of smoke rising above the spiky hedge from the direction of the house, then orange flames bursting into the sky, like the torches on the night of the party.

'Please,' I say. 'Please just let me –'

But before I can get the words out I hear the sound of faint voices and the crackle of a radio. It's coming from behind, from the entrance to the maze. The police are in here, trying to find me. He hears it too. He stares at me with unblinking eyes then twists me round to face him.

Fear, like nothing I have ever felt before, grips my body, paralysing me. I try to scream but nothing happens. It's like I've been immobilized by some invisible force.

'This is it, Iris,' he hisses, placing his hands round my throat. 'This is where it ends.'

I try to yank him off me but he's too strong. White spots appear in front of my eyes and my chest constricts. I'm going. I can feel it.

Then I hear a loud cracking sound and a female voice calling my name. I feel the weight of him lift away, hear the crunch of his shoes on the uneven ground. Yet I stay where I am, too terrified to move.

Then I hear the noise of many feet running towards me. I lift my head and see a stream of uniformed police officers. And at the back of them, her red hair wild and dishevelled, her face twisted with fright, Lottie.

39. Now

Six hours later

Georgie clutches my hand as I sit in the living room listening to DS Bains. When the police found me they tried to make me go to hospital to be checked over but I assured them that the man hadn't hurt me.

He'd run away as the police had closed in on the maze. They are searching for him but so far there has been no sign.

'We were completely unaware that Mr Rivers's son was living with him,' says Bains, cradling a mug of tea in his hands. 'In fact, those who came into contact with Geoffrey said that he made no mention of having a son. It was so many years ago that he disappeared from public record that our investigation didn't unearth anything – then today my colleague, DS Lindsay, discovered a death notice for Mr Rivers's wife, which mentioned a "beloved son, Gabriel".'

It's the first time I've heard his real name.

'When we searched the upper floor of the house we found his phone,' says Bains, placing his empty mug on the table. 'It contained graphic images of Geoffrey Rivers's dead body as well as many, many images of you, Miss Adams, which had been taken from your social media pages. It seems he was rather obsessed with you.'

I have already told Bains about the childhood connection with Gabriel, the party, the letters, his subsequent stalking campaign.

'The call log shows a call made to your mobile last night,' he continues. 'Did you speak to him, Vanessa?'

'He . . . he told me he was a police officer,' I say, recalling the West Country accent on the other end of the line. 'And that I was to attend West Hampstead police station at 1 p.m. today.'

Bains nods his head and writes something in his notepad. Beside me, Georgie squeezes my hand tightly.

'We also found a collection of journals,' says Bains, looking up, 'in which Gabriel Rivers wrote about ways to kill his father. It's clear that Gabriel had serious mental health problems.'

I sit in a daze while Bains gets up from the chair. I hear him say something about getting some rest and how I must still be in shock, but I don't answer. All I can think about is Gabriel and his silent, sad life. Though he nearly killed me, there's a part of me that still sees the small boy he must've been. The boy that rescued me that night at the party.

'I'll see you out, DS Bains,' says Georgie, ushering him to the door.

I hear her, out in the hallway, telling him that she will keep an eye on me, that it's all been such a terrible shock.

'Is it safe to come in?'

I look up and see Lottie. She and Jack had been sidelined to the kitchen while Bains spoke to me and Georgie.

'Of course,' I say, patting the sofa next to me. 'Oh, Lottie, I've missed you so much. It's been hell without you.'

'I know,' she whispers, hugging me. 'I can't imagine what you've been through being stalked like that.'

I pull away from her and put my head in my hands.

'I'm so sorry, Lottie,' I murmur, tears blinding me. 'About everything. I messed up. I know I did. I let you down but . . . why were you with Connor this morning when you'd asked me to meet you? I don't understand.'

'I didn't ask to meet you,' she says, grabbing a tissue from the box on Georgie's coffee table and handing it to me. 'You texted *me* to meet you at that cafe. You said it was really urgent. When I turned up and saw Connor I thought the two of you were up to something.'

'A message from me?'

'I thought it was a bit strange,' she says, brushing her hair from her face. 'Because it was through Messenger but the name came up as Vanessa Iris Adams and I knew that wasn't your middle name. The profile photo was different too. But then I clicked on the page and it looked like you'd just set up a new account. All your friends were on there and all your holiday photos. So I replied and said, okay, I'd be there.'

'Gabriel,' I whisper, remembering how he talked about my online life, how he could build a world around what I had put out there. 'But Connor?' I say, my head throbbing. 'Why was he there?'

'Same as me,' says Lottie. 'He said you'd messaged him asking to meet at that coffee shop at the same time.'

What was Gabriel doing? What was he trying to achieve? I wonder just how much he had discovered through the information I had put out. He obviously had some plan for bringing Lottie and Connor together and to have me see them. Then I realize: he was trying to make me think they were together, that the two people I had been closest to were not to be trusted. That way he could have me all to himself.

'You know I've never really liked Connor. But I thought you'd come soon, so I was making awkward small talk with him,' she says, her voice shaking. 'Then he said that you two had split up, that you'd gone crazy and basically had a nervous breakdown. He said he'd almost called the police on you because you slapped his mother. He told me I should leave too, that you were unstable, dangerous. It was crazy, Nessa. I didn't know what to think. It didn't sound like you at all but then I hadn't seen you for so long . . . Maybe you'd . . . I don't know, changed.'

I feel light-headed as I listen to her. I went crazy? No, Connor, you tried to make me think I was.

'But then he said something,' says Lottie, shuffling in closer. 'And it made me go cold. He was about to leave and I asked him what had made you go crazy, what had happened. I had to ask. You were such a steady, calm person, Nessa. It didn't make any sense. And then . . . then he told me.'

'What did he tell you?'

'He said that you'd got really drunk one night at a club and that when you got back to the flat you'd jumped on him,' she says, clutching my hand in hers. 'He said that the next day you accused him of forcing himself on to you. He said you were mentally ill and needed help.'

My eyes brim with tears as I listen to her, remembering that night and the horrors that followed. Remembering his mother jumping to his defence, telling me that I was harming her son, remembering those pills, the blood, my life slowly falling apart.

'He's lying,' I say, my voice barely audible. 'I swear to you, Lottie.'

'I know,' she says, and with those words I feel my whole body go limp. She believes me. My best friend.

'How did you know I was at Holly Maze House?' I say, remembering the relief I felt when I saw her running out of the maze.

'We were waiting outside the cafe,' she says. 'Connor had just told me all that bullshit and I didn't know what to think. Then we saw you. Connor got up straight away and ran after you, but I was in shock for a minute. Next thing, this big black Range Rover comes out of nowhere. A man in a balaclava jumped out of it and grabbed you from behind. I was yelling at Connor to do something, but he was just standing there, frozen to the spot. It all happened in seconds. Once I caught up, the man had bundled you into the car and driven off. I told Connor to ring the police, but he just shoved past me, said he wanted nothing to do with it, and ran off. Then this woman came over to me, she'd taken a photo of the licence plate. We called the police and . . . well, you know the rest.'

I think of Gabriel and his sad eyes, the way he lit up when he thought there was a chance we could be together. I think of those letters, the fact that he liked my sadness because it made him feel less bad about his own. He could have had a happy life, if only he'd been allowed. But then I think about my mother. About my father. How we all have to overcome our childhoods somehow.

'Right, who fancies a takeaway?'

I look up and see Georgie standing by the door. Jack appears behind her, puts his arm around her waist and smiles.

'I don't know about you lot but I'm starving,' he says. 'Prawn ramen for you, Lottie?'

'How did you remember?' she says, laughing.

'Well, you always were a creature of habit.'

I smile, allowing myself to sink into the bosom of my family for a few moments, but there's a feeling of unease that I still can't shake. I think of Connor running away from the scene, remember his face as he pressed down on me. I look at Georgie as she snuggles up to Jack to order the meal and I realize that the time has come.

I have to tell her what happened.

40. Now

After supper Jack washes the dishes then heads up to bed, leaving me, Georgie and Lottie sitting in the living room.

'Anyone fancy a top-up?' says Georgie, holding the bottle of red aloft.

'Not for me, thanks,' I say, placing my hand over my glass. I need to have a clear head for what I'm about to say.

Beside me, Lottie lets out a sigh.

'God, what a day,' she says, squeezing my arm gently. 'You must be completely shattered, Ness.'

I nod my head.

'There's something I need to tell you both,' I say, my hands trembling. All these months and this is the first time I will actually articulate what happened to me. It feels surreal.

'What is it?' says Georgie, her face all concern. 'What's happened?'

I realize I can't look at them or else I'll lose my nerve so I stand up and walk over to the Grimshaw painting. Fixing my eyes on that lone figure, I begin to speak.

'I –'

My voice catches in my throat. I take a deep breath and start again.

'I – I think Connor raped me.'

There. Out it goes. Out of my head, where it has plagued me these last few months, and into the world. I feel my body crumple with a mixture of terror and relief.

'What?'

Lottie's voice rips into the silence. I turn. She is sitting there open-mouthed. Georgie is quiet, but I see that she is clasping her hands so tightly her knuckles have gone white.

'What happened, Nessa?' she says, looking up at me. 'Tell us.'

I turn my head and tell them every little detail, not just of the night in question but everything leading up to it: the mind games, the control, the way he described his ex, Sam, as a psycho, the subtle undermining of everything I said and did. When I'm finished I feel a hand on my shoulder. I turn and fall into my sister's arms.

'Oh, my darling girl,' she says, kissing the top of my head. 'How could I have let this happen to you?'

'Georgie, this isn't your fault,' I say. 'You've been there for me all my life. When Mum died you were invincible.'

'It's these last few years I'm talking about,' she says, shaking her head. 'I became selfish, got absorbed in my own life.'

'Georgie, you've never been selfish. I'm a grown woman,' I say. 'I chose to be in a relationship with Connor. No one could have foreseen this happening.'

'The only person at fault here is that bastard,' says Lottie as we join her on the sofa.

'He made it seem normal,' I say, putting my head in my hands. 'And then he made me feel like I was losing my mind, like I couldn't function. That's why it's taken me so long to realize what actually happened. I couldn't be sure. All I kept thinking was what if he's right? What if I am having some sort of breakdown and accusing a man of doing something terrible, something he didn't do?'

'Oh, Ness,' says Lottie, putting her hand on my shoulder. 'It's what abusers do. They make you think it's you. They play the victim.'

I nod my head, recalling his tears the morning after the burlesque.

'I know. But I just never thought that's what was happening to me. I couldn't see clearly. In a weird way, Gabriel made me see sense,' I say. 'His life had been destroyed by his father, a man who was adored by millions. His childhood had been stolen from him and put up for public consumption. He'd been violated and he was angry, so angry he ended up killing. I realized that Connor had done something similar to me, he'd violated me when I was at my most vulnerable. But I don't want to be like Gabriel. I don't want my life to be destroyed by anger and hate.'

'It's not going to be,' says Georgie, crouching down in front of me. 'And you know why? Because tomorrow morning, after we've all had a good rest, you're going to call the police. This man has to be stopped before he does this to someone else, darling. You know that, don't you?'

She takes my hand in hers and looks me straight in the eye.

'Yes,' I say, tears blurring my vision. 'I know that, but I'm scared, Georgie.'

'I'll be right here next to you, as will Lottie and Jack, and we'll be with you every single step of the way.'

'This is it, Vanessa,' says Lottie, squeezing my hand. 'This is the moment you take back control.'

41.

Wimbledon Magistrates Court
5 March 2019

I watch Connor's face as the jury files back into the court-room. He doesn't show any sign of emotion, just stares straight ahead. The dazzling smile and bravado that has carried him through life, has charmed men and women alike, convinced them to do as he asked, to believe his version of events, has deserted him. He looks small, diminished.

The last seven months have brought me to the very limit of what I thought I could endure. Once I made the call to the police I thought the hard part was over, that the weight of the legal system would come down on Connor and relieve some of the anxiety and fear I'd been feeling. Little did I know that the hardest part was still to come.

When Connor was arrested he not only protested his innocence but repeated the lies he had told to Lottie: that I'd got drunk that night then I'd woken up the next day, hung-over and regretful at having blacked out, and decided to accuse him of rape. He pointed out my subsequent decline, leaving my job, my 'unhinged' spree of visiting houses under different guises and, of course, Geoffrey Rivers's death. Even though I was cleared of that entirely, he maintained I wasn't as innocent as everyone thought.

With Connor refusing to admit what he had done, I was faced with the decision of whether to go ahead and face a trial that could see every aspect of my life dragged out and scrutinized. As nicely as she could, my barrister pointed out that I would be painted as an unreliable witness: a woman in a seemingly stable relationship, with an Instagram page full of loved-up photos of the two of us at the time of the alleged rape, a woman who went on to dupe estate agents in a bizarre game that got me tangled up in a murder case.

The odds were stacked against me, but I decided to proceed. I needed to prove that what Connor did to me that night was wrong, criminally wrong, and to do that I would have to be brave. I thought of my mother, how she hid those headaches from us because she didn't want to worry us, didn't want to cause a fuss, and I tried to imagine what she would say if she were here. She would want me to stand up for myself, want me to have the life she never had, a long and healthy one, free of fear. I knew it was going to be daunting, but I knew I had Georgie and Jack and Lottie behind me. I had no choice, I told myself, I had to see this through, had to see justice served.

Still, the odds continued to be stacked against me as the trial began. Connor's mother had paid for an expensive barrister, an intimidating giant of a man with gold cufflinks and a permanent sneer, who spent the first two days ripping me to shreds. I spent each night curled up in the foetal position on Georgie's sofa, my sister rubbing my head and bringing me cups of tea, telling me, just as she had done in the days and weeks following my mother's death, that everything was going to be fine. 'The good will out, my darling,' she told me as we drove back to the court the following day.

I couldn't see how it possibly would. But when we arrived at court that morning I was met by my barrister, Nicole Jones, a softly spoken but deadly sharp young woman. She told me that, following a tip-off from one of Connor's ex-colleagues, they had managed to track down Cathy Cooper, a woman who had worked with Connor and accused him of date rape, before he'd intimidated her into leaving the firm. She'd relocated to Brussels, but when my legal team tracked her down and explained what I had gone through, she felt she had to speak out. 'She'll be appearing in court, as a witness for the prosecution,' said Nicole as we stood in the corridor, huddled up against a wall. Neither of us dared say it but we knew that Cathy giving evidence could change everything.

I'll never forget the look on Connor's face when Cathy stepped into the witness box. Until then he had been ultra confident, laughing with his legal team, flashing that beaming smile up to his mother in the gallery, answering every question without a flinch. But when he saw Cathy – a tall young woman with blonde hair, pale-blue eyes and a light voice that never wavered, even as Connor's barrister tried to rip her story to shreds – the colour had drained from his face. He knew, in those moments, that his trail of abuse had come to an end. It was all over.

Like me, Cathy had been a confident, well-balanced, happy woman when she met Connor but after the date rape she had suffered from depression, which was so bad her employers had wondered if she was having a nervous breakdown. When this was revealed in court I thought back to that conversation with Connor where he'd told me about a friend of his who'd had a breakdown. 'We were all so worried about her,' he'd said. In reality, he'd stood by and watched as the woman he'd attacked was ground down by the horror of what he'd inflicted on her. And yet, despite her own trauma, Cathy had been brave enough to come forward. I will never forget that and will always be grateful to her.

As the foreman of the jury – a middle-aged man with receding hair and thick, heavy-rimmed spectacles – stands to deliver the verdict, I feel Georgie's hand clasp mine. This is the moment. This is what I have been waiting for. The man stumbles slightly as he begins to speak, coughs and then says the word we have been hoping for, but never thought would come.

Guilty.

Georgie sweeps me into her arms. Behind me, I hear Connor's mother hiss some expletive. I feel strangely calm, almost numb.

A couple of minutes pass in a blur and as the verdict sinks in I recall the Victim Impact Statement I had written with my barrister, Nicole.

I'd like to say that before I met Connor Dawkins I was a happy, vivacious person without a care in the world but that would not be true. The fact is that I was a victim before I ever met this man. In 1996, my mum, Penny Adams, suffered a brain haemorrhage while driving home from the shops. She died instantly. And when she died she took a little bit of me, and my sister, and my dad, with her. We would never be the same again. Before that day in July 1996, I had been a happy child with a loving family and a secure home, and I would spend my early adult life looking for a replacement.

It was my search for that feeling of home, for the love and security and warmth that come with it, that put me in the path of Connor Dawkins. When he rushed me into making our relationship official, telling friends, moving in together within a couple of months, I took that as a sign that he loved me and that I had finally found someone to build a life with, a home, a family. I had trusted Connor Dawkins completely but that trust had been misplaced. When he met me for a drink on our first date, he hadn't seen a potential life partner, a woman he could love and marry and start a family with. He saw another victim. And in my vulnerable state I was an easy target. To the outside world, our relationship looked blissful. But behind his dazzling smile lay a toxic trail of lies, deceit and mind games, which Connor Dawkins hid so skilfully he managed to fool not only me but his family, his friends and his colleagues. 'A good man,' was how most of the people who came into his orbit would describe him. 'A charming man, a team player, one of the lads.' And I had thought the same of him, even when he was gaslighting me, telling me that I didn't know my own mind, that I was imagining things, that my suspicions were those of a crazy person, a 'psycho' – which is the term he used to describe his exes. And because I was a trusting person, because I desperately wanted to see the good in him and our relationship, I made the mistake of letting Connor

Dawkins control my mind to such an extent that I no longer knew what was real and what was just in my head.

I continued to do that right up until the morning of 29th May 2018, when I woke up to find that Connor Dawkins had raped me. Yet, even then, I let him try to tell me that it was all in my head, that I was the bad person for accusing a loving boyfriend of committing such a heinous crime. I knew, instinctively, what had happened, but I tried to block it out by losing myself in other people's lives. My short-lived coping mechanism was to view expensive houses using various aliases, which the defence has used to paint me as a dangerous fantasist, a mentally unstable woman who doesn't know her own mind, who lives in a dream world, and who would be quite capable of inventing a story accusing an innocent man of a terrible crime. But during my lost months of trying on other people's lives, I made a discovery. No one, not your mother, not your father, not your lover, has the right to violate you, to control you, to 'take' your life from you and twist it to shape their own ends.

Because what I didn't know when I fell under the spell of Geoffrey Rivers and his books, as a traumatized ten-year-old, and again when I fell under Connor Dawkins's spell all these years later, is that for some people, love means power, it means ownership and control. These people would have you believe that you have no voice, no right over your own life. They chip away at your self-esteem, at your judgement, at your very essence, until there is so little left you might as well be a ghost. Yet Connor Dawkins didn't break me fully. With the support of my family I summoned the courage to go to the police, knowing that he would very likely deny the charges and therefore put me through the ordeal of being cross-examined in court. Most victims would lose their nerve at this point and drop the charges. I very nearly did. To anyone in this position, I would like to say I am with you and I understand your fears, but your silence makes it possible for people like Connor Dawkins to carry on destroying lives. If you can find it in you to come forward then you might help other people like you, like me.

Someone told me recently that the 'good will out', that truth and honesty and fairness will always prevail. It will take me a long time to believe that, to trust people again, to let someone else into my heart. But I hope one day to recover from the ordeal this man put me through and to rebuild the life he tried to destroy.

The room remains hushed for a few moments. Up in the public gallery, Connor's mother gets to her feet and noisily exits, while her son sits with his head in his hands.

Outside the court, Lottie suggests we go and have that celebratory drink before heading home. I smile at her but decline the offer. This is not about celebrating. This is about justice being done. Now it has been, I can sleep peacefully in my bed and I can get on with my life.

Epilogue

Two years later

'As you can see, Miss Adams, it's a stunning view.'

I watch as Phil, the estate agent, opens the wooden shutters. A stream of sunlight bathes the living room, giving it a honey glow.

'The garden needs a little work but if you're happy to roll your sleeves up you could easily add an extra 50k to the value of the house.'

I nod my head politely as I step towards the window and look out. Phil is right, the garden is in need of some attention, but adding value to this house is the last thing on my mind. If I've learned anything these last few years it's that family and friends are what matters, not fancy houses or picture-perfect lifestyles.

I think back to the woman I was two years ago and I barely recognize myself. In the months after the trial I was a nervous wreck. I was plagued by nightmares where Connor would be on top of me, pinning me down, his face contorted with rage and hate. I'd wake up in a sweat then reassure myself that he was in prison, that he could not hurt me, or any other woman, again. He was sentenced to five years in the end and, though I've been told that he will likely only serve half of that, it was enough for me to see him receive punishment for what he did to me and Cathy, however lenient the sentence might be.

Sometimes my thoughts wander to that strange man with the piercing blue eyes, the man who set all this in motion. The police got in touch with me at the end of last year to say there had been possible sightings of Gabriel in Melbourne and Sydney. Part of me was happy for him that he could be having adventures, living the life his father had denied him all those years. Yet another part of me felt uneasy, remembering his hands around my throat, the glee in his eyes as he told me he'd killed his father. The fact that he could be on the other side of the world is reassuring, though when it comes to him, I will never feel truly safe.

Through all of this, my sister has been a tower of strength. 'I'm so proud of you, Nessa,' she'd told me, the night after the verdict, as we sat in her kitchen, Radio 2 blaring out of the Roberts radio. She and Jack have had their troubles but they're still together, still going strong. Of course, they still quarrel but they find a way to work through. As Georgie often reminds me, 'We're not perfect, but then, who is?'

Perfection. It's an odd thing to crave, isn't it? Particularly as, by nature, humans are messy and complex and impetuous and changeable. They are anything but perfect. Yet that is what we're constantly being told to pursue: the perfect house, the perfect body, the perfect children, marriages, jobs, even bloody plates of food. When really, what all of us needs is something very simple but equally elusive.

Happiness.

Looking back at my life, there are two distinct moments when I felt truly happy. The first was that morning when I'd sat in the kitchen watching Mum singing along to Barbara Dickson, knowing that it was the first day of the summer holidays and I would have her all to myself for six whole weeks; in reality, it would turn out to be our last day. The second was the morning Anne offered me the job at Luna London. In the months after the trial I felt like I needed to recalibrate, to find out who I truly was without the filters and hashtags. So I deleted all my personal social media pages, removed the property app from my phone and set about dismantling the idea of pushing a perfect life on to other people, bombarding them with images of a life that doesn't exist. And I set about reclaiming the happiness I'd once had. I got back in touch with Anne and, over a long lunch in her beloved Chelsea Arts Club, decided to return to what I love best, this time as Senior Partner of Luna London. I now have shares in the business with the option of buying Anne out when she decides to retire. Some would say working in the beauty business feeds into those toxic ideas of unattainable perfection but, as I remember Mum once telling me as she sat at her dressing table getting ready for a night out, make-up is not about hiding behind a mask but about being the best version of yourself and feeling empowered. As always, she spoke a lot of sense.

And it was with Mum in mind that I set about reclaiming that first moment of happiness. Once I'd got my job back, I spent the next two years living as frugally as possible until I had enough saved for a deposit. With the small sum Mum had left me added to those savings, I was finally in a position to buy. Though I loved living with Georgie, the time had come to find a place of my own. Still, the thought of scouring property websites made me feel ill, like a recovering alcoholic trapped in a wine cellar. In the end, I didn't need to bother with any websites as I found the house by chance as I drove back from a meeting in Oxford. Curiosity had got the better of me and I'd decided to take a detour through Caversham, the place where I'd grown up.

I'd stopped at the local florist to buy some flowers to put on Mum's grave and as I drove to the churchyard I'd passed a house I recognized from childhood. It was the house my mother used to point out to me when we went to feed the ducks. Located opposite the park, it was unusual as, unlike the other houses in the terrace, this one had a white clapboard exterior and a yellow door. My mum used to call it the sunshine house as it always made us smile.

My eyes had filled with tears as I parked up outside the house and saw the 'For Sale' board. The white clapboard was now grey and dirty, the yellow-painted door badly chipped, but those imperfections made it even more appealing. Even before I found out that the house was in my price range, I knew it would become my home. There was something fated about the moment, something right.

When Phil comes back into the room I'm still standing by the window, memories of Mum and toast and jam and Radio 2 and Geoffrey's voice flooding my head. *This is it*, I think to myself, *this is the place*. As Phil resumes his sales pitch, I switch off and let my thoughts wander. I have seen many houses and have come to realize that none of what Phil is talking about matters – expensive paint, room for expansion, all the marketing guff I've heard along the way. No, what matters is the feeling I had when I walked into this little house today. And that is why I make Phil an offer on the spot. I've spent so long living through other people, adopting different identities, taking different names, that somewhere along the line I forgot who I was. I guess I was afraid of who I might find if I dropped the act and looked in the mirror. But now I realize that there was no need to be afraid, that to be truly happy, to truly live, I don't need to hide behind stories. I just need to be me. Vanessa. And that, as my mother always told me, is enough.

Acknowledgements

I would like to thank my amazing editor, Katy Loftus, for believing in me, and this novel, from the start.

Huge thanks to Victoria Moynes for your excellent insight and suggestions. It has been such a joy to work with you.

To the magnificent team at Viking Penguin. Thank you Ellie Hudson and Georgia Taylor for all the hard work you have put into the digital and marketing campaigns for my novels. I appreciate it so much.

Thanks so much to Karen Whitlock for your meticulous copy-editing.

Heartfelt thanks to my agent, Madeleine Milburn. Eight years on, you are still the greatest inspiration and support.

Thanks also to Giles, Hayley, Rachel, Georgia, Georgina, Mark and all the team at the Madeleine Milburn Literary, TV & Film Agency.

I want to take this opportunity to thank the eternally glamorous Anne Bryce for giving me an insight into the world of property and house viewings and for welcoming me so warmly to Harrogate all those years ago when I was a young mum.

I also owe a debt of gratitude to the children's fiction that shaped my own childhood and introduced me to the wonder of reading. Here are just a few: *Orlando the Marmalade Cat* by Kathleen Hale, *The Children of Green Knowe* by Lucy M. Boston, *Moondial* by Helen Cresswell, *The Wind in the Willows* by Kenneth Grahame, *The Dark is Rising* by Susan Cooper, *Danny, the Champion of the World* by Roald Dahl, *The Worst Witch* by Jill Murphy, *The Tailor of Gloucester* by Beatrix Potter and *A Traveller in Time* by Alison Uttley.

Love and warm wishes go, as always, to my family for all their love and support.

Thanks to my mother, Mavis Casey, for inspiring the character of Penny. Those childhood memories of sitting in the kitchen with you, eating toast and listening to Terry Wogan, before school, will stay with me for ever.

All my love and thanks to my father, Luke Casey, whose voice I hear in my head every time I sit down at my desk to write. You are, and always will be, the person who inspires me most.

A huge thank you to my lovely son, Luke, not only for surviving my attempts to teach you chemistry during lockdown but also for bringing so much love and laughter to my life. You have the biggest heart and you make me proud every day.

Finally, thank you to Jason. My love, always.

NUALA ELLWOOD

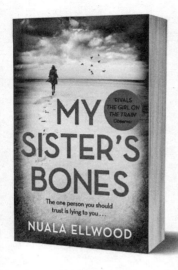

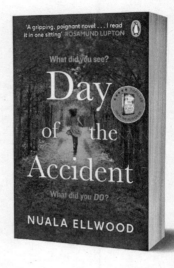

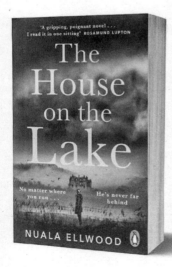

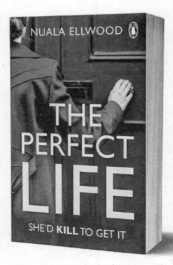

Have you read them all yet?

NUALA ELLWOOD

The House on the Lake

No matter how far you run . . .
he's never far behind.

Lisa needs to disappear. And her friend's rambling old home in the
wilds of Yorkshire seems like the perfect place. It's miles away from the
closest town, and no one there knows her or her little boy, Joe.

But when a woman from the local village comes to visit them,
Lisa realizes that she and Joe aren't as safe as she thought.

What secrets have Rowan Isle House – and her friend –
kept hidden all these years?

**And what will Lisa have to do to survive,
when her past finally catches up with her?**

'Gripping, poignant'
Rosamund Lupton

'Eerily haunting'
Jane Corry

'I literally couldn't put it down'
Emma Curtis

NUALA ELLWOOD

MY SISTER'S BONES

If you can't trust your sister, then who can you trust?

Kate Rafter has spent her life running from her past.
But when her mother dies, she's forced to return to Herne Bay –
a place her sister Sally never left.

But something isn't right in the old family home.
On her first night Kate is woken by terrifying screams.
And then she sees a shadowy figure in the garden . . .

Who is crying for help?
What does it have to do with Kate's past?
And why does no one – not even her sister – believe her?

'Couldn't put the lights out until I'd finished it!'
Emma Curtis

'Rivals *The Girl on the Train* as a compulsive read'
Guardian

'Twists and turns until the last page'
Tammy Cohen

NUALA ELLWOOD

Day
of the
Accident

WHAT DID YOU SEE?
WHAT DID YOU *DO*?

**Sixty seconds after she wakes from a coma,
Maggie's world is torn apart.**

The police tell her that her daughter Elspeth is dead. That she
drowned when the car Maggie had been driving plunged into
the river. Maggie remembers nothing.

When Maggie begs to see her husband, Sean, the police tell her that he
has disappeared. He was last seen on the day of her daughter's funeral.

What really happened that day at the river?
Where is Maggie's husband?
**And why can't she shake the suspicion that somewhere,
somehow . . . her daughter is still alive?**

**'A clever, twisty plot that takes psychological mind
games to a new level. Nuala Ellwood has done it again!'**
Jane Corry

'This clever, multi-layered novel is simply stunning'
Dinah Jefferies